"THE DEAD MAN WAS NO KURDISH TERRORIST."

"Are you sure about that, Aaron?" Brognola asked, his interest rising as he began to consider the implications.

"The bullets taken from Haquim, plus samples fired from all those M-16s used by our forces, were flown to the U.K. I had the Yard send me all their findings."

Kurtzman keyed up more photographs, shots of the various bullets, magnified and classified. The striations and grooves stood out clearly on each.

"We have the U.S.-fired bullets here. Against each one is an indentical photo of the bullets taken from Haquim."

"They don't match?"

"No way. Whoever shot Omar Haquim, it wasn't one of our guys. He was shot with an M-16, sure enough, but not one belonging to anyone at Incirlik."

And Hal Brognola had to wonder who it was that had come up with that red herring....

DON PENDLETON'S

MACK BOLAN®

STONY MAN®

EXTREME
MEASURES

A GOLD EAGLE BOOK FROM

W🌐RLDWIDE®

TORONTO • NEW YORK • LONDON
AMSTERDAM • PARIS • SYDNEY • HAMBURG
STOCKHOLM • ATHENS • TOKYO • MILAN
MADRID • WARSAW • BUDAPEST • AUCKLAND

First edition October 2001

ISBN 0-373-61939-1

EXTREME MEASURES

Special thanks and acknowledgment to
Michael Linaker for his contribution to this work.

Printed in U.S.A.

EXTREME MEASURES

PROLOGUE

There were no absolutes. Nothing was carved in stone. The chances of something going wrong were clear to see. It was a lesson Falil had learned many years ago as a young man, and the images of ill luck turning quickly to tragedy had stayed with him through to his adult life. Then it had been his father and elder brother, dying when one of them had stepped on a land mine. The day erupted into searing fire and horror as it exploded. In that same moment he had felt the shards of metal tear into his own legs, leaving him sprawled in the dust, numbed with pain. His agony came later, but he had to lie there in the dirt and see what had happened to his family. Such images weren't easily forgotten. Falil only had to close his eyes and recall that hot, dusty day, and the horror came back with startling clarity. He had never seen anyone die violently before, and at fifteen years old the brutal, sudden extinction of his father and brother became the stuff of his nightmares. In that shattering moment, hearing the explosion and the pain-filled screams of his father and brother, Falil left childhood behind and was cruelly pushed into position as head of the family. In the dusty hills of the Palestinian homeland, where a daily battle was fought not only with mortal enemies, but also with the rapacious climate, a fifteen-year-old boy becoming a man overnight was nothing new. In Falil's mind it became the turning point in his life. A place from where he never looked back, nor even wanted to. His destiny was bound up with the need to stay alive, fighting the hunters from across the border and trying to maintain some semblance of community. It was all his people had. Their devotion to one another in a world that had become successively more alienated toward them. So they looked inward, asking for nothing, begging for nothing, placing their backs to the wall and standing firm against a treacherous world.

The deaths of his father and brother were only the beginning. In the space of the next six months he watched his grieving mother die from the loss of her husband and son. His uncle, turned bitter by the death of Falil's father, joined one of the resistance movements and died weeks later during a furious encounter with Israeli troops.

Falil's already fragile world collapsed about him. He was alone now, still trying to get over his wounds.

He emerged from that black period of his life scarred in his mind as well as his body. The explosion, though it had spared his life, had left him with a shattered left leg that never healed correctly. He walked with a limp, and the leg plagued him with recurring pain. That pain became part of him, reminding him who he was and adding to the bitterness that grew with the passage of time. Falil looked out on the world through eyes that saw daily the injustice heaped upon his people. The injustice that refused to allow them to settle, always on the move because one of their many enemies had chosen that time to harass them. Or again attempt to destroy them. He sat and watched and listened, and realized that all the promises made to them were as nothing. They had little more substance than the dusty wind drifting across the barren slopes. They were all the same, he began to see. The Americans. The British. The West. Their words held nothing. They looked on Israel as the promised savior of the region, and everything went to the Zionists.

He looked and saw through the eyes of a young man, but within his heart was the wisdom of experience, and the seeds of bitterness against an uncaring world forced his mind and body to turn inward. He rejected the material world and found his comfort in the calmness and tranquillity of his religion. He embraced it with a vengeance, immersing himself in the Holy Book, devouring the words and molding his life in their image. He used his natural skills as an orator to convince those who were like-minded that their world was in danger of being destroyed, not only by the infidel nations of the world, but by those he saw as traitors to their way of life within the borders of the Islamic nations. The ones who had sold out to the West. Who broke the laws of God by giving in to temptation. They sold their oil. They allowed the infidels to live and work within their borders, and as the Westerners came so did their poison. Slowly, insidiously, the infidels began to erode the solid foundations of the true Islam. Customs were relaxed. Laws openly flouted, and Falil saw a creeping disease beginning to take hold.

He favored the religious men, the ones who held great power and had the ability to change the thinking of the masses. His youth and his fervor brought him their confidence. He worked tirelessly to do their bidding, while all the time cultivating his own growing circle of powerful, influential sponsors. And over the next few years Falil's devotions and his skill in secrecy and guile drew him ever closer to the more outspoken clerics, the ones who advocated resistance to the West, who wanted nothing to do with the weakening of Islamic law. As time passed, he used his growing influence to gather a loyal group around him. They stayed isolated, away from all they believed evil, and they began to lay their plans for a strike against the enemies of Islam. Not just the West, but against all those who were allowing the destruction from within.

It took time.

It also took money. Falil's supporters, under his guidance and his growing strength, branched out, and with careful orchestration they brought in backing from those who were silently in favor of Falil's expanding agenda. Their wealth and their influence helped immensely. Many of them were men who had once held positions of great authority, but due to political changes they had been ousted. They had retreated, waiting for the time when they could return, and they saw Falil's skills at bringing together likeminded Islamics from a number of countries as a way of regaining their former positions.

Falil's plan was simple, direct, and if it went as expected would bring them all together as a powerful Islamic cadre. His scheme was intended as a twofold operation.

The first was to create unrest among the weaker Islamic regimes by coordinating a state of siege and multiple strikes against chosen targets within the Middle East. They would attack in a series of crippling operations against oil pipelines, power sources, individuals. Small, well-equipped cells, in place well before the appointed date, would lead the strikes. If the operation escalated, creating a longer-term conflict, then they would accept that as God's decision. None of them had any reservations about turning back the clock if the need arose.

Better to be a free man living in a tent, following the word of God, than a betrayer of Islam residing in a mansion, Falil had told them. They were all descended from noble tribes who had created a rich and devout society long before the infidels came and sullied the very air they breathed. If it was the will of God that they return to that way, then so be it.

His use of the Holy Book took hold. Falil used his power of persuasion well, measuring every word he spoke to bring his followers closer to his vision. His art was in the way he delivered his oratory. He spoke only from his heart, and any man who listened saw the truth in his words.

The second part of their battle would be against the greatest enemy Islam would ever face.

Here the hatred that had been created the day his father and brother died came of age. Over the long years it had been festering deep within him, and though he had outwardly embraced the cloak of his religion and presented a picture of lucidity, beneath the skin he daily fought the festering rage that burned inside. The need for revenge isolated him from the needs of other men. He neither desired nor sought the pleasures of the flesh. He disdained liquor because he knew it might distort his rational thoughts, or worse, loosen the careful control he maintained over the spoken word. His physical needs were few, and to the faithful who followed him he was a role model, the perfect Islamic leader. Little did they suspect that his denial was less spiritual strength and rather more a condition brought about by his all-consuming desire for vengeance on a despised world.

The infidel West and its lapdog, Israel. Again Falil had devised a long-term strategy. He was aware that to take on the West in an all-out battle would be foolish. They had the superior weaponry and the ability to maintain a prolonged conflict. His plan was to attack from within and to concentrate on the most evil of the nations—America itself. Falil's cunning was in his plan to deploy his cells to attack from within. To make the American people suffer as had the peoples of Islam over long years. He would attack the very fabric of the nation—its civilian population, the soft, pampered millions who considered themselves safe from any harm. Let them become the victims and they would see how quickly the U.S.A. would fall apart.

They would all have to become warriors, fighting for Islam against an enemy who was both clever and evil. The infidels lived their lies every day. Falsity was their creed. Truth was a stranger to them. Yet they possessed great power. They had vast reserves of material to sustain themselves.

But even they needed the oil of the Middle East. Denied that, they might think again who had the greater power. Falil had considered his plan from every angle.

His first move was to create a diversion. Something that would engage the interest of the West and its allies, and while that took place Falil and his people would begin their operation. He knew that his deception would only hold for a while, but even a short time would help, and by the time the West had realized what was going on his operation would be nearing fruition.

CHAPTER ONE

The War Room, Stony Man Farm, Virginia

"Go through that again slowly," Calvin James asked.

"Echelon is a means by which surveillance has been taken to an ultrasophisticated level. The basics are that the system can monitor all kinds of communications, including electronic mail, sift it through a program that is coded to recognize key words or phrases, repeated data, and collate that information into recognizable patterns."

James nodded as Aaron Kurtzman paused.

"Then this data is examined by security agencies and it can let them know something is happening, or going to happen?"

"Simplistically, yes. There's a whole lot more to it, but in effect Echelon is a big ear scanning the electronic message lanes, picking up gossip."

Hal Brognola chuckled softly. "I wouldn't let too many people hear you describing it that way."

"In layman's terms I'd class it exactly like that. But the important thing is what it's been picking up over the past month or so, information that has been coming and going, back and forth, between the U.S., Europe and the Middle East. We seem to have a dialogue going on that has raised some concerns.''

"This was dropped in our laps because the President believes we could be looking at some kind of heavy plot involving extreme Islamic groups. And we mean extreme. Never mind your average terrorist. These people don't even like their own. I mean that in the sense they believe certain Islamic regimes are going soft, allowing a drift away from the strict word and deed. Like reform parties who want to bring Islam into line with the new millennium.''

"Still Muslim but easing back on some of the more restrictive practices?'' Rosario Blancanales said.

"A desire to lower tension. Concentrate on creating a better environment for their own people,'' Brognola said. "Nothing that is going to turn them away from their religious or ethnic lifestyles. Nothing we would want them to do, anyway.''

"But these extremists see that as a crime?'' Encizo asked.

Brognola nodded. "They read the same book as everyone else. Only their interpretation of the words comes out differently. In their eyes the purity of Islam is being tainted by the liberals. The reformists. They refuse to accept that. Our information has it that they would be prepared, no, *they are prepared,* to take that extreme view and make it a reality.''

"I don't like the way this seems to be going,'' Barbara Price said. "Are we talking about armed aggression here? Hard strikes against nominated targets?''

"It looks that way. Our intel, aided by the data

Echelon has dredged up, allows for a scenario that could very well slide into full-scale conflict.''

''They see the world going to hell so why not help it along?'' David McCarter said. ''These people are so frustrated and pissed off by all the changing allegiances and policy making they figure maybe it's time to have that mother of all battles, as Mr. Hussein put it. Drag in the whole bloody world and let's see who comes out the other end.''

Yakov Katzenelenbogen leaned forward, adding his comments in his quiet, authoritative way. ''Look at it from their angle. They have a society that is devoutly religious, and it's not the way some in the West see religion. We have deeply committed people, of course, but not in the Muslim way. For them all existence is directed toward their faith. It is what they live for. It makes them what they are and I have no quarrel with that. In their way they are far more true to their devotions than we are. That doesn't make people good or bad in either society. Each to his own. That should be an end to it, but we all know it isn't as clear-cut. There are those of the Muslim faith who look on our society and see something depraved and sick, a culture based on a greed for money and personal gain. There are those who see America especially as the root cause of their problems. America interferes, tries to tell them how to run their affairs. America attacks them. Desert Storm has been viewed by many as an affront to their way of life. I could go on, but the point I'm making is that the differences in our cultures have brought us to an impasse. Moderates will sit down and talk. They will put aside religion and discuss the future. But others refuse. They disbelieve every word we utter. There isn't anything we can say to alter their feelings.''

''Is that what we're up against here?'' Price asked. ''The tone in those messages we deciphered was direct enough. They spoke openly of making America suffer as they have suffered and making the world aware that the U.S. has been negotiating with their enemies to wipe them out. That we aren't to be trusted.''

''It's the kind of rhetoric that will stimulate aggression. Make people sit back and think. We have a Muslim presence in this country. The great majority are hardworking, solid citizens. But there has to be a percentage who are, for whatever reason, out of the mainstream. It may not be their fault directly. No work. Ill health. The root cause doesn't matter. But they are the ones who can easily be converted into believing that they are deliberate victims of injustice. And remember they are still Muslims, firm in their belief, always loyal to the religion that supports them. Anyone looking for followers would generate enough support from those people to see the logic of their argument and flock to the cause.

''The feeling is, according to our Middle East experts, that there's a lot of discontent within certain factions. As David suggests, there is a lot of frustration, rage, feelings that everything is falling apart, and there's a growing need to do something about it. Ultraextremists are making big speeches about the new millennium, telling the masses that this is a new century and it should be *their* century. My contacts in Israel have been confirming this. They have justification to be worried. Being in the front line of any potential crisis that might erupt gives them a unique perspective on the matter.''

"I've asked Katz to go and meet with Ben Sharon,'' Brognola said. "See what they can conclude when they compare notes.''

"Give him my best,'' Calvin James said.

Phoenix Force had worked with Ben Sharon, Mossad agent, on a couple of earlier missions, and he had been invaluable in the field with his intimate knowledge of the Middle East.

"You can tell him yourself,'' Brognola said. "I want you and T.J. to go along and watch Katz's back.''

"Found your vocations at last,'' McCarter said with a smile. "Nursemaiding the old guy. Don't forget his warm blanket and hot milk when you tuck him in.''

"Us tuck *him* in?'' James said. "You want to rethink that, David?''

The Israeli's age hadn't diminished his capabilities. He might have retired from full-time active duty in the field, but in all other respects Yakov Katzenelenbogen was no slouch when it came to the social graces. His reputation as a connoisseur of fine wine, food and beautiful women hadn't lessened in the slightest. And when it came to assessing field operations and strategy, he could leave them all at the starting gate.

There was a person in the War Room who believed David McCarter's words were anything but an affectionate dig at Katz. Smiling to himself, Brognola slid another printed page from his file. "Included in the information we had dropped in our laps were some details concerning the existence of extremist cells operating within the U.S. There are reports processed from FBI field agents. They make scary reading.''

Brognola passed the data to Carl Lyons, Able Team's commander.

''Look into it, people. We need to find out if there's substance to those reports, and if there is do some digging. See if the suggested links to the Middle East factions are true.''

Lyons nodded. ''Anything else for us?''

''Not right now, guys,'' Price said. ''Come see me when you're ready to move out.''

Able Team left the War Room. They would find themselves a quiet place within the Annex facility where they could go over the data and plan their strategy.

''David, I want you, Gary and Rafael to go and see this man.'' He slid a photograph across the table. ''His name is Abu Talik. The man is a respected Kurdish Mullah. He was in Washington a couple of weeks ago, in secret talks with the President. His visit came after that abortive attack at Incirlik. The one claimed by the KHP.''

''They tried to blow up U.S. aircraft, didn't they?'' McCarter said.

Brognola nodded. ''Using stolen LAWs. They might have gotten away with it if they hadn't tripped alarms. Soon as they were spotted they made a fight. Still tried to take out aircraft but only hit a fuel bowser. One U.S. aircraft tech died and another suffered bad burns. When the military arrived at the launch spot they found two unused LAWs, one dead Kurd and some pamphlets inside the guy's tunic telling the world about the KHP and its aims.''

"And?"

"As far as Abu Talik is concerned, he knows nothing about this KHP. The group doesn't exist within the framework of known Kurdish political and or freedom fighter groups."

"Surely splinter groups exist within Islamic terrorism?" Price said. "Same as they do with, say, the IRA? Members who don't agree with general policy who go off and do their own thing."

"Not according to Abu Talik," Brognola explained. "The Kurds aren't that disparate. They tend to stay in touch. Follow the party line. And why hit U.S. targets? Okay, we could have done more to help them. On the other hand we haven't worked against them."

Katz raised his hand. "Maybe that's what motivates these people."

"In what way?"

"People who are ignored for the greater part, and who are nevertheless suffering at the hands of oppressive regimes, sometimes reach a point where they say enough is enough. Let's show these great powers what it feels like to hurt. To suffer like we suffer. They see the rest of the world going about its business, growing richer. Stronger. Enjoying life while they live in fear. The oppressed must get tired of living with their backs to the wall."

Brognola pondered the Israeli's words.

"This isn't the first act perpetrated by this so-called KHP. Information forwarded when the President handed this to us shows a number of attacks directed toward U.S. citizens and business interests. All in the Middle East, Turkey. Even Israel."

Hawkins scanned the documents scattered across the conference table.

"Why now? What's so significant about now?"

"Too many things happening to be a coincidence," Katz agreed. "There has to be some kind of agenda behind all this."

"Which is why I'm sending you guys out to look into it," Brognola said. "The President wants us to handle it because he feels there are too many interagency rivalries going on in the background."

"And maybe some covert interests at work," James suggested. "Wouldn't be the first time."

Brognola slumped back in his chair, running a big hand through his hair. "Here's where we hit one of our first snags. The NSA is doing some breast-beating because they say they have undercover people placed in sensitive areas. They are extremely reluctant to name names or even point in the general direction. It's the same old story. All in the national interest. You sometimes have to do A to protect B. If a few wrong people get hurt in the process it becomes a sustainable loss."

"Tell that to some poor bugger's wife when he gets offed on a business trip," McCarter said bitterly. "All that is a crock. Just excuses for lazy management."

"Or some guy trying to climb the ladder over anyone who gets in his way," Manning said.

"As far as we are concerned it just makes the job that much harder," Brognola said.

"What's the word on interagency cooperation?" McCarter asked.

"Until we receive word otherwise don't expect too much," Price said.

"The President wants us to handle this our way," Brognola explained. "He's looking into certain areas where he doesn't feel he's been getting the right answers from some agencies. Until he has that cleared up he wants to keep things separated. You'll get all the backup you need from us, with additional clout coming directly from the Man himself."

"Anything else we should know?" McCarter asked.

"I was saving the best for the end," the big Fed said. "The feelings are that if there's some kind of internecine flare-up in the Middle East, the U.S. is going to get dragged in. It's bound to happen. We have too many commitments. Alliances. Business interests. If the Islamic world starts hitting on one another, who knows where it might end up? Let's face it—there are a lot of nervous people and places out there. If the extremists gather enough support, we could have brushfires springing up across the whole damn area. Remember, too, that we have some sensitive states with fingers hanging over nuclear buttons. If somebody feels threatened, the big mushroom could be the finale to the whole thing."

"Mission briefs here," Price said, passing out folders to each man."

David McCarter scanned the printed sheets inside his folder, a smile playing across his lips as he absorbed the text.

"I've always liked Kurdistan."

"Send us a photograph," Brognola said. "You need to talk to Aaron before you leave. He's got a few items you might find useful."

"Hope he has return tickets in the package," McCarter said.

"What we need is some proof about this KHP. Do they exist, or is the whole thing just a scam put on to distract us. You'll link up with a group of Kurdish resistance fighters. Led by a guy named Hanif. They'll do what they can to help. Find out what's going on out there, David. But don't forget the Iraqis are liable to put in an appearance. If you tangle with them we could have a hell of a job pulling you out. If you need to kick ass to save your skins do what you have to do. KHP or not, the Iraqis are hunting the *peshmerga* on a regular basis."

"I get the message, Hal."

"Nice? The South of France?" Katz inquired as he spotted his destination.

"It's where Sharon wants to meet," Price said. "His intel suggests there could be some use in looking over that area."

"Fine by me," Manning said. "I could do with a little warm sun."

"Man, why not," Calvin James said. "I need to work on my tan."

Brognola stood. "Watch your backs out there, guys. This is starting out a little hazy around the edges, so you're going to have to pick up the pieces as you go."

Computer Room, The Annex

AARON KURTZMAN handed McCarter a book-size GPS unit. The Briton checked it out, making sure it was fully functional. Kurtzman watched him with a glint in his eyes.

"I wouldn't give it to you if it didn't work," he said, finally unable to keep silent.

"And if I took it without giving it the once-over, you'd chew my ass for that, too," McCarter replied without blinking an eye.

"Long as you use NRO radar maps you'll be able to locate yourself to within inches."

Kurtzman swung his wheelchair to his workstation and tapped away at his keyboard, bringing up a satellite picture.

The imagery, courtesy of satellite surveillance, was sharp and defined. The advanced digital cameras on board the military orbiter had been designed to give the best reproduction possible. Photographs obtained using the sophisticated equipment installed in the satellites were able to take close-up images of objects at ground level and enhance them to the point where it was hard to miss the finest detail. Providing the weather conditions were stable at the point of taking the photographs, there was little problem. Inclement weather conditions, where cloud cover and ground mist could interfere with the imagery, were the enemies of satellite surveillance. Despite the major advances in technology, nature could still hold the upper hand, sometimes rendering even the most expensive digital camera redundant.

Kurtzman had checked prevailing weather conditions, waiting for the clear point before he accessed the satellite and put the orbiting bird through its paces. As always, he achieved the optimum results for his people, refusing second-best, and had come up with superb shots.

"General area where you'll be meeting your guide. Pretty rough country out there. Mountainous area between Turkey and Iraq. Don't expect much except local Kurds and goatherds. No burger bar around the corner if you get hungry. Those people survive on goat meat and rice. On a good day you might get mutton."

"You taken up writing travel articles, Aaron?" Rafael Encizo asked.

"Just trying to provide you with as much data on your destination as I can," Kurtzman said. "I know you think we just sit here all day and night drinking coffee and watching movies over the Internet, but we sometimes do a little work."

"Cut it out, you guys," James said. "Anything you come up with is useful, Aaron."

Kurtzman clicked to more images.

"You could run into Iraqi patrols. See there. Couple of trucks and armed soldiers. I tracked them yesterday. They came up from Kirkuk, moving up this trail, and did a scouting run along these ridges and down through this valley." His finger traced the route. "Sometimes they use choppers."

"Those vehicles look like BMP personnel carriers," McCarter observed, peering at the screen. "They carry 73 mm cannons and light machine guns. They aren't fast and they have crappy armor. Crew of three, plus seven-man squad of troops."

"According to our intel," Huntington Wethers said from his workstation, "the Iraqis have a few T-72 class tanks in the mountain patrols."

He brought up a screen image of the Russian-built tank. Using the three-dimensional scan of his program, he was able to rotate and alter the image of the tank, giving the team a full view of the machine. Clicking keys, he moved in close, zooming in on the tank's weaponry, scrolling up text that described in detail the full complement of main armament as well as the secondary weapons. If necessary, he could have taken them inside the tank and shown them the controls and how to drive the thing.

"Wasn't that the one the Israelis took out in the '82 conflict?" Encizo asked.

Wethers nodded. "The Israelis were using the Merkava tank. The T-72s just couldn't match them. It's an easy tank to handle. Has a top speed of 50 mph, but has weaknesses in its armor. Firepower comes from a 125 mm gun, a 12.7 mm antiaircraft machine gun and a 7.62 mm coaxial machine gun."

"This gets to sound better all the time," James said. "They got Rambo as a backup man?"

"Hi, guys," Carmen Delahunt said as she entered the Computer Room. "Got you some new communications units."

"Be nice to have someone to talk to when it gets lonely and cold up there in the hills," McCarter replied.

"Digital radios," Kurtzman said, taking the units from Delahunt. "These will give you far better reception than anything you've used before. Good range, too. We've had fifteen miles out of them. Still good reception. No crackling or background fuzz. They'll work as handheld sat-com units for personal contact in controlled setups. When you fit a headset you've got your hands-free unit for combat situations."

McCarter weighed the compact transceiver, turning it over to examine the detail. The unit had few controls. It had the look of something that would be efficient without being complicated to use.

"No weight," he said. "Looks easy to operate."

McCarter passed the unit to James as the rest of the team gathered around.

Kurtzman handed over the lightweight headset with its curved microphone.

"Radio in your belt, headset on, you won't know you have it. But you'll pick up every word clear as day."

"Dolby stereo?" McCarter asked.

Kurtzman grinned. "You won't need it with these babies. Batteries will last for days. One in each radio and a spare for standby. I'll make sure they're fully charged before you guys leave."

"Pretty handy when you've got your hands full," Manning said.

"They have to be better than the old stuff," Hawkins observed.

"Any drawbacks?" James asked.

"As far as you guys are concerned, no. All I have to do is worry about the cost. We've been testing the things for the last month. Not one failure. Straight reception, even inside a metal structure. You won't get any interference. Haven't tried, but I'd bet these damn things would work underwater."

Kurtzman drew a second carton toward him.

"New cell phones if you need to phone home or when the hand units are out of range. Speed-dial number has been encrypted so you can access home at the press of a button." He held one up for them all to see. "These are the best we can get our hands on. They work on Tri-Band technology. Means you can call us from anywhere in the world. They can receive e-mail messages. We send and the phone lets you know there's a message waiting. All you do is access the e-mail menu and read the message. Connect to a laptop, and you can even send and receive faxes.''

''Bloody hell,'' McCarter said. ''Is there anything it doesn't have?''

Kurtzman smiled. ''A sense of humor.'' He handed over one of the phones for the men of Phoenix Force to inspect. ''I'll run a final check on all this stuff and have it ready when you guys are moving out. Let Able know I'll have the same for them.''

''What happens if we lose all this stuff?'' McCarter asked.

''It gets docked from your pay,'' Kurtzman said, keeping a straight face.

''Somebody else who doesn't have a sense of humor,'' McCarter said as he walked out.

ROSARIO BLANCANALES sat back, rubbing his eyes. He pushed the file away and poured a fresh mug of coffee.

''Too much,'' he said.

''What?'' Schwarz asked.

''Intel. Paperwork.''

Lyons nodded. ''Hate to admit it, Pol, but you're right.''

''Okay, ladies,'' Schwarz said, ''that's it for the sympathy. Now let's see what we have and get the hell out of here.''

Blancanales grinned. He took a swallow of coffee, tapping the pad in front of him.

''My money goes on this guy here. Mustapha Ashar. Iranian. Been in the U.S. for almost four years. For the past eight months he's been on the FBI list as a possible suspect in a smuggling racket. No proof. No evidence. But this case report from a field agent is strong on gut feeling.''

''How the hell do you figure that from a written report by an FBI suit?'' Lyons asked.

''Maybe my gut feeling.''

''Oh, great,'' Schwarz said. ''All the high-tech stuff that goes into compiling these files and we have to rely on Pol's motivational gut feeling.''

Lyons had picked up the report in question and scanned the data.

''This guy, Ashar. Seems to do a lot of traveling back and forth between the States and Canada. Why?''

''Appears he has family connections up there. Some uncle who lives in Ontario. Seems the guy isn't too well and Ashar goes to see him on a regular basis.''

''He been stopped at all?''

Blancanales checked further into the FBI report. ''A few times. Nothing was ever found. After the fourth time he threatened legal action against the cops. Apparently they received a letter from Ashar's lawyer a few days later accusing them of harassment, and if they didn't leave his client alone proceedings would follow.''

''Lawyer?''

''Some guy named Fariq. Egyptian born. Been here for most of his adult life. He has a practice in New York and an associate office in Toronto.''

''Anything known?''

''He's big on helping his Islamic brethren. Works on retainers from a number of Islamic groups.''

Lyons sat back. ''Okay, we'll look at this Ashar first. Could be he'll turn out to be free and clear. Pol, you want to have a word with the FBI agent who wrote the report? See what's at the back of his gut feeling.''

"FINISHED RUNNING these through a test program," Kissinger said, holding up the new night vision goggles. "Advanced technology incorporating infrared and light amplification. Standard NVGs work on a constant brightness level, and don't vary. Give the eyes a hard time trying to process what's coming in when you're moving from dark to lighter conditions. These new models monitor the light source input constantly, taking the strain off."

"Sounds good," Blancanales said, checking out the set Kissinger was holding.

"What's the power expectancy?" Hawkins asked.

"Fitted with a couple of AA batteries, it should give around thirty hours. The setup will allow a forty-degree view field, with a 25 cm-to-infinity focus spread."

"These must be the absolute top of the line," Calvin James said.

"There's a manual adjuster on the headpiece," Kissinger explained, pointing out the item. "You guys want to take them away, or should I mail them home?"

"Trot them out, chum," McCarter said. "And while I'm here, don't you have something for me?"

"Ready and waiting," Kissinger replied. He turned away and returned shortly with McCarter's beloved Browning Hi-Power.

McCarter had left the weapon with Kissinger for a thorough overhaul and to have the trigger pull reset. It had started to feel a little rough, according to the

Briton. Kissinger had stripped the pistol to its bare frame, replacing springs and working on the fittings until he had the weapon in pristine condition.

McCarter took the pistol, snapped in a clip of 9 mm rounds and walked down to the firing range where he spent the next half hour putting the Hi-Power through an exhaustive firing procedure.

"Well?" Kissinger finally asked.

McCarter had cleaned the Browning before he raised his eyes to meet Kissinger's stare.

"Bit of advice," he said. "Take this up as a living. You're bloody good, mate."

Kissinger grinned. He followed McCarter to the exit, handing him the new NVGs and armament.

"Take care out there," he said as McCarter left to rejoin the others who had already taken their gear.

McCARTER HAD the coordinates logged into the GPS unit. It would allow him to pinpoint their drop zone when they parachuted into the mountains. They would meet with Abu Talik, who would ask them to make contact with one of the genuine Kurdish resistance movements in Kurdistan. A U.S. Air Force plane would fly them from Incirlik and they would free-fall in. Their mission was covert with no prior warning except to their contact, named Hanif. He would take them in and it would be his input that would confirm or deny the existence of the so-called KHP.

"At least you'll be able to go in fully equipped," Price said. "You got everything you need from supply and armory?"

McCarter nodded.

"How soon do we ship out?" he asked.

Price glanced at the wall clock. "First thing in the morning," she said.

"Time to get married and put in for leave of sympathy?" McCarter asked.

"Not quite," Price said, grinning.

IT WAS THE SMALL details that bugged Aaron Kurtzman. The Stony Man computer expert, who also possessed a probing mind, had the capacity to see things others missed. It was no mystical quality. More due to dedication to his particular job. Kurtzman always looked beyond the first layer of any problem, searching for that small detail others ignored. And he usually found it.

In this case it was a security video from the air base at Incirlik, and a precise moment that had caught his eye the first time he saw it. Kurtzman had made no comment on the first showing, waiting to see if anyone else noticed what he had seen. There was no comment from anyone, so he assumed the moment had slipped by. After the briefings and the final meetings with the SOG operatives Kurtzman had retreated to his workstation, taking a quiet time when all the others were on a break to look again at the tape. When he had reached the particular point of interest he had paused the tape. Using the high-tech spec of his computer, Kurtzman had isolated the section of the image he wanted and had blown it up, sharpening the image as best he could. He spent some time reconfiguring the portion of the tape until he was satisfied he had the best image possible. Then he made high-quality copies, saved the enhanced image and went back to the original tape, rerunning the section again and again until he was absolutely sure he had it right before he took the next step.

Only then did Kurtzman start to make a number of telephone calls that took him late into the night. Even when all the others had been long gone Kurtzman was still working, kept awake by endless mugs of his infamous coffee. It was in the early hours of the next morning when Kurtzman took a break, sleeping for a few hours before returning to his workstation. He carried on with his own investigation while still directing the rest of the cyber team as they monitored and handled the other business of the Stony Man covert action teams now that they were in the field.

It was the evening of the second day when he called Brognola and Price, asking for a meet in the War Room where he had all his evidence ready and waiting for them.

"Something I picked up from the security videotape copy we received from Incirlik bugged me," Kurtzman explained, "so I worked on it. This is what I found."

He used a remote to run the tape on one of the big wall monitors, then sat back and waited until it reached and passed the section he knew off by heart. Brognola and Price said nothing. Kurtzman rewound and played the section again.

"Aaron, we give up," Price said. "We obviously missed the point."

Kurtzman grinned at her. "Okay, no more crowing."

He reran the tape, this time at slow speed, using his laser indicator to highlight the exact moment he wanted them to see.

"See it now?"

"Only thing I spotted were three small white flashes."

"Right," Kurtzman said. "That's exactly what I wanted you to see."

Brognola glanced across at Price. "He gets more like Jessica Fletcher in *Murder She Wrote* every damn day."

"The three flashes are from the muzzle of an autorifle. Three shots that killed the Kurd terrorist the military found after the abortive attack on the base."

"We know that," Brognola said. "How is it so important?"

"Because it proves that the dead man was no Kurdish terrorist. Or a KHP member. In fact I'd stake my reputation it goes to show that the KHP is nothing more than a scam."

Price looked from the screen to Kurtzman.

"This is going to be good. I can feel it."

Kurtzman nodded. He had their attention now, and before anyone could say more he explained his theory.

"The dead man has been identified as Omar Haquim, Kurdish national. According to information received, he was no extremist and an unlikely candidate for a reactionary group like the KHP. He was, by all accounts, a moderate."

"People change," Price said.

Kurtzman nodded. "Agreed. But if that's so, then this guy made the quickest conversion on record. Within a week he changes sides, vanishes for three days, then turns up dead at the site of a KHP raid on Incirlik."

Brognola shifted in his seat.

"Aaron, what is all this leading to?"

"I'm getting there. During the attack the U.S. personnel at Incirlik got off a fair number of rounds. They were firing blind for the most part. Remember it was dark during the attack. The only real light came from security lights around the perimeter, which the raiders stayed beyond range of. Okay?"

"So far."

"The setup wasn't best suited for world-class targeting, but when Haquim was found dead he'd been hit three times. All in the heart and in a tight grouping."

"So maybe they do have a marksman at the base," Price said.

Kurtzman wagged a finger at her.

"There were only three shooters involved from the U.S. side. They were all pretty adamant, when interviewed, that they had been surprised when they found out one of the terrorists had been taken out."

"Modesty?"

"Military types? I don't think so," Kurtzman replied. "Something wasn't gelling. So I did some checking and spoke to the doctor on the base at Incirlik. He took another look at the body and came up with a couple of unusual items."

Kurtzman tapped in instructions, and one of the other monitor screens burst into life. It showed a series of body shots of Haquim. Kurtzman used his laser pointer to indicate what he was trying to show.

"When the medic ran the additional checks he came up with this first. The three shots that killed Haquim were proximity wounds, fired from a range a lot less than they would have been if our boys on the other side of the fence had done it. Now look at this picture, a close-up of Haquim's wrists. See the faint marks in the flesh? Lesions left behind by cord bound around his wrists. Omar Haquim's wrists were bound together some time before he was killed. You can see the formations on the right and left surfaces where the wrists were crossed together. There are lesser lesions on his upper arms. His clothing would have reduced the impact on his flesh.''

''You certain about this, Aaron?'' Brognola asked, leaning forward now, his interest rising as he began to consider the implications of the findings.

''Yeah. I got the doc to put it on his computer and I downloaded it into my system. Then I spent some time digitally enhancing the images so I knew I wasn't seeing things. I also got him to agree to keep this to himself for the time being.''

''I take it there's more?'' Price asked.

''The best is yet to come. The bullets taken from Haquim, plus samples fired from all three M-16s used by our guys, were flown by Air Force jet to the UK. I'd already pulled some strings there, and they linked up with Scotland Yard's forensic department. Those Brits pulled out all the stops for me on this, Hal, so we need to send a big official thank-you letter. I had to use your name and influence to get this moving so you can chew me out later.''

Brognola grunted. ''Prove your point and you can have a cigar.''

''I had the Yard send me all their findings. Downloaded it and this is what we have.''

Kurtzman keyed in more photographs. They were shots of the various bullets, magnified and classified. The striations and grooving on each stood out clearly. Kurtzman's laser beam flicked from each set.

"We have the U.S.-fired bullets here. Against each one is an identical photo of the bullets taken from Haquim."

"They don't match?"

"No way. Whoever shot Omar Haquim, it wasn't one of our guys. He was shot with an M-16, sure enough, but not one belonging to anyone at Incirlik."

CHAPTER TWO

French Riviera

"Is the cloak and dagger necessary?" Yakov Katzenelenbogen asked.

Ben Sharon smiled. The Israeli Mossad agent, associated with Phoenix Force on a number of previous occasions, had always struck Katz as a no-nonsense type. This current guise, with Sharon constantly checking whether he was being watched, or perhaps even followed, puzzled Katz.

"If it wasn't needed, I wouldn't be doing it," he said.

"So what's the story?"

"You know about the information collected by Echelon? Our tie-in with U.S. intelligence agencies identified that we had been picking up similar themes via our own feedback from agents and suchlike."

Katz had to smile at the way Sharon referred to Mossad's methods as *suchlike*. The Israeli intelligence network was one of the most intricate and widespread in the world. There was little they didn't know about in one form or another.

"For some time we've been gathering data that

suggest the existence of a rogue Kurdish terrorist group called the KHP.''

''Kurdish Hope Party. Yes, we've heard of them.''

''And?''

Sharon watched closely, seeing nothing in the other's expression that might indicate he knew anything further. But Sharon also knew Katz well enough to know the experienced man would give nothing away unless he wanted to. He picked up his cup and drank some more of the rich coffee, biding his time while he studied Katz.

''Our analysis of the KHP suggests they don't really exist,'' Katz said finally, letting Sharon off the hook.

''Our feelings exactly. The only thing we do know is this group is claiming responsibility for a number of atrocities. Attacks against vulnerable targets that make for high profile results and maximum publicity.''

''So we assume the KHP is made up of non-Kurdish people? If so, what's the reason?''

''That's the piece we haven't been able to fit into the puzzle,'' Sharon admitted.

''I did some thinking about that on the flight over. Ben, why would you want to put the blame on someone for things they haven't done?''

''Revenge. To achieve some political gains.''

''Risky when you consider the repercussions in the area,'' Katz suggested. ''You only have to look at the recent past to understand how fragile the peace is.''

''Which is one of our main concerns. It wouldn't take much to send the whole of the Middle East up in flames.''

"Exactly," Katz said. "That's my theory."

"An all-out war? That's what this is all about? I think you'd better explain, Katz."

"It's only a theory. Remember that."

Sharon knew about Katz and his theories. The man carried a lifetime of knowledge and experience around with him. His long life had involved him in many and varied situations. He'd been in war himself and knew the price a man had to pay. And he knew people, their thought processes and the deep urges that drove them. His wisdom came from the heart of battle and the dissection of the human experience. Ben Sharon would have opted for one of Katz's theories over the spoutings of so-called think tanks any day.

"The Kurdish terrorist thing could be nothing more than a smoke screen, a false problem created to occupy our time while something far more serious is being organized."

"But what?"

"A grand scheme to destabilize the entire area. To goad nervous factions into aggression against one another."

"Who benefits from something like that? Apart from the arms dealers."

"If I was a cynical type I might say you've got your answer. I believe this goes deeper than profit. I'd take a guess and say an extreme group so deep into the philosophical morass of their own agenda that they believe, and I mean they truly do believe, that the only way to purify the Middle East is to set its people against one another in an all-out confrontation. A purging of the nonbelievers. The interlopers. The foreigners and the ones who have strayed from the path. They want to rid the region of anyone and everyone not of the true blood.''

"So they set this off by having a group of non-Kurds acting like maniacs? Killing and destroying just to set the first fires?''

"Nothing new, Ben. Deception. Trickery. Subterfuge. They all go hand in hand when it comes to creating an illusion. Something to draw the attention from the real trick going on right before their eyes. And at the same time it gives them some small victories to bolster their followers' ego.''

Sharon raised a hand and called the waiter across. He ordered fresh coffee for them both, and they waited in silence until the cups came, each deep in thought over the specter Katz had raised.

"The thing is you're most probably right,'' Sharon said. "I saw the signs but I didn't read them. What we need now is to identify the *real* terrorists.''

"Up to now they've stayed well in the background. It's helped that we haven't been looking for them. Our efforts have been on these *Kurds,* putting the blame on the nation as a whole instead of looking beyond to the real problem.''

"Someone out there really has it in for us,'' Sharon said.

"And if this thing really gets steam up we could all be in trouble,'' Katz said.

"I HAVE SOMETHING for you, by the way,'' Sharon said.

They were in Sharon's car, a dark-colored BMW, moving along the waterfront. The Mossad agent opened the glove box, took out a package and handed it to Katz.

Inside the wrapping was a shoulder rig holding a 9 mm 92-F Beretta. There were a couple of extra magazines, and when Katz checked he saw that the pistol already had a magazine in place.

"Am I going to need this?" Katz asked.

"Past history suggests yes," Sharon said. "By the way there are a couple more in the trunk for the others."

Katz nodded his thanks. They hadn't been able to bring weapons into France. The time frame hadn't given Stony Man the opportunity to arrange anything. However, Sharon had said he would provide what was needed.

"So who are we going to see?"

"His name is Alexi. He has an interesting background. Worked for the French in Algeria until a few years ago. Has connections with Mossad. Buys and sells information, among other things. Odd thing is for a wheeler-dealer is his honesty. He never plays tricks."

"Why the contact now?"

"He called me three days ago and said he wanted to see me about some Middle East information he had come across. That was all. He said he would get back to me, but he hasn't. Once I knew you were joining me I decided it was time to take the initiative and go to see him."

"Is he reliable?"

"He hasn't let me down before. I don't think he will this time."

"I hope not," Katz said.

"By the way, what are your friends driving?"

Katz had let Sharon know about Hawkins and

James. They had dropped him off so he could walk to his rendezvous with Sharon.

"White Citroën."

Sharon glanced in the rearview mirror and read out a license plate to Katz.

"That's them."

"Just the one car?"

Katz nodded.

They headed out of Nice, following the coast road for a while before turning inland. Sharon took a narrow road that led into the hills. He drove fast, but with an eye to the winding course of the road. Katz glanced in the mirror now and then, picking up the Citroën a couple of hundred yards behind them.

Out the corner of his eye he noticed that Sharon seemed to be slightly more nervous than he had been on previous occasions.

"Ben, why don't you tell me what's wrong?"

"Is it showing?"

"Yes, it is."

"Okay. I was certain I'd lost the tail that's been on me the past few days. Now I'm not so sure."

"So?"

"I don't want to be responsible for letting you walk into a problem."

"The day I worry about that I'll quit and settle down in an old folks' home," Katz said.

He fished the compact sat-com unit from his inner pocket and contacted Hawkins, who was carrying the other set.

"We might have a shadow on our tail. Keep your eyes open."

"Roger that."

"Feel better now?"

Sharon eased around a slow bend, then opened the throttle and sent the BMW surging up a steep section of the road. He swung in at a narrow entrance and up a short drive, pulling to a stop outside a single-story villa surrounded by lush, colorful vegetation. The villa, a sprawling, white-painted affair, stood on a high spot with views over the city and the placid sweep of the sea beyond.

"Nice spot," Katz commented as he and Sharon climbed from the car. The heady scent of flowers filled his nostrils. The sensation was almost overpowering.

As they approached the villa, Katz noticed that there was an open window at the front. Gauzy white curtains wafted through the opening, moving in the gentle, warm breeze that came off the surrounding high ground.

"Stay sharp," Katz said into the sat-com unit.

The Citroën had parked in the road outside the entrance to the villa. When Katz glanced over his shoulder he could see Hawkins lounging beside the parked car.

Sharon had almost reached the door to the villa.

"Ben," Katz warned.

Sharon looked over his shoulder at his companion. Katz had the Beretta in his left hand, the muzzle pointing down at his side.

"Cover me," he said, and Katz nodded.

The giveaway was the front door, which stood ajar. Sharon paused for a few moments, listening, but no sounds came from the interior other than the gentle tinkle of water. He recalled there was an ornamental fountain in the entrance hall. Sharon toed the door open, easing to the side as it swung wide.

Katz, standing to one side, was able to see inside. No movement. Not even a telltale shadow.

They went in quickly, each man breaking to opposite sides of the door, covering the hall. Nothing. Only the glittering spill of water in the fountain.

Then Katz noticed an overturned potted plant. Thick soil had spilled from the container across the floor, and the green leaves and bright flowers of the plant that had been in the pot had been crushed underfoot.

"Damn!" Sharon muttered as he moved deeper into the house, searching for any sign of Alexi.

They found him in the sunny lounge, sprawled faceup on a white rug that now had a dark spread of dried blood marring its pristine weave. The blood had come from the deep, curving gash in his throat. It was obvious from the condition of the body and the hard-dried blood that Alexi had been dead for a couple of days.

Katz knelt beside the body and checked it. He saw other marks on Alexi's body—knife cuts and burns on the man's chest and in his groin. There were also signs of hard blows to the ribs and face. The left cheek was distorted where the bone had been broken. Alexi hadn't died easily.

"Come on in, guys," Katz said into his com unit.

James and Hawkins joined them a minute later. They surveyed the grim scene without saying a word.

Sharon moved through the house.

"Let him go," Katz said. "He knows the place better than we do."

"You think this had anything to do with what we're here for?" Hawkins asked.

Katz stood, shrugging. "Hard to know at the moment," he said. "Someone like Alexi would have mixed with a lot of hard people. In his business it would be easy to upset any number of them. Let's remember he dealt in information—the kind people don't always want broadcast."

"Maybe his luck just ran out," James suggested.

Sharon returned to the lounge. "Whoever was here rifled through his files."

"And there's no way of knowing if they found what they wanted or not," Hawkins said.

"Are we treading on toes around here?" James asked. "Could be Alexi did have something he needed to tell us."

"Could explain your tail, Ben," Katz said.

"Just what I was thinking. And maybe they've been holding off until I met up with anyone else."

"Meaning us?" Hawkins said.

Sharon raised his shoulders in a gesture of apology.

"No need for that," Katz said. "We didn't take up this work because we wanted a soft option."

"By the way, what do I call you this time around?" Sharon asked James as he moved to shake his hand.

"Just call me Morris."

"And I'm Lee," Hawkins said.

They exited the villa and returned to their cars. Sharon turned the BMW around and set off toward Nice with the Citroën close behind.

BACK AT THE HOTEL where Phoenix Force had rooms, James opened the laptop he'd brought with him, plugged in the lead to the phone line and sent an e-mail to Stony Man. The message was short and without frills:

Contact made with Israeli companion's information source. He has expired. With prejudice. We are unharmed. Will contact when we have more to say.

"Ben?"

Sharon was standing at the open window, staring across the water. He turned at Katz's voice and took the drink the Israeli handed him.

"Thanks."

"Any thoughts?"

"Plenty. But not what you want to hear. The only thing I can come up with now is we could go talk to a guy called Nefu. He and Alexi go back a long way. He was one of the few people Alexi trusted. He might know what Alexi had been up to recently."

"It's better than standing around doing nothing," Hawkins said.

"This Nefu easy to find?" Katz asked.

"No, but I can get to him."

"Do you want us all to come along?"

"It would probably scare him off if he saw me with all this backup." Sharon thought for a moment. "Just you, Katz. But stay back until I call you in."

"Looks like you pair will have to find your own amusement for a while," Katz said.

"In Nice?" James said. "Gee, that's going to be a challenge."

"I'm sure you'll bear up," Katz said, smiling.

HAWKINS GLANCED at his watch.

"They should be arriving soon."

"T.J., relax and have another drink," James said.

They were sitting outside a busy café on the waterfront. The street was thronged with people. Boats drifted across the harbor. Others were moored, their occupants seated under awnings, taking in the sights as they sipped drinks.

"This is another world," Hawkins said.

"Enjoy it," James told him, "because it's as close as we'll ever get."

Hawkins smiled and picked up his glass.

ACROSS THE STREET two men, sitting in a red Audi, watched the Phoenix Force pair. One of the watchers fidgeted nervously, and his companion nudged him.

"Are you that eager to make your kill?"

"No. I feel exposed. For all we know the police could be watching us."

"Why should they? Tourists enjoying the scenery. Eyeing the pretty girls in their bikinis. The French may be idiots, but at least they understand about women."

"Those women are Satan's whores. They will burn in hell for their sins."

"No doubt. But it seems a shame not to appreciate what they show in the meantime."

"I would sooner die than touch them."

"Really? We are all going to die sooner or later. Why not enjoy our time in this life while we can?"

"Have you forgotten why we are here?"

"With you to remind me? No. I have not forgotten, my brother. Tonight we kill those two Americans. And our brothers will kill the two who have gone seeking Nefu. Despite my lustful thoughts I have not forgotten. The beauty of those women has not blinded me to my task.''

''CAL, YOU WANT to take a turn around the block?''

James nodded. The Phoenix Force warriors finished their drinks and left some money on the table. Together they strolled along the waterfront, then turned away from the water, wandering the narrow streets and enjoying the casual mood that drifted in with the warm breeze. Many shops were still open, doing a steady trade as the tourists spent their vacation money. For James and Hawkins it was a pleasant break from the norm. They seemed to spend most of their time chasing around the globe, taking on violent enemies intent on killing them. They were both aware that by the morning they might well be thrown back into the arena. In the meantime they decided to make the most of the lull.

Neither of them noticed the red Audi parked at the curb behind them. The two men who exited the vehicle were clad in light, casual clothing. They fell in behind the Phoenix Force commandos, staying in the jostling crowd until it began to thin out.

James and Hawkins realized they had walked away from the main tourist area and were on a quiet street with less than adequate lighting.

It was James who picked up the sound of footsteps behind them. He touched Hawkins's arm, warning his partner.

''I hear them, buddy.''

It was at that moment that the pace of the footsteps increased.

James and Hawkins turned in time to see two men closing in fast.

One had a slim knife in his left hand. The other held a thin wire garrote, and he lunged at James, trying to circle the Phoenix Force pro's neck with the deadly loop.

James ducked under the lunge, driving a solid punch into his attacker's lower stomach. He hit hard, putting all his muscle behind the blow. The attacker grunted, his breath exploding from his mouth in a hot gust. As he stumbled, trying to suck air back into his lungs, James sidestepped and came up behind the man. The tall black man snapped his left arm around his adversary's throat, simultaneously ramming his knee into the small of his back and applying pressure. The attacker felt the pain, became instantly aware of what was happening and began to struggle frantically. His arching did nothing to relieve the tension. James increased the pressure until the man let out a terrified half-scream, then spasmed as his spine snapped. Instantly a deadweight, the man slipped through James's hands and dropped to the ground.

In the seconds it took James to dispatch his would-be assassin, T. J. Hawkins had feinted to the inside of his attacker's knife slash. His right foot struck hard, slamming into the man's groin, crushing his testicles in an instant, engulfing the man's lower body with scalding pain. The knife man let out a shrill squeal. He was totally disoriented for a few seconds, and that was long enough for Hawkins to lock the knife wrist under his arm, trapping it at his side. Hawkins twisted, slammed the palm of his free hand up and under the man's jaw. The blow snapped the man's head back, his teeth shattering as his jaw smashed shut. Blood spurted from the suddenly slack mouth. Hawkins kept up the momentum. He locked his hands behind the guy's head and whipped it forward. There was a soft crunch as something snapped. The knife man sank to the ground and lay still.

"Wallets," James said.

They bent and went through the dead men's pockets, then eased into the shadows, tracing their way back to the waterfront.

James took out his sat-com unit and spoke to Katz.

"We just made contact. Two guys tried to take us out, one with a knife, the other had a garrote. These were no muggers. Stay cool, guys."

Once they were back with the crowds on the waterfront, James and Hawkins found themselves a spot where they could check out the wallets they had taken from their attackers.

"Plenty of cash money," Hawkins said. "Driver's license. This guy was Iranian. Address in Paris. Few business cards."

"Same here," James said. "But I also got this."

He held up a small, compact cell phone. The instrument was one of the state-of-the-art flip-open type. Once closed it was barely larger than a credit card.

"Think we can pull anything from it?"

James smiled.

"Won't be from lack of trying," he said.

In the distance, back the way they had walked, came the wail of police sirens. The French cops were moving in on the scene.

They found another café, sat at a table and ordered drinks while waiting for Katz to join them.

THEY HAD DRIVEN to a small village a few miles along the coast. It had retained its native appearance, shying away from the tourist trade as much as was possible. The man called Nefu lived in a former farmhouse on the outskirts.

It was full dark by the time they arrived.

"What exactly is this Nefu's line of business?" Katz asked, already anticipating the reply.

Sharon didn't disappoint him. "Nefu will trade in most things illegal, apparently. Except drugs."

"A crook with morals." Katz mused. "It's becoming the thing."

"And you get more cynical every time I see you."

Katz chuckled. "It comes with age and wisdom, my boy."

"Is that right? Hope I live long enough to gain that state of mind."

Sharon stopped the car a few hundred yards from the rambling old house. He switched off the engine, and he and Katz sat listening to the night sounds—insects, the rustling of small animals making their way back and forth through the grass and undergrowth.

"Nothing seems to have disturbed them," Katz said. "Maybe Nefu has avoided contact with the people who killed Alexi."

"Could be they were concentrating on your boys."

"Might be a good idea to make ourselves known to Nefu before a backup team shows," Katz suggested.

They left the car and walked to the house, weapons out and ready.

Soft light showed from the house, and music drifted from an open window. As Katz and Sharon reached the front door, the relaxed voice of a man reached them as he passed on the other side of the door. A woman's voice, young and full of laughter, answered him.

Sharon knocked.

The woman said something in French. The man replied. Then the door rattled as it was opened.

Nefu was tall and lean, his skin dark, long black hair thick against the collar of a cotton shirt. He held an open bottle of wine in his left hand, and though he appeared relaxed his right hand remained near his waist, fingers curled. Katz guessed he had a pistol tucked in the waist of his trousers. Sharon had put his weapon away as they approached, and so had Katz. Now the Mossad agent held out both his hands. He spoke in French.

"Good evening, Nefu. It is Sharon."

Nefu leaned forward until he was able to recognize the Israeli. He nodded, then glanced at Katz.

"This is Mr. Levi, a friend. Nefu, we need to talk. It is important."

The Algerian stepped back and invited them inside. He led the way to a large, low-ceilinged room filled with comfortable furniture, rugs strewed on the stone-flagged floor.

A slender, beautiful young woman, who wore her jet black hair to her waist, turned away from the radio she was listening to. Her smile was angelic.

Nefu introduced Sharon and Katz. The girl's name was Celine.

"Would you make coffee for us, please?" Nefu asked. "There is something I need to discuss with these gentlemen."

Celine nodded. "Of course. Excuse me," she said

and left the room, the perfume she wore remaining as a gentle reminder.

"So, Mr. Sharon, to what do I owe this visit?"

Sharon glanced at Katz. It was obvious that Nefu had no knowledge concerning Alexi's death.

"There is no way I can make this easy, Nefu. Alexi is dead. We went to see him earlier today and found his body. He had been killed, and not easily."

Nefu stared at him, shock visible in his eyes. He held out a hand as if seeking support, then turned and sat in a large leather armchair.

"When you say he did not die easily…?"

"It appeared that he had been beaten and someone had used a knife on him," Katz said gently.

Nefu digested the information. After a few moments he looked at Sharon. "I warned him not to deal with those damned Iranians. I said they were trouble. He wanted me to meet with them. Arrange to supply them with weapons. I told him no. Not after what I had heard."

Katz chose a chair close by Nefu.

"I did not know Alexi," he said, "but I share your loss. No one should need to die the way he did. I'm here with Ben because we are looking for the men who killed Alexi. It is possible they could be planning other deaths. Perhaps many. We would be grateful for any help you might be able to offer us."

Nefu's expression didn't change. He continued to study Katz closely, as if by etching the Israeli's image in his mind he could dissect it and look deeper.

"How did you lose the arm?" he asked.

"In the Six-Day war," Katz told him.

"And since then?"

"I have fought my enemies, and I have grown old doing it."

"And still you fight?"

"Only a little in the field now. I spend most of my time advising these days."

Nefu picked up glasses from a small table. He was still holding the bottle of wine. He offered the glasses to Katz and Sharon, then poured red wine for them.

"Nefu, what can you tell us about the people who wanted to trade with you?" Sharon asked.

"They made me nervous. There was something about them. In their words. The way they looked. They were very...extreme. Intense. Even the way they carried themselves. I met them twice. Each time I came away counting myself lucky to still be alive."

"Did they give you any indication who they were?" Katz asked.

"Nothing. They were extremely cautious."

"What where they looking for exactly?"

"Weapons, of course. But then they started to inquire about other things. Communication equipment. Cell phones. The most advanced available. Laptops. With the highest specification."

"How did you leave the negotiations?" Sharon asked.

"I told them I would need time to find out about the electronic equipment. I said I would get back to them. I wanted to stall them. Yesterday they phoned and said they needed to meet again."

"Did you arrange anything?"

"I told them I would meet with them in the hills above Nice."

"Were you going to keep that meeting?" Katz

asked. "From the way you talked I imagine it's not something you want to do."

Nefu drained his glass and poured himself some more.

"I'm no coward," he said, "but I'm not a fool, either. If I ignore these people, they could very well come looking for me. Now I know what happened to Alexi I'm damned sure they will."

Katz considered the situation.

"May I suggest something?"

"What?"

"What time is your meeting?"

"Eleven o'clock tomorrow morning. Why?"

"Are you going to meet them?"

"I have to. If only to try and get myself off the hook. I can tell them there is no way I can get the computers or phones fast enough to meet their deadline. The thing is, that's the truth."

"Ben will go along, stay out of sight as backup in case of problems. My team will be on hand, as well. If you will allow me, I will take Celine and get her out of the area. No point giving these people the chance to use her against you."

Nefu nodded. He saw the wisdom in Katz's words. When Celine arrived with the coffee he took her aside and explained the situation to her. She made little protest.

"Celine is going to pack some things," Nefu explained. He poured cups of the rich, aromatic coffee she had made. "Even when I use the same coffee grounds, in the same pot, I can never make it like she does." He smiled. "I am going to miss her."

Nefu went to find the woman, leaving Katz and Sharon alone.

"He's already decided he's lost her," Sharon said. "I think he's in over his head this time."

"We at least owe him the chance to get out in one piece."

"From the little I know of this group I'd hazard that isn't going to be as easy as it sounds."

"Ben, I want you to take my people along tomorrow. Let them help you. I'll be in touch as soon as I get Celine settled in a safe place."

"You watch your back," Sharon said. "These people could be watching this house right now. They might come after you and the girl."

Katz nodded, aware of the situation.

"Why the hell are they so jumpy?" Sharon asked. "First Alexi, then the pair going after your people tonight. What is it they need to keep under wraps?"

"Maybe we'll find out tomorrow."

THEY SAT in the airport coffee shop. Celine, dressed in a light gray suit, toyed with her spoon, constantly stirring her coffee.

"My friends will meet you at Heathrow. They know who you are and they will take care of you, Celine."

"I understand," she said. "Nefu told me from the start that something like this might happen one day. I suppose I should be grateful you showed up last night. If you hadn't..."

"I can't promise that we will be able to protect Nefu, as well. He must make his own decisions how to handle the situation. But he is trying to help us."

Celine looked away for a moment, her eyes betraying her feelings. When she turned back to look at Katz there was a shadow of regret in her expression

"I understand what you are saying. We always used to joke about something like this happening, but now that it has, it is not the same."

"I wish I could tell you different."

She placed a cool hand over Katz's. "No. You are honest and that is what I want. Thank you for that."

Celine's flight was announced a few minutes later. Katz walked her to the check-in desk and waited until she had boarded. He didn't fully relax until her plane was in the air. He located a pay phone and put through a credit-card call to his friends in London.

"The plane took off a few minutes ago. As far as I can tell, the girl wasn't followed. Fine. You have the flight number and arrival time? Good. I'll be in touch. Goodbye."

Katz left the airport building and hailed a cab to take him into Nice.

He sat back and tried to make some sense out of everything that had happened since his arrival in France. There had to be a logical reason for it all, something to justify the sudden eruption of violence coming from the shadowy group they had encountered. From small beginnings the affair was rapidly escalating, and annoyingly for Katz, he had yet to pin down the reason for it all. He hated unfinished puzzles. He preferred answers. Cold, clear explanations were far more acceptable than vagaries.

He still felt the Kurdish connection was little more than a teaser, something to occupy the interested agencies while something far more sinister went on in the background. The Kurds, according to the information being filtered through, were acting completely out of character. With luck McCarter's trip to Kurdistan would reveal exactly what was going on. If McCarter was pointed in the right direction he might separate the fact from the fantasy. Expose the reality of the situation.

But what reality?

Exactly where did the fantasy end and the real agenda begin?

Katz recalled Nefu's detail about the buyers asking for cell phones and laptops. Nefu had expressed surprise at the request. Those two items weren't usually found on the list of merchandise he was asked for. Katz's curiosity was aroused. He needed to know why the buyers wanted such high-tech equipment.

He stared out of the cab window, not really seeing the scenery go by. His mind was somewhere else. With James, Hawkins and Ben Sharon.

SHARON HAD A TRACKER fitted in his car. A small transmitter fixed under the rear of Nefu's car showed as a blip on the monitor unit. Hawkins watched the screen from his seat beside Sharon. James sat in the rear of the car, keeping an eye on the road behind them.

"I got him on-screen," Hawkins said. "Going south along the coast road. Let's go."

They had allowed Nefu to leave ahead of them, waiting a few minutes before they set off. Sharon accelerated and pulled onto the road, following in the wake of Nefu's Renault. Once he had closed the distance Sharon eased off the pedal, allowing the BMW to slow. He didn't want to get too close to the Renault in case Nefu was being watched. Using the tracking device made it easier. They could maintain observation of Nefu's vehicle without actually having it in their sight.

Thirty minutes later Hawkins called a halt. "He's stopped just short of a road that takes off across country."

Sharon pulled to the side of the road and waited for Hawkins to instruct him further.

"What's he doing?"

"Nothing. Just sitting there."

"And so are we," Sharon said. "Maybe he left the car. Moved on foot."

"Let's get in closer, then," James suggested.

Sharon drove until they reached the last curve in the road before Nefu's parked car. Easing off the road, the Israeli cut the engine. They climbed out of the vehicle and used the cover at the edge of the road, crouching behind the embankment and checking out Nefu's position. The man was leaning against the side of his vehicle, casually smoking a long, slender cigar.

"Hope he doesn't look too casual," Hawkins said.

"I hear a car," James stated.

Hawkins picked up the sound, too, then spotted a thin cloud of dust misting the air along the side road close to where Nefu had parked.

"Here they come."

A dark-colored BMW rolled into sight, driving slowly as it approached the junction with the main road. Nefu pushed away from the side of his vehicle and watched the approaching BMW. It came to a stop yards from Nefu. Dust drifted in a fine cloud, almost hanging motionless in the still air. Nefu stayed where he was. He expected the passengers in the BMW to come to him. For a while both sides played a waiting game. Then one of the BMW's rear doors opened and a man stepped out. He was tall, lean, dressed in a pale suit. The bright sunlight gleamed against his bald head as he adjusted the garish tie he wore. He moved away from the BMW, taking a few steps toward Nefu.

"They're talking. That's all I can tell you," Hawkins said. "These guys speak soft."

Without warning Nefu ended the conversation. He made sharp gestures with his arms. His voice rose as he yelled something to the man in the pale suit. It brought no reaction. The man simply smiled and backed away, holding his hands, palms out, in a gesture of acceptance. Or so it seemed. As he turned his back on Nefu, his right hand slipped under the folds of his coat. It came out holding a large autopistol. The man turned, raising the weapon.

Nefu had already moved to get in his car, so his back was partly toward the gunman. When the first shot was fired it caught Nefu under his left shoulder, angling in through his body and bursting out the wall of his chest. The impact of the heavy slug bounced Nefu off the side of the Renault. Blood spattered the gleaming paintwork and the tinted window glass.

The gunman stepped in close and delivered three more shots. Two to the body and the final one to the back of Nefu's skull, blowing his brains across the door of the car. Nefu, his body jerking in ungainly spasms, slithered to the ground. He hunched over in the dust, pressing against the rear wheel of the Renault. It had all happened in a few seconds of time. Too fast for anyone to stop it.

"Bastards!" Sharon swore, pushing to his feet, snatching his autopistol from under his jacket.

Hawkins and James followed close behind, clearing their weapons.

Sharon raised his pistol and lined up on Nefu's killer as the man, attracted by the Israeli's appearance, began to turn.

The first shot caught the man in the upper chest, Sharon's second and third following through and finding the man's heart. Knocked off balance by the impact, the guy went down hard, his body twisting in pain.

James and Hawkins tackled the car as the startled driver hit the pedal. The BMW fishtailed as the power spun the wheels.

One of the rear windows slid down, and the muzzle of an autorifle was poked through. The weapon was triggered instantly, a heavy stream of slugs cutting the air. The shooter dropped the muzzle, the next burst kicking up dirt as the slugs struck the ground ahead of the Phoenix Force pair.

Hawkins and James parted company. Each put his pistol on the car and triggered into the windows. Glass starred, then shattered. The driver jerked sideways as he caught a couple of shots that shattered his collarbone. Out of control, the BMW spun in a half circle. The rear doors swung open and figures tumbled out. Stumbling, trying to maintain their balance, they left themselves wide open.

James hit the guy on his side with a quick three-shot burst that put him down hard. The man on Hawkins's side of the BMW had Sharon in his sights. He didn't seem to be aware of Hawkins, giving the Phoenix Force pro a clear shot. The 9 mm slugs hammered into the guy's skull. He pitched facedown in the dust and lay still.

The BMW came to a sudden stop as it struck the front corner of Nefu's Renault.

The silence that followed the short, brutal confrontation was almost as startling as the sound of battle.

Sharon crossed over to kneel beside Nefu, checking him out, knowing before he did there was no hope. Nefu was dead.

Hawkins and James carried out similar examinations of the four men from the BMW. The driver was the only one still alive, but his life was ebbing away swiftly as blood pumped steadily from a severed artery.

The only thing they found in the BMW was a slim laptop. James lifted it from the rear seat.

"Could be useful. Maybe our people can pull something from it."

They checked the pockets of the BMW's passengers, checking their wallets, as well, and taking anything they thought might yield information. Then they returned to their own vehicle and left the scene, not wanting to be seen by any passing motorists. Sharon took them through the back roads, and they were outside the hotel in less than an hour.

"I'll call the police from a pay phone down the street," Sharon said. "At least Nefu will be taken care of. Then I need to talk to my people. I'll join you later."

James and Hawkins made their way up to their rooms. In James's room Hawkins opened the laptop, found a power cord in the case and plugged the computer in. While it booted up James called Stony Man, asking to speak to Kurtzman.

"Check out the case and see if there's a modem

link cable," Kurtzman instructed. "Yeah? Good. Connect the computer to the phone line and log on. After that you can leave it to me."

Hawkins unplugged the telephone and connected the computer modem cable to the socket. He logged on to the Internet and keyed in the Stony Man link. Once that was established he left it to Kurtzman and his cyber skills. There would likely be some kind of lock denying access to the files, but Kurtzman was no beginner. And he wouldn't quit until he had the data downloaded into the Stony Man information banks. In fact it took him less than an hour to crack the lockout. With the information safely in his electronic hands Kurtzman sent an e-mail to James and Hawkins, thanking them for the information and telling them what he could do with the redundant laptop. Hawkins smiled as he read the message. He shut down the connection and unplugged the computer.

Now it was down to Stony Man to decipher any information they might find in the downloaded files.

James and Hawkins took the belongings they had found on the BMW passengers and started to go through them.

They had barely got into the task when one of the sat-com units came on-line and Katz came through.

"I'm on my way back from the airport," he reported, "and it looks like I have just picked up company...."

CHAPTER THREE

Kurdistan

The high-altitude U.S. Air Force plane had already turned, heading back to Incirlik, before Phoenix Force landed. The only sound they made came from the soft rippling of their chute canopies. Once they had come together, gathering their parachutes and concealing them, McCarter used the GPS unit to establish their position.

"Spot on," he said.

They made a quick check of weapons and equipment. Clad in black jumpsuits, caps and boots, with backpacks holding extra equipment, the commandos were ready for whatever might confront them.

"Hope this Hanif is on time," Manning said.

"He will be," McCarter replied.

"He is!"

The voice came from the shadows, followed by a dark shape moving quickly to settle beside them.

The man was tall and lean, his brown face wreathed by a thick beard. Even in the semidark his eyes glittered with a fierce light. He wore thick, loose pants, and a wool shirt was secured at the waist by a broad leather belt. A well-worn long coat made of goatskin swept around him like a great cape. His head was covered by a loose turban. A curved knife was tucked into the belt he wore, and he carried an AK-74.

"I am Hanif." He turned to McCarter. "You are the English?"

"I'm Jones. This is Brown."

Manning nodded.

McCarter pointed at Encizo. "Green."

"Pah! Idiot names." Hanif banged his hand against McCarter's shoulder. "Come with me, English, and bring your friends Brown and Green."

The Kurdish *peshmerga* led them away from the LZ, moving with the agility of a mountain goat. He made no concessions to the three Phoenix Force warriors, assuming they were capable of keeping up with him as he darted from place to place, covering the treacherous mountain slopes at a fast pace.

They traveled for the next three hours, stopping only once. Hanif grinned as he watched his guests catching up, then quickly moved on again once they were close.

The sky was growing paler by the minute when Hanif finally led them along a dry, dusty streambed and through a tangle of thorny brush. On the other side was a clutter of tumbled rocks and boulders. The Kurd led them through a narrow defile, pushing deep into the rock face beyond, and after a few hundred yards it opened onto a semicircular basin.

They found themselves in a *peshmerga* camp, with a dozen of the robed, bearded fighters, men who spent their lives battling against their natural enemy—the Iraqis. They fought the soldiers of Saddam

Hussein, who hunted them day after day, hounding and harassing the fierce, proud warriors of Kurdistan. Ill-equipped, outnumbered and for the most part forgotten by the outside world, the Kurdish fighters refused to surrender to the Iraqi threat. They preferred a quick, honorable death in battle to a drawn-out agonizing one as captives of the invaders from Baghdad.

Hanif took them through the camp where small fire pits heated the food and water. There were no tents or lean-tos to shelter the *peshmerga* at night. They simply slept in their clothes, wrapped in blankets they carried with them. These men had no permanent camps. They were constantly on the move, refusing to establish comfortable dwellings that would be spotted from the air when the Iraqi helicopters flew over. The Kurds carried everything they needed with them, replenishing their ammunition and food whenever the occasion presented itself. They had organized supply lines, meeting places. And of course there were also the supplies they gained from dead enemies. Nothing was wasted out here in this inhospitable land.

"Here," Hanif said abruptly, pointing to places around one of the fires.

McCarter squatted on the stony ground, Manning and Encizo following suit.

"This is the life," Manning muttered under his breath.

"It's why I joined up," Encizo said, trying to find a reasonably comfortable spot.

"You blokes are always moaning about something," McCarter said, obviously enjoying himself.

"You see, that's his trouble," Manning said to

Encizo. "These Brits are all the same. Once they've seen *Lawrence of Arabia* they go native. Can't wait to pull on a robe and bed down with a camel."

"Wait until they bring you some goat stew." McCarter grinned.

Encizo tapped the side of his head. "Loco."

Hanif returned shortly, accompanied by two older men. They were dark, fierce warriors, with bandoliers of ammunition crisscrossed over their chests, heavy knives tucked behind the thick leather belts around their waists. Each carried a battered, well-used Kalashnikov. The weapons were laid across their knees when they sat down. One of the men, the elder of the two, stared directly into McCarter's eyes, fixing him with a stern look.

"Why did you not destroy Hussein when the opportunity presented itself?" he asked in clear English. "Why did the Allies end the war before they reached Baghdad?"

"I think they lacked the wisdom of the *peshmerga*. And there were too many reasons not to go on. I believe they were wrong. They should have removed that bloody madman and given the people of Iraq the chance to work their own destiny. But we will never know. Right or wrong we will never know."

"Hussein still wields power. He crushes any resistance. And still he kills the Kurdish nation." The old man leaned forward, the flames from the fire dancing across his face. "Why do Washington and London not help us? Can you answer that, English?"

McCarter shook his head. "I'm not a politician so I can't give you an answer. For myself I'm shamed by what they allow to happen to you."

The old man considered McCarter's words.

"Have you come to count our dead, English?"

"No. But I have come to put down this lie that says the Kurdish are attacking Western targets and killing our people."

"Would you blame us if we did?"

"I would understand why, but if I was sent to stop you that I would also understand."

The old man allowed a ghost of a smile to play across his seamed features. His only response to McCarter's reply was a soft grunt.

"You do not believe we are doing these things?"

McCarter shook his head. "Above everything I know the Kurdish people to be honorable. What has been happening isn't. We have come here to try to find out what lies behind the deceit."

The old man held his hands up in a gesture of frustration.

"What could we gain from attacking Western targets? Only your anger. And if we did not stop your bombers would come and wipe us out. Then you would have done Hussein's work for him."

"That is one hell of a point," Manning said. "Maybe it's not far from the truth. Someone out there causing mischief and laying it on the Kurdish people."

"There's another angle," Encizo said. "If enough of this goes on, the West might eventually get angry enough to step back and say okay, we've had it. Let Saddam deal with the Kurds. We'll stop giving him grief over it if it stops them hitting us."

"We are not a powerful nation," the old man said. "We have little in the way of money, or weapons." He held up his Kalashnikov. "We fight with these because we have nothing else. Hussein has an army.

Tanks, planes, rockets. The *peshmerga* have nothing but what we carry on our backs. What would be the gain to make enemies of the West? We fight Hussein because *he* is our enemy. We want nothing more than our own land. That is why we fight. That is why we will continue to fight. No matter how long it takes.''

Hanif produced battered tin mugs and poured generous helpings of coffee from a blackened pot standing in the embers of the fire. He handed them round to everyone, then sat back.

"Tomorrow, English, you will come with us and see how we fight our war. It will help you to understand why we fight. And why we must never give in.''

"THIS IS WHAT we wanted you to see,'' Hanif said. "This is one of the reasons we wage our war with Iraq.''

Below, moving along the dusty, rutted road, was a convoy of fuel tankers. They were flanked by outriders in smaller vehicles, open-backed and armed with heavy machine guns capable of a high cyclic rate of fire.

"These go through three, maybe four times a week. Through our territory into Turkey. There the oil is sold on the black market. These are your lawbreakers. We fight for our land. Our freedom. For recognition from the world. All we want is what belongs to us. Not to that thug Hussein. I still say you should have finished him during the Gulf War. Not stopped at the final moment and walked away.''

McCarter had no answer to that. He had expressed his feelings during the campfire session the night before. He still felt that the Allied war machine should have marched on up to Hussein's front door and kept on going. But his was one voice, it was his opinion, and he knew that the world didn't operate like that. The top brass had made their decision, rightly or wrongly, and everyone had to accept it. McCarter could understand Hanif's feelings. The world had deserted the Kurds on more than one occasion, so they had a right to be slightly aggressive over the matter. Despite the setbacks, the Kurds were still battling on, refusing to sit back and accept the seemingly inevitable. McCarter hoped they did win out eventually, because they deserved their peace. He wasn't too optimistic about it happening for some time yet, if ever. There was too much stacked against them, and the Iraqi dictator had a nasty habit of reaching out every so often and knocking them off their feet.

He lay now, alongside the Kurdish fighter, and watched the snaking convoy of vehicles as they progressed up a long, winding section of the road, flanked on either side by arid, dusty hills.

"Hussein is laughing all the way to the bank," Hanif said. "The sanctions laid down by the Americans and the UN mean nothing to him. He is selling oil to anyone who will buy it. What you see here is only a small part of his operation. Most of his production goes out from Basra, controlled by the Iranians. The whole operation is masterminded by Russian Mafia. They have the black market in their hands. There is no problem selling the oil. The world is hungry for it. And Hussein pockets the money then uses it to finance his wild schemes and buy the loyalty of his personal army."

"Iraq, Iran and the bloody Russians working together?'' McCarter shook his head. "The world's gone crazy.''

Hanif clenched a fist and banged it against the ground. McCarter glanced at him and saw a wild rage in the man's eyes.

"What is it, Hanif?''

"To my shame I have to also tell you that there are Kurds down there. Traitors who have sold their honor to those bastards. They allow the convoys to travel through our territory in exchange for money. So you see, English, some of what I told you last night was a lie. Some of my people walk beside the enemy.''

"Like I said. This is getting hard to believe.''

Hanif smiled, stroking his thick beard. "English, you are laughing at me. Are you thinking that I am a fool? A simple Kurd who knows nothing of the world?''

"What I'm actually thinking is you've got a better idea of what's going on around here than the whole of the bloody American and British security services.''

"That is because they are too far away while I am sitting on top of a hill watching it happen,'' Hanif said. "We had a man from some American agency here a few weeks ago. He came with his wallet full of money and his promises.'' Hanif spit in the dust. "Pah! He was an idiot. I believe he thought he was some kind of James Bond. Even when we showed him what was going on he behaved as if we were stupid. I did not like him or his companions. He treated us as if we were the strangers in our own land, and he told me we should stay away and do nothing. That this was not our business. *Not our busi-*

ness! Here we had Hussein's thugs delivering oil to some black market thug and this fool tells us to leave it alone. He said there were bigger things taking place and we were to stay away."

"How did your people take to that?"

"What would you have done, English?"

"Probably thrown him out of the bloody window."

"Unfortunately there was no window handy. So I had my men kick him out of the door."

McCarter smiled. He understood exactly how Hanif felt. Help from a foreign source was one thing. Aggressive interference from a foreign agency was something else. Whatever the agenda being pursued by the American agency, it had no bearing on Hanif's running battle with the terrorist force using his country as a staging post for some insidious scheme liable to involve the whole of the Middle East.

"When I tried to show him photographs of dead Kurdish civilians, woman and children, he brushed them aside. He called them acceptable losses. Casualties of war that *he* could live with." Hanif's face darkened with the anger still boiling inside. "*He* could live with it, English. He spoke as if those dead were nothing but specks of dust in the wind. My people. My flesh and my blood, English. Would he have been so willing to accept if those dead were American? If the killing had been on the streets of New York?"

"Might make him think differently."

"He asked me what I was going to do about the oil smugglers, but I refused to tell him."

"What *is* your answer, Hanif?"

"I have saved that until now," the Kurd replied.

"We have waited until the time was right." Hanif reached out and picked up the walkie-talkie he had been carrying with him. He spoke into it briefly, then turned to McCarter. "This is my answer, English."

McCarter heard the throaty whoosh of sound. Out of the corner of his eye he saw the thin trail of flame and pale smoke from a launched missile. It streaked down out of the rocks above the road. Seconds later it struck one of the oil tankers in the lead of the convoy. The tanker unit exploded in a burst of fire, expanding into a huge ball that swelled skyward. The heavy thump of the blast brought the convoy to a panicky halt. A number of vehicles hit the ones in front as drivers reacted slowly. The debris from the first strike was still in the air when more rockets were released, adding further chaos and destruction to the stalled trucks. Even if they had broken from the ranks there was nowhere to go. The road was narrow, flanked on either side by undulating, rock-strewed ground. The smaller vehicles carrying the machine guns began to sweep out from the main line of the convoy. They were able to maneuver across the bumpy ground, but although their gunners opened up, raking the high slopes with heavy fire, they were unable to pinpoint the attackers. The Kurds were well concealed and also able to move around behind the rock formations. They were on home ground here, and it gave them the edge.

Streams of heavy-caliber fire from the machine guns peppered the slopes and rocks. The continuous crackle of autofire was punctuated by more rockets. The screams of the injured rose above the gunfire. The convoy line was quickly being turned into one great blaze. The tankers became glowing skeletons of metal, even their tires burning away to the steel wheel rims. The drivers who were too slow at exiting their cabs were burned at the wheels of the vehicles.

With the convoy dealt with, the Kurdish missile men turned their attentions to the circling machine gunners. Three of the vehicles were hit in quick succession. Exploding ammunition added to the general mayhem as the vehicles blew apart.

The whole attack only lasted a few minutes. It didn't take long for the convoy to be reduced to a state of complete destruction. The solid thud of the missiles faded away and was replaced by the crackle of autoweapons as the Kurds began to pick off the convoy's handlers.

Hanif glanced across at McCarter. "Well, English, what do you think of my answer?"

"I think you got your message across."

Hanif grinned, his teeth white behind his dark beard. "Did I not, English? And we will do this to every convoy Hussein dares to send. If he wants to play games, then he can do it on our terms. Tell your people, English, that this is *our* war. Not the pretend game these KHP impostors play. Nor do we dance to the tune of American agencies."

One of the *peshmerga* crawled across to reach Hanif's side. He spoke to him rapidly. Hanif nodded, turning to McCarter.

"We have picked up Iraqi radio messages. They are calling in additional troops. And helicopters."

Hanif looked down on the scene of devastation. Vehicles still burned. Autofire was still being exchanged between the Kurds and the people in and around the convoy.

"We have what we came for," he said.

McCarter's keen ears had picked up a familiar sound.

"Hanif, I have a feeling you're going to get something extra."

The air pulsed with sound as a swooping shape came into view—a helicopter carrying the markings of the Iraqi military. The machine dropped suddenly, putting itself on a level with the Kurdish positions. Heavy machine guns opened up, the sweeping volley splintering rock and kicking up dust as the bullets whacked into the *peshmerga's* cover. Some of the bullets found human targets, spinning the stricken Kurds, bodies punctured and bleeding, clothing shredded.

"Another one," Manning yelled, indicating a second helicopter striking from the far side of the Kurdish positions.

Hanif, ignoring the spray of bullets, pushed to his feet and began to order his men back. The *peshmerga* retreated, firing as they went.

McCarter turned on his side and caught Manning and Encizo watching him.

"This is rock and a hard place time," the Canadian said. "Whichever way we go, those Iraqis will try for us."

"Tell me something I don't bloody well know," McCarter said. "Let's see if we can get the hell out before they do."

The Phoenix Force trio scrambled from the ridge, weapons ready as the dark shape of the helicopter loomed large. The pilot had brought the aircraft in as close to the ridge as he could, allowing his door gunner to get a clear shot.

The chatter of AK-74s broke through the beat of

the rotors. A hail of slugs clanged against the side of the helicopter, forcing the pilot to spin the machine out of range. The frustrated door gunner opened up, sweeping the ridge with heavy volleys.

"Come, English, and bring your friends," Hanif yelled, replacing the empty magazine in his Kalashnikov. "Those Iraqi dogs will be back."

The men of Phoenix Force followed the hardy band of *peshmerga* into the rugged tumble of rock and scraggy brush strewed across the landscape. There was little good cover for some distance, this slope of the barren hills being open and exposed.

McCarter, his admiration growing rapidly for the Kurdish fighters, watched as they made directly for the narrow defile that had brought them, via a long climb, to this high ground overlooking the convoy road.

Behind them the helicopter returned. The pilot, seeing that the Kurds had drawn away from the ridge, powered his machine in a shallow swoop, closing rapidly with the retreating enemy. His gunner angled his weapon around and fired ahead of the helicopter, bullets crackling against the rocky ground, creeping ever closer to the moving figures.

Manning and Encizo, close together as they ran, found the bursts coming too close for comfort.

"The hell with this!" the Canadian muttered and dropped to the ground. He lay hugging the earth as the chopper overflew him, then came up on one knee, his H&K snug against his shoulder. Manning aimed quickly, holding his moving target for a few seconds before stroking the trigger and sending a short burst of 9 mm slugs into the helicopter's tail rotor. The sharp clang of bullets against metal was followed by the thumping sound of the damaged blades running off-center. With the rotor damaged the pilot was suddenly flying an uncontrollable aircraft. He tried to correct but the damage had been done and the chopper began to arc in dizzying half-circles. With his head ruling his hands, the pilot put the helicopter down and cut the power once the machine was earthbound.

The crew scrambled out, weapons firing. Now they were on the Kurds' home ground and they were outnumbered. The pilot and the gunner went down in the first few seconds. The radio man threw his weapon on the ground and stuck his hands in the air.

Surrounded by *peshmerga,* the Iraqi searched for a friendly face. He found none. His hopes were dwindling fast when he saw three figures at the rear of the Kurds. They were dressed in military-style jumpsuits and carried better weapons than the Kurds. The Iraqi turned toward them.

Hanif stepped in front of the man, his face taut with the anger he carried for any Iraqi.

"Do not look at them. You are *my* prisoner. And in my court you know the penalty."

Hanif reached for his belt and pulled out a 9 mm Browning autopistol. He raised the gun and triggered two swift shots into the head of the Iraqi. The man went down, still kicking against the indignity of death, his blood splashing the ground.

Hanif turned, tucking the pistol behind his belt. He saw the Phoenix Force trio watching and crossed to where they stood.

"He was Iraqi. Our enemy." The *peshmerga* leader studied the three faces of the Westerners. "You do not approve?"

"It wasn't why we came, Hanif. This is your war. You wage it as you wish," McCarter said.

"Yes!" Impatience crowded the single exclamation. "But would you have done the same?"

"No. He would have been my prisoner."

"And you would have had to spend time looking after him so that no harm came to him. We do not have the luxury of such indulgence, English."

"He surrendered," Encizo said. "Didn't that give him rights?"

"Ah! So we are talking about rights? The rights allowed to the women and children who died in the Anfal. The ones Saddam Hussein wiped out with chemical weapons back in 1988. Who asked them whether they should live or die? No one. Did you see the pictures in magazines? I saw the real thing. How they died in agony. The young ones without having even lived part of their childhood. Every one of them who died was part of the Kurdish nation. They were denied even the right to die with dignity. And you ask should I give that Iraqi his life? These Iraqis have forced us to live like nomads. When they finished using the chemicals in 1988 they rounded up those who remained and killed them. Destroyed our villages so there was no trace left of whole communities. The survivors fled and were left to roam these mountains like a pack of stray dogs that the Iraqis might kill when they want. Do not ask again how we deal with the Iraqis. It will be something our worlds will never agree about."

The *peshmerga* had held back from their flight at the sight of the Iraqi helicopter coming down. Once the crew had been dealt with the Kurds climbed all over the chopper, stripping it of every usable item.

Weapons and ammunition were cleared from the cabin. The Kurds even freed the door-mounted machine gun and took it and its ammunition boxes with them.

"You see, English," Hanif said. "Nothing is wasted."

When the Kurds moved on, the helicopter was set alight by the simple expedient of fracturing the fuel line, allowing fuel to spill to the ground. When enough had been drained from the tanks the fuel was ignited and the flames rose to confine the helicopter in a ball of fire.

As the Kurds began to move into the defile, the chatter of rotors indicated the imminent arrival of a second helicopter. This one was larger, swinging over the lip of the ridge with ponderous slowness. It was a troop transport, and as it hovered above the ground, armed Iraqi soldiers jumped out and began to pursue the *peshmerga*. Once again the Phoenix Force commandos came under fire as the Iraqis started shooting in the direction of the Kurds.

"Get your people under cover, Hanif," McCarter yelled, dropping to a firing position just short of the defile, followed by his partners.

"How will...?" Hanif began to ask.

"Get the hell out of here, you bloody idiot," McCarter shouted.

Manning and Encizo dropped flat to the rocky ground, returning the Iraqi fire. Using steady aim-and-fire techniques, they cut a swath through the front group, dropping three and wounding two more. The Iraqi squad, not expecting such concentrated resistance, fell back, crowding the remaining troops from the helicopter.

McCarter used the diversion to free a couple of grenades from his webbing. He pulled the pins and released the levers, holding them for a few seconds before he lobbed the missiles at the Iraqis. They began to scatter, but the twin explosions still had the power to reach a number of them.

Alarmed by the sudden blasts, the pilot of the helicopter juggled the controls and began to lift the machine away. He ignored the yells from the grounded troops, swinging out from the ridge. A couple of Iraqis managed to scrambled inside before the helicopter distanced itself from the edge of the rocks. A third tried but didn't make it. He slipped over the edge of the ridge and fell out of sight, screaming briefly before his falling body hit the rocky slope.

McCarter turned his H&K on the aircraft, triggering short bursts that clanged against the outer skin and the canopy, starring the Plexiglas.

Discarding his H&K, Encizo added a pair of his grenades, causing more disruption to the remaining Iraqis. Following through, Manning set off smoke grenades that sent thick clouds of white rolling across the area.

The Phoenix Force team took the distraction to ease into the defile, moving quickly to catch up to Hanif and his group. Using the Kurds' intimate knowledge of the terrain, McCarter and company lost themselves in the inhospitable mountain landscape of Kurdistan.

THE KURDS TRAVELED far during the rest of the day and well into the night. As they tramped the treacherous mountain slopes with the ease and surefootedness of goats, the *peshmerga* talked about the attack on the convoy and the subsequent fight. Hanif, acting as a mobile translator, kept Phoenix Force informed on the details, relating with a grin every mention of the three Westerners who had scattered the Iraqis like chaff in the wind.

"They will talk about this for years," Hanif said. "How the three foreigners, led by the English, fought in battle alongside them. Do not be surprised if they ask you to marry their daughters. You would make good husbands. Not as good as a real Kurd, but I think they would tolerate that just for the honor."

McCarter chuckled at the thought.

"If the suggestion comes up, Hanif, explain to them that as honored as we would be, our work takes us to many corners of the world. It would not be fair to make any woman wait for us."

"English, are you not a politician in your country, because you have the silver tongue of such a creature?"

"Hey, he's seen through you there, *English,*" Encizo said.

Toward dawn they arrived at yet another of the *peshmerga* camps. Buried deep in a vast ravine where neither vehicles nor helicopters could penetrate, this base had been used for many years by the roving bands of fighters. After they had passed through the sentry posts, wending their way down into the dark and cold of the base, where vast overhangs created wide, open-fronted caverns, the Phoenix Force commandos were invited to share the warmth of fires shielded from prying eyes by the ceiling of soot-blackened rock.

Hanif brought them mugs and they dipped into a deep pot of bitter, scalding coffee. They were offered bowls of rice and hot, greasy goat stew. Without a moment of hesitation they ate the offered food, scooping it from the bowls with their fingers, grateful for the nourishment and acutely aware that the Kurds had divided their meager meal to include the newcomers.

McCarter held up his empty bowl to the assembled *peshmerga* and nodded his thanks.

"Hanif, tell them their hospitality is something we will always remember."

When Hanif spoke the words there was a murmur of appreciation from the group.

A little while later, as the Phoenix Force commandos relaxed, enjoying a second mug of coffee, a figure detached itself from the deep shadows at the rear of the cavern and crossed to join them. The robed figure squatted in the space between McCarter and Hanif, reaching out to fill his tin mug.

"So now you understand why this so-called KHP is nothing more than a device of troublemakers," the man said in English.

McCarter glanced at him as the man drew the folds of the robe from his face. He was no Kurd, despite the sun-browned skin of his face and the thick black beard.

"To save time I'll introduce myself. Lev Badr. Mossad. I know Ben Sharon well, and he speaks highly of you and your partners. Right now I wish I was in Nice with him and your one-armed friend."

Hanif smiled at the expression on McCarter's face. "For once you have no words, English."

"Not ones you'd like to hear," McCarter said.

He turned to Badr. "You want to explain what this is all about?"

Lev Badr had been working under cover in Kurdistan for almost three years. He was there to protect the interests of Israel, as well as gather and pass along any information liable to be of interest to any of the Western allies. Badr had a good knowledge of the area and the people. He lived and fought alongside the *peshmerga,* accepting the risks his presence brought. The intricacies of the Middle East, plus the changing allegiances and the political about-faces, meant there was always something bubbling away beneath the surface. Israel, a lone nation surrounded by many potential enemies, needed to have its finger on the pulse on a permanent basis. Things had a habit of changing very quickly, and Israel had to maintain its guard if it wanted to survive.

Badr had become aware of the KHP and had played a part in bringing it to the notice of interested parties. Linking this with the information gathered by Echelon, the decision was made to take action.

"What have you learned about this KHP?" Badr asked.

"Information reached us just when we were ready to leave Incirlik that the raid on the U.S. air base was set up to look like the Kurds had done it," McCarter said. "Our people found out that the dead man was shot by his own people, using an American M-16, to make it look as if the security at the air base had done it. It also looks as if the dead man was a plant, kidnapped and deliberately murdered."

Badr nodded slowly as he digested the information.

"Stranger and stranger," he said.

"Since we've been here, out with Hanif and his people, we understand how they feel. I don't believe for one minute they've been attacking Western targets. So that leaves the question why?''

''I've been doing some looking at the background to all this,'' Badr said, ''and I think I've found something that could explain a great deal. Supply bases being set up. But we need to move quickly.''

''How quickly is that?'' Encizo asked.

''We can get some sleep first,'' Badr said.

CHAPTER FOUR

New York

Dan Delacort was tall, spare, with a good-natured expression concealing a sharp mind. In all other respects he was the epitome of an FBI agent. Neat gray suit. Pressed white shirt and dark tie. His shoes were polished to a frighteningly high degree.

"Jesus," Blancanales muttered, "he makes me feel like a bum."

"Pol, you *are* a bum," Schwarz said.

Lyons ignored his partners and moved to meet Delacort. The team commander held out his badge wallet, showing the Justice Department credentials provided by Stony Man.

"I'm Kane," Lyons said. "My partners are Johnson and Craddock."

Delacort nodded. He didn't believe for a minute that these were the trio's real names, but he understood the need for security. His superiors had informed him about total cooperation, and Delacort saw no reason to ask questions.

The FBI agent took Lyons's outstretched hand.

"Good to meet you."

Lyons led him to the table and Delacort sat facing the men of Able Team.

"I've been instructed to accommodate you in any way I can," Delacort stated politely.

Blancanales gave a tight smile. "I bet that hurt."

Delacort glanced at him, held the man's stare, then grinned.

"You'll never know how much," he replied. Visibly relaxed, he asked, "So what can I tell you guys about Ashar?"

"Is he up to something we should know about?" Schwarz asked.

"I'm damn sure he is," Delacort said. "Trouble is, I don't have enough to move on. Not legally, and you know the way we have to operate."

"We don't have to worry about that," Lyons explained. "You understand?"

"As far as I need to. Can I speak off the record?"

"That's what we need."

"I don't believe he's working on his own. I figure he's part of a cell operating within the U.S."

"Any thoughts where they might be?" Lyons asked. "I know that's asking a lot."

"It's a reasonable question. To be truthful I have no idea. Ashar has little contact with anyone outside his working environment. He runs a small bookshop in Brooklyn. We've been watching him for weeks, monitoring his visitors. We ran a tap on his phone, but he doesn't use the damn thing except to order stock for the store. His main occupation out of work hours is taken up by his trips to see his *sick* relative in Canada."

"So if you don't have anything on the guy, hard

evidence, what makes you believe he's doing the business?''

Delacort leaned back, rubbing his jaw with a long finger.

"There's something about him that makes my skin crawl. Can't tell you what it is or put it down on paper. But I damn well know he's up to his ass in some kind of deal, and it scares the hell out of me.''

"What about your bosses?'' Schwarz asked. "What do they say?''

The FBI agent smiled wistfully. "Ever cautious, they just tell me to back off. I don't have probable cause. Ashar hasn't broken any laws. He doesn't openly consort with known or suspected individuals. So there isn't a thing we can do.''

Lyons glanced at his partners. It would have been easy to dismiss Delacort as an overzealous Fed, determined to prove his gut feeling was giving him better information than all the FBI machinery could. On the other hand the Stony Man operatives had played hunches themselves on many occasions. There was a lot to be said for instinctive reactions. Delacort had put his finger on the point when he'd said he was unable to explain why, or describe his determined stance as far as Ashar was concerned. Gut feeling had little to do with substance. It was something in the air, transmitted from the hunted to the hunter by a look, an attitude, even a gesture.

"Looks like they made you the Lone Ranger on this one,'' Blancanales said.

"You said it. At least he had Tonto to back his play.''

"We'll go and take a look at these guys,'' Lyons said. "See if you've read the signs right.''

"Sounds reasonable to me," Delacort said. He passed Lyons his card. "You need anything just call. Day or night."

"Okay," Lyons said. "Fill us in with everything you have on these people."

Delacort opened his briefcase and took out a manila file. He slipped a number of eight-by-ten blowups of surveillance photographs and passed them around.

"This is Ashar. The car he drives. Next up is Fariq, our lawyer friend. This guy has at least three cars. Shots of all of them for ID. Fariq's office in New York and the one in Canada. This is of a guy we have no name for at the moment. He began to show himself recently. Since he showed on the scene he's been visiting Fariq regularly. So what's unusual about that? I'll show you. He's also been seen in the company of one Mr. Mustapha Ashar. This was taken exactly a week ago in Central Park. Just two regular guys out for a stroll. The next day Mr. No Name took a flight to Canada to see Mr. Fariq. This one shows him going in to Fariq's Toronto office. Next one has them getting into Fariq's car and being driven back to the airport."

"Busy people," Blancanales said.

"You tracking this guy down?" Lyons asked.

"Yeah. His photo is being run through the system right now. Nothing yet."

"Could be in the country illegally," Blancanales said.

"That angle is being covered."

Delacort handed the photos to Lyons.

"All yours now," he said.

"Thanks for that."

THE STREET WAS deserted. The torrential downpour had driven pedestrians under cover. Cars still rolled by, trailing silver spray in their wake. Rain coursed down the fronts of buildings, splashed off awnings and swelled the drains to capacity. The storm had washed the litter off the sidewalks.

The small bookstore where Mustapha Ashar worked had all its lights turned on, even though it was early afternoon.

The men of Able Team, seated in a diner situated across the street from the store, were on their third coffee refill. Steam from behind the counter had misted the windows, and Blancanales used the sleeve of his leather jacket to clean a patch.

"If this guy is as unsociable as Delacort said, we could be here for a long time," Schwarz said.

"Don't remind me," Lyons muttered.

The big ex-LAPD cop was, as usual, getting restless. He hated sitting back, waiting. He preferred it when things happened. It was alien to his nature to sit and observe. He was an action freak, and having to curb his natural exuberance only made him bad company.

"What do you want to do? Go knock on his window and ask him to meet you at high noon?" Blancanales asked lightly.

Lyons scowled at him. "Gary Cooper had the right idea. Identify the bad guy and deal with him face-to-face."

"All we need is Gene Autry singing in the background," Schwarz said.

Lyons glanced at his watch. "If he stays to the end of his shift," he said, "it gives us four hours clear before he gets back to his apartment."

"You want to go and check it out?"

Lyons nodded at Schwarz.

"One of us stays here. If Ashar leaves, he can use his cell phone to alert us."

"Okay, I'll order the special and risk my health," Blancanales said.

"You are a hero, my man," Schwarz stated as he stood and followed Lyons out of the diner. "My buddy will pay," he added as he passed the counter.

THE APARTMENT was small, incredibly tidy and yielded a number of unexpected surprises. There was a corner of the main room where Ashar had arranged his area for prayer. In the same room, sparsely furnished, with a worn carpet covering the floor, Schwarz discovered an expensive laptop hidden under the couch. It was in a zipped soft case, concealed beneath the floorboards. Schwarz had spotted the hiding place when he had moved the couch as part of his room search. The floorboards had moved when he had stepped on them. Schwarz had pulled back the thin carpet and discovered that two of the boards had been cut so they could be lifted. He had raised the boards and found the computer lodged in the space beneath.

"Hey, look at this," he said.

Lyons joined him, and they inspected the laptop, not touching it until they had made certain there was no booby trap or alarm fitted. When they were sure, Schwarz gently eased the case out of the gap and carried it to a table standing under the apartment's window.

Schwarz examined the case again before he unzipped it and exposed the computer.

"If the guy has a computer like this why leave it at home?" Lyons asked. "If he hides it for safety, why not take it with him?"

Schwarz had raised the cover section of the laptop. He examined it again.

"If there is anything fitted as a safeguard I can't see it. It could be inside the damn machine. Activates when you switch on."

"Nothing we can check?" Lyons asked impatiently.

Schwarz shook his head. "Not until it's powered up and the program opened."

"Damn!"

Lyons was itching to get his hands on the computer. If it had been left to him, he would have switched on and downloaded all the data directly to Stony Man. He knew, though, that any tampering with the machine might be picked up by Ashar next time he operated it. If Delacort was correct and Ashar was part of some covert cell, realizing his computer had been breached might easily cause a shutdown of the cell. If that happened, there would be no chance of locating anyone else in the cell.

"There's something we can have checked," Schwarz said. "The serial number. Might give us a lead as to where it was bought."

Schwarz wrote down the model and serial number on the small label fixed to the rear of the case.

"Okay, put it back," Lyons said.

Schwarz put the laptop back in its case and returned it to its hiding place. He replaced the floorboards and the carpet. Easing the couch into its original position, Schwarz made sure there were no signs showing that the place had been disturbed.

They spent the next twenty minutes checking out the rest of the apartment. It revealed only one other interesting item—a 9 mm autopistol with two extra loaded magazines. Lyons found it when he checked the bathroom. The pistol, wrapped in plastic, was hidden in the water cistern of the toilet. He didn't remove the wrapped package. It was easy enough to identify the contents of the package even though it sat in the water. Lyons replaced the top of the cistern.

"Guy has a handgun hidden in the bathroom," Lyons told Schwarz when he returned to the living room.

"For a simple bookstore manager he has some unusual hobbies."

"Yeah? Simple bookstore manager, my ass," Lyons muttered. "Okay, let's get the hell out of here before he decides to come home over the rooftops and really scare us."

They left Ashar's apartment as they had entered, through the door, Lyons keeping an eye out while Schwarz used his lock pick to secure it. They made their way out of the building and crossed to where they had parked their car by the curb. Once they were inside the rental Lyons took the wheel while Schwarz called Blancanales on his cell phone.

"Finish your apple pie. We're on the way back for you."

"Make it fast. One more cup of coffee and I'll be able to fly home without a damn plane."

BLANCANALES SETTLED in the rear of the rental.

"What was the special like?" Schwarz asked.

"Everything but. You find anything interesting at the apartment?"

Schwarz explained what they had found.

"Maybe the guy is a porn freak. Has it all down-loaded on his laptop and keeps it hidden so his secret stays safe."

"What about the gun in the cistern?"

Blancanales shrugged. "He doesn't like cock-roaches? Maybe it isn't registered so he keeps it out of sight."

"You on his side or what?" Lyons asked.

"No. Just looking at the flip side of the coin."

"I think you're doing it to piss Carl off," Schwarz said.

Blancanales looked crestfallen. "Seen through my plan again. Hey, Carl, you're not pissed at me, are you?"

Lyons raised his eyes to stare at Blancanales through the rearview mirror.

"Oops! He is."

Still smiling to himself, Schwarz used his cell phone to call Stony Man. He connected with Kurtz-man and told him what they had found.

"The guy could have access codes, alarms or both set to register if an illegal user tried to get into it," Kurtzman said. "Give me the serial number and I'll run it through the system. See if we can come up with anything."

THEY DROVE IN SILENCE until they reached their hotel and went inside. In Lyons's room they considered their next move.

"So we've established this guy is definitely a suspect," Schwarz said. "Where do we go from here?"

"How about this relative he visits in Canada?"

Lyons suggested. "Maybe we should check that end."

"We still need to keep an eye on Ashar," Blancanales said.

"How about asking Delacort for a hand?" Schwarz said. "He's got the backup. We could ask Hal to get an okay for us."

Lyons nodded. "Let's do it."

Stony Man Farm

Carmen Delahunt watched the information flash onscreen. She checked it out, nodding in satisfaction as the data gave her exactly what she needed to know. She printed it off, then saved the data on disk.

"Hey, Barbara, I think we hit lucky here."

Barbara Price read the printout, smiling as she reached the best part.

"That is great," she said.

"I thought you'd like it."

"What do we have there?" Kurtzman asked.

"The laptop Able Team found in Ashar's apartment is part of a consignment stolen from a New Jersey warehouse three months ago. It was taken along with a dozen other laptops. According to the crime report filed by the New Jersey police, nothing else was taken, even though the warehouse was stacked up with computer equipment worth hundreds of thousands of dollars."

"Somebody had a shopping list," Akira Tokaido said.

"Anything else?" Kurtzman asked.

"Prints were taken at the scene. Nothing on file in the U.S. Carmen had them sent via the NJPD fingerprint division, and she ran a make through all our sources. British Secret Service, Interpol. Mossad.''

Brognola had entered the room quietly, a mug of coffee in his hand. He leaned against the wall, listening to his people.

''The Brits and Mossad both came up with a name and picture ID,'' Delahunt said. ''Our guy is Joseph Haruni. He's Lebanese. The Brits want him for questioning about a car bombing in Yemen about three years ago. Mossad want him for a number of terrorist acts in their region. According to information, Haruni is listed as extremely dangerous. He's not your run-of-the-mill terrorist, if they could ever be termed that. This guy is an extreme terrorist, dedicated to the point of being ultrafanatical. He has been linked to an organization every Western agency would like to pin down. This group is into one-hundred-percent pure Islam. The analysts term this as a desire to return to Islam as it was in the beginning. They want to sever all connections with the West, and they mean all connections. No Western influence at all. Business, cultural, financial. It all has to go. Any Islamic individual who has become part of another culture would be termed a betrayer of the faith.''

''This group makes the Taliban sound like pussycats,'' Price commented.

''The next question is what are these people doing in the U.S.A.?'' Brognola asked, including himself in the conversation for the first time.

''When I read the data,'' Delahunt said, ''that was the question I asked.''

''Is there anything on the group as a whole?'' the big Fed asked.

''Pretty vague,'' Delahunt said. ''They don't make

many claims about what they've done. That doesn't appear to be what they're about. Publicity isn't on their agenda, so pinning them down is difficult.''

''Unusual for a terrorist group not to want its deeds to be known,'' Price said.

''Reading between the lines,'' Delahunt said, ''this particular group is single-minded. They want Islam back on track. They don't have any connection with other terrorist cells and make no claims or demands.''

''The only other thing we need to know about them,'' Price said, ''is that this group is pretty international as far as the Middle East is concerned. It comprises rank and file from a number of Islamic countries.''

''Who runs this group?''

''He's something of a mystery. The data has him down as being Palestinian. His name is Falil. And that,'' Price said, ''is all she wrote.''

ACCORDING TO the information provided by Delacort, Ashar's uncle, Nasram Ghosh, lived on a farm in Ontario. The farm, according to the FBI data, was less than a model of efficiency. Ghosh reared chickens and raised some cereal crops. There wasn't much more to go on.

Able Team had plenty of time to digest the scant information on the flight to Canada. There were also the data from Stony Man based on what had come up from the serial number on the computer found in Ashar's apartment.

''All this from a serial number?'' Blancanales said, thumbing through the printed information.

"Good job we didn't find the guy's telephone book."

"At least it gives us some idea what we're up against," Schwarz said.

"And what exactly is that?" Blancanales asked. "Okay, so we have some unidentified terrorist group in the Middle East. Doesn't exactly give us intel on what they want here."

"Nothing good." Lyons said. "Come on, Pol, if these guys are on American soil you can bet they haven't come to take in the sights."

Blancanales scrubbed his hand across his face.

"Hey, don't listen to me, guys. I think I need a vacation."

"So don't fret, buddy," Schwarz said. "We're heading for Canada."

"Funny," Blancanales replied. What made it worse was Lyons chuckling at Schwarz's remark.

Ontario, Canada

THE CHARTER PLANE landed at a small local airfield about an hour's drive from the farm. The bright-eyed young woman at the airfield office handed over the keys to a dark sedan she had been holding for them. It had started to rain as the plane descended to the airfield. By the time Able had loaded their gear into the trunk of the car and started off along the highway, the rain was falling heavily.

Schwarz was driving, Lyons beside him. Blancanales had the rear seat all to himself, and he opened his map and checked out where the farm was.

"Keep heading north," he told Schwarz. "We need to go about thirty-five miles along here. Closer to the place there's a feeder road that heads into the country proper. The Ghosh place is six or seven miles in from the main highway.''

Wind began to bounce the rain off the car. Schwarz had the wipers going on high, but he was finding it hard to peer through the heavy downpour.

''Hey, there's a diner up ahead,'' Blancanales said. ''You guys want coffee or anything?''

''I'm fine,'' Schwarz told him.

''Me, too,'' Lyons agreed.

Blancanales grunted. ''Good thing I didn't need anything then,'' he muttered.

''Hey, Pol,'' Schwarz said.

''What?''

''There's a diner up ahead. You want coffee?''

''Or anything?'' Lyons added.

''Funny guys. Keep it up and I'll leave you in Canada and go home myself.''

Off road, the going was harder. The constant downpour had turned the feeder road into a muddy ribbon. Schwarz had to drive slowly, working the wheel as he felt the car backsliding every now and then as the tires lost traction on the mud.

They traveled for almost five miles before Schwarz eased the car into the shadows among a stand of trees and cut the engine. Blancanales climbed out to open the trunk. He brought the equipment cases, and Able Team prepared themselves for a soft probe. They shed some of their civilian clothing and pulled on camouflage fatigues. Combat webbing was donned, and onto the various hooks and clips went grenades—fragmentation and smoke—while into the zippered pockets went ammo clips for their handguns and the Uzi SMGs they were taking along. Each man had a razor-sharp knife tucked into a boot sheath.

They clipped their communications gear to their belts, fitting the headsets in place, and checked that the units worked.

They exited the car, pulling on baseball caps against the rain. Lyons took point, moving ahead, with Blancanales in the middle and Schwarz bringing up the rear. Conversation was kept to the minimum. They covered the distance to the farm perimeter in good time despite the soft terrain and the poor vision caused by the rain.

Nearing the fence boundary, they stopped to survey the spread of farm buildings. There was a scattering of machinery around the yard.

"Doesn't look like there's much going on," Blancanales commented.

Lyons had pulled a small pair of binoculars from his side pocket. They were compact but had strong magnification. He spent a few minutes scanning the area.

"Only movement I can see is inside the house. Lights on. People moving around. Nothing in any of the outbuildings. No. Wait a minute. Somebody's coming out of the big barn, carrying a rifle. And it isn't the kind you go hunting squirrels with."

Lyons turned to face his partners.

"That guy didn't look like any farmworker I ever saw. He handled himself more like a damn soldier."

Schwarz had taken the binoculars so he could take a look around himself. He checked out the farm and the surrounding terrain. His scanning paused, and he returned to a spot he had been looking at moments before.

"Hey, looks like we're not the only ones interested in the old homestead."

He handed the glasses to Lyons.

"Check out the barn. Go way left until you see that split fork tree. Got it? Now look beyond."

"What the hell?" Lyons muttered.

"It's either a surprise party, or we have a posse of the local law moving in," Schwarz said.

"I know we were supposed to be handling this back home," Schwarz said, "but somebody forgot to tell the Canadians."

"Shit!" Lyons snapped. "What the hell are they doing?"

"Probably the same as us, Carl," Blancanales said. "Just remember they're legal. We're not."

"Those guys bust in like SWAT, and we could have a war on our hands," Schwarz said.

"Hey, what's all this *we* business?" Blancanales asked. "This is recon. Remember?"

The rattle of autofire reached Able Team. Raised voices sounded from different locations, then more shooting added to the confusion.

Lyons snapped the glasses into position and started to scan the area. He made out armed figures moving back and forth, around the house, coming from beyond the farm perimeter. As both sides exchanged fire, Lyons was able to make out muzzle-flashes. He saw one man go down, but there was no way he could identify which side he belonged to.

The roar of an engine added to the noise. A battered panel truck careered out of the barn, slithering on the wet ground as the driver tried to maintain speed and control. He lost as far as control was concerned. Off to one side someone opened up with an autoweapon, peppering the side of the panel truck. The vehicle, still moving, blew apart as a solid explosion took place. A gigantic rolling ball of flame reached into the rainy sky, and debris from the truck was scattered in all directions. The stripped carcass of the truck rolled for a few feet before coming to a halt, flame and smoke still rising from it. Chunks of metal slammed to the ground around the burning wreck.

A number of figures went down, flailing in agony. More than one staggered around with clothing alight.

The rattle of gunfire went on for some time. Each side seemed to have found its place to stand, and cover for the combatants meant that the confrontation took on a static atmosphere.

The crash of window glass was followed by clouds of thick smoke issuing from the main building. A smoke grenade had been lobbed inside the farmhouse.

A door was flung open. Smoke billowed out, followed by armed figures, firing as they moved. The exchange of fire went on for a little while longer, then petered out. Silence fell across the battleground.

"Time we moved," Lyons snapped.

CHAPTER FIVE

Sanctuary

Falil had them now. He could see it in their faces. Each of them gave his full attention, put all other thoughts aside. Their world—their very universe—was Falil. His words enveloped them, cloaked them with rhetoric as powerful as anything in the Holy Book.

To an outsider Falil might not have made much of an impression. He spoke softly, measuring his words and pausing for effect, letting his audience digest each phrase to the fullest. Never once did he raise his voice. He didn't rant or make grand gestures. He never prepared his speeches. Each came directly from his heart.

His way was simple, but entirely effective. He sat before them and spoke. And his gathering drank in his words with reverence, as if the words had come from the lips of God himself.

Falil told them of the need for unity against their enemies. The time of Islam had come. They had the opportunity to strike.

"My brothers, the time is right. We of the faith

do not fear death because it is no more than a portal to the great life beyond. Our enemy is not worthy even of our contempt. He is without honor. Without purpose. He exists only to take and defile. His life has no meaning save his own aggrandizement. Wealth upon wealth. He lives on greed and creates sickness.

"We must strike, and as we strike against the followers of Satan, the time is upon us to do the same to those of our faith who are treading the path of the infidels. Those who have fallen into the pit created by the enemies of Islam, those who have taken his money, who look upon the corruption of the West and sip from its vile cup. They have tasted Satan's poison and now they look upon the world of God and question it. They desire to bring in new ways, diverting from the true path and allow the stench of the West to taint our air."

Falil paused, gazing around the upturned faces, and saw the glow of their awareness. He nodded slowly and went on.

"This must not be allowed to continue. If we fail to act we will be swallowed and consumed by the great Satan. But if we stand firm we will prevail. God will not desert us. He looks down upon us and sees the faithful. He will guide us and will prepare our way to paradise."

Falil held out his hands, inviting questions. A young man, bearded and in the robes of a cleric, leaned forward.

"How should we begin?"

"We have already begun, my son. God, in his wisdom, bade me to instruct our warrior brothers to make attacks on American targets. Small at first.

Here and there. Enough to make the Americans wonder. Then we staged the raid on the air base at Incirlik. This was twofold. To hinder the Americans and to strike at the traitor Turks who allow the great Satan to fly his planes from there to bomb our people.''

The young cleric had another question, but he was nervous about asking. Falil knew what it was and took the responsibility from the man.

"God willing, the Incirlik raid failed in its main purpose. No American aircraft were destroyed. However, a fuel truck was hit and we left two American casualties. Although we did not fully succeed, we must accept that time will reverse this setback.''

"One of our brothers died,'' the cleric said.

"Yes. A true believer who sacrificed his life for the cause. Yet in doing so he provided the Americans with evidence that the raid was the work of a Kurdish group calling itself the KHP.''

He didn't enlighten them about the circumstances that surrounded the death of the Kurd. At this time he had decided they didn't need to be burdened with the truth of that part of the raid. Suffice it to say it would prove to be something he might regret later, but at the moment Falil was content to let it rest.

"No one here has any knowledge of such a group,'' a man said.

Falil smiled, waving the general round of chatter to silence.

"Of course you have not heard of them,'' he explained. "It is because the KHP does not exist.''

Confusion showed on a number of faces. Falil calmed the murmurs.

"The Americans are easily fooled. They will see

the signs we have left for them and will simply follow the false trail. While they do this, we will be able to put our actual plan into operation. By the time the gullible American agencies have realized the truth, we will be ready and able to strike. Many American targets will be destroyed and lives lost. They will start to learn how it feels when the gutters run red with American blood. Let them see that even their beloved nation is not invincible. That the home of the great Satan can taste the smoke and fire of retribution.''

''And the other targets you talked about?'' someone asked.

''As the strikes against the Americans begin so will those against the traitors in our midst. At the head of the list will be the lair of the Zionist trespassers. The time has come also for the Israeli puppets to dance to a different tune than the one the American piper plays. And then will follow those of the faith who make a mockery of it.''

''A word of caution,'' a scar-faced man said. He wore black, flowing robes, and as he stood to speak he rested on a walking stick. ''Justice against our own traitors may cost us dear. We could see the region in flames if the price becomes too high.''

''Do not believe I have not thought of the consequences,'' Falil said. ''But to regain what is rightfully ours, to return to the word of the great book, we must rid ourselves of the weak and the corrupt. I would be happy if I had to return to the desert and live in a tent, secure that I was living the way God had decreed. I would willingly burn every oil well and abandon the capricious nature of the life we now lead if it meant a return to the real meaning of God's word.

"To gain what is in reach we must be prepared to risk everything. My brothers, we can do this. The Americans could not. Without their automobiles and their television sets and their vast supermarkets they would perish quickly. We are a warrior people. We came from the desert. We ruled the desert and the world admired us. Now they see us as providers of the oil the West needs to survive. Strange people who wear robes and ride camels. This is no longer a state we can tolerate. If it requires that we fight to the death, so be it. This time had to come. If we look into our hearts we know it to be so."

Once again Falil let his words do his bidding. He waited just long enough before he spoke.

"My brothers, we stand on the brink of a great abyss. Do we simply wait until it opens wide and swallows us? Or do we unsheathe our swords and challenge whatever lies at its darkened depths? Here, now, I pledge myself to take that challenge. But I need the strength and the courage of my beloved brothers beside me. Will you offer me your hands?"

Falil knew their response before they uttered it. He listened to their uniform cheers and he felt a tear of pride in his eyes.

They came forward, pressing their hands to his. They murmured their thanks and gave him their support.

"God is great!"

The exultation was repeated over and over.

Falil nodded and smiled, thanked his brothers and joined their prayers.

LATER, AS HE SAT alone in the silent, cool room, his mind filled with the details of what lay ahead, he realized that if everything came to pass as planned, then there could very well be a new era for the Islamic nations, a time of fulfillment, of rebuilding and planning. A world that should have existed long ago.

First the enemy had to be defeated, driven out of the Islamic nations and back to his own shores. If that was achieved and the inner decay removed, then there might very well be a twenty-first-century Islam.

Falil cleared his thoughts. Before any of that would have to come the struggle. It would be hard-fought, long and bloody, but no victory came without cost. What lay ahead would require skill and courage. There could be no hesitation. Actions would have to be swift, decisive, The time had come for extreme measures, a cleansing flame of true Justice.

THE TWO Iranians faced him across the plain wooden desk, their faces mirroring the concern in their hearts.

"Six dead in France," the spokesman said. "All from our group. Murdered by Mossad and their henchmen."

"Connections?"

"Both dead. Killed by our people before they themselves died. "

"So there is no one left who can link us to this matter?"

The Iranian was shocked. "I would consider the deaths of our brothers to be our prime concern. What are we supposed to do? Brush them aside?"

Falil raised a hand. "Of course not. I meant no disrespect. But we must look at the practical considerations. Your people were negotiating with the Algerians in Nice not only for weapons, but for computer equipment and electronics. An unusual request when you look at who we were dealing with. I hope they did not pass too much of that information to others.''

''I feel safe in the knowledge that our brothers handled everything before time elapsed,'' the Iranian said. ''This is becoming an expensive matter.''

''Yes. And where our brothers are concerned they have paid the highest price. For this I will never forget them. They will be remembered as martyrs to our cause. Brothers who sacrificed their lives for the continuation of Islam.''

There was a protracted silence, Falil sitting with his head bowed, the Iranians following his devotions and waiting until he spoke again.

''Arrange for the names of their families to be sent to me. They will be cared for as befits the relatives of brothers who have given their lives.

''Now, do you understand the next phase of the operation? What is required from all of you in the coming days? If there is anything you need, ask for it. Nothing must be left to chance.''

''What about the equipment we failed to purchase in France?''

''That has already been taken care of. There are always backup plans ready to be utilized. The moment we were informed about the unfortunate occurrence in Nice, the second team was activated, and the matter is well in hand.''

The Iranians asked more questions, and Falil answered them with his stoic calm, allaying their fears and offering once again heartfelt words of recognition for the losses.

After the Iranians had left he sat back and considered the next phase of the operation. His mind had moved beyond concerns over mundane matters. The discovery of the French cell was unfortunate. It wasn't catastrophic. Neither the world nor their long-term planning would be devastated. The Iranians were bemoaning the loss of six members from their group. They would need to understand they could lose even more before the strategy began to take full effect.

Falil had accepted there would be many deaths in the coming weeks and months. Despite planning and careful preparations there would be losses. A war, no matter how big or small, would create loss on both sides of the conflict. Anyone who expected otherwise was a fool.

What mattered in the end was who emerged victorious. In Falil's eyes that had to be Islam.

Their judgment as to the cost and how that victory took shape differed widely from the Americans, for example. The U.S.A. saw victory as the defeat and surrender of the enemy, his material world crippled and his capacity to reform erased. The Islamic victory could still be won even though much of their land became barren and standards were lowered. For centuries the Islamic countries had, by choice in may cases, seemingly faltered in advancement. That was because the Americans saw progress in terms of wealth and property and superior weaponry. Islam was based upon its religious propriety. A man could be wealthy in his faith, despite living in a crude dwelling in a harsh land. The gathering of personal riches and status wasn't overly important to the world of Islam. If civilization as the West defined it crumbled, the faithful of Islam would remain as they had for decades—a society of people rich in their faith, able to move about and gain what they could from the land, disdainful of the false trappings the West held so dear. Electronic devices such as television and refrigerators, expensive clothes and great automobiles, these had been denied to millions of the faith, yet they bore their lives with pride and held on to what they truly believed would be their reward in the afterlife. How could a people such as these be defeated by cultures that concerned themselves with the superficial? What did the lack of a neighborhood fast-food restaurant weigh against the simple desires of an Islamic villager who only wanted to serve God?

The fight they would wage against their satanic foes would be as a breath of wind across the desert. Islam could wage this war for years, taking it directly to the West, slowly eroding their security. Striking here and there, moving on, striking again, taking away the smug feelings of a fat and lazy society that had little moral strength for such a drawn-out conflict.

Within the country there were already disparate groups who isolated themselves, standing alone against the dictates of the federal government. They called themselves survivalists. True Americans. They hoarded weapons and supplies and existed in lonely places throughout the vast country, waiting for the day when the reigning power base began to crumble. The fragmentation of America, initiated by Falil and his cells, could help to initiate the start of internal conflict. The isolationists would see this as the beginning of the end and might initiate their own resistance against a government that allowed such things to happen. There were no guarantees this would follow. But if Falil and his force continued their attacks on a permanent basis, shredding the security of Americans within their own borders, who could tell what might take place over the long term. Added to that would be the internal battle, fought against the betrayers of Islam. The wavering regimes who pandered to their Western masters. They were guilty of weakening the structure of Islam and damaging the faith of those they ruled. In some ways they were a worse enemy than the West, defiling the good name of Islam for their own ends, steering the faithful from the right path. Their day of reckoning was coming. It would be hard and it would be final, clearing the way for Islam to become pure again.

The Holy War—the jihad—they were soon to wage wouldn't be fought on a grand scale across a vast battlefield. No, this would be a war of erosion, carried out by small groups who would strike and hide, then strike again. This way they would be able to create unrest and chaos. Bring fear into the very homes of the American masses. Allow them to experience the shock and the mental desolation when they saw stricken communities and shattered families. It would give the complacent Americans a taste of the sheer horror that followed the destruction of their homes and businesses.

Falil's cells operating in America, small and well-equipped, would move from place to place, working to a laid-down plan of action. They would strike at communities all across the American continent, not just the big cities where the local authorities were aware of terrorist activities. Even these were still open to attack as the Americans still found it difficult to defend themselves from isolated terrorist incidents. The opening phase of the operation would involve as many as twenty devices being set and detonated in widely differing locations across the continent. Falil had yet to decide on the targets. They would be smaller locations, and as such wouldn't be expecting anything. The devices would be placed, primed and detonated all at the same time. By the time this occurred Falil's people would have long been gone from the locations.

The effect would leave the country reeling from the death and destruction, the authorities shocked by the events. Medical services would be swamped with emergencies, and across the country the unthinkable would have become reality.

America's impregnable status would cease to exist. The most powerful nation on Earth would be as vulnerable as the lowliest village in the Middle East.

And it would be only the beginning. Within days a larger target would be hit. This time with something far worse than high explosive. New York would suffer the effects of a deadly bacteriological weapon that would leave thousands dead. It would demonstrate that no matter how powerful the Americans imagined they were, in reality they were vulnerable. An ultramodern military couldn't combat the flexible, near-invisible small terrorist cell. A single man, armed with a small bioweapon, had the advantage of anonymity, the freedom to move among the population and deploy his weapon where and when he desired. That was the key. And it would be that which would ultimately defeat the Americans, and any other target Falil chose.

Falil drew his laptop across the desk, keyed in his

code and opened the program. On the screen was his cell deployment and timetable of events. He read through the sequences slowly, making adjustments here and there. He still wasn't happy with some of the key elements. He spent the next couple of hours working on the layout, absorbed in his task as he made certain that nothing had been overlooked. This initial demonstration of Islamic solidarity had to perform to the letter. There was no margin for error. Once he had the current changes completed he saved the information on a disk, made a second copy for safety and removed it from the computer. Both disks were placed in a safe set into the floor of his office.

Toward the end of the session he logged on to the communications modem and e-mailed a simple message to each of the cell leaders in the U.S.A. and throughout the Middle East, then waited patiently until they had all acknowledged his communication. The cyber connection was most important to the whole enterprise. Through it Falil could issue his instructions quickly and to everyone at the same time. This meant he had total control over the entire cell network, and they were all in a position to act in unity at his command. He still needed additional computers to equip more of his people. Once he had them and they were distributed, the operation could go ahead.

Again the flexibility of his conceived plan was in its time phase. Falil wasn't working to a predetermined commencement. He wouldn't initiate his full strike until he was satisfied that everything was just right. His people had been instructed in this manner. Patience would have its own reward, because when they did strike the effect would be catastrophic. Like a falling arrangement of dominos, one press of a computer button would topple all the others. One by one, slowly at first, but with increasing speed, they would all fall.

When all the replies had been received Falil logged off and shut down his laptop. He closed the machine and sat for a while, simply gazing at the machine. So much knowledge contained in such a small item. The data stored in the machine and on the disks he had removed would be responsible for setting in motion the greatest strike of the Islamic front. The technological creation of the West would be used against them. Falil smiled at that.

It was somehow very just in its irony, he thought.

FALIL REMAINED at his desk, suddenly bowing his head as pain began to pulse inside his skull. He had been aware of the dull ache coming on slowly but had chosen to ignore it while he worked. His concentration helped him bear the increasing pressure, but once he ceased and sat back the severe ache increased its intensity. As the minutes passed the pain grew stronger, as it always did, and soon he was almost incapable of coherent thought.

It had been almost a week since the pain had plagued him. His schedule had been so full, every hour of the day and night taken up by the ever-increasing responsibility he shouldered, that any sign of the headaches had been pushed aside. Always, though, he knew the agony would return. It was something he tried to ignore, to push to the very back of his mind, hoping that the last attack would be that—the last. He was only fooling himself. The headaches always returned, and each time their in-

tensity increased. There was little he could do to escape them. Medication did little once a headache had
established itself fully. Sometimes if he took the tab-
lets he had been given by the doctor in Lebanon, the
pain would subside. Mostly he had to endure the
hours of raging depression when the pain was so
great he would have gladly struck his head against a
wall to make it stop. When those times were upon
him he would, if possible, excuse himself from any
business and retire to his rooms, using the excuse
that he needed time for prayer and solitary contem-
plation. Such was the devotion he was held in by his
followers that they bent to his will without question.
Not that any of them would ever have questioned
anything Falil demanded of them.

He was held in great reverence by all who came
into contact with him. His humble manner and his
total devotion to God and the word of the Koran,
which he never reminded them of, was the power he
wielded. His complete and unshakable faith couldn't
be challenged. In the eyes of his followers Falil
proved the greatness of God, the truth of God's word
and the absolute and unquestioning certainty of paradise yet to come.

Falil pushed to his feet, gripping the edge of the
desk until he felt confident enough to stand. He
crossed to the door and secured it. For a time he had
to press himself against the cool wall as wave after
wave of pain filled his head. It felt as if it might
burst. He raised his hands and pressed his palms
against the sides of his skull. Tears of pain filled his
blurred eyes. He moved slowly away from the wall
and crossed the office, pushing open the door to his
private room.

It was unadorned, plain, furnished only with a single bed. He shed his robes and kaffiyeh, letting them fall to the floor as he limped to the bed, dragging his crippled leg. Normally he was able to cope with the badly stiffened limb. Yet when his head pained him, as it did now, the crippled leg became awkward and he found himself experiencing difficulty when he walked.

He fell across the bed, his head striking the pillow. Even the cool feel of the cloth beneath him failed to ease the pain. He lay, eyes closed, trying to rest. Sleep evaded him. Sometimes when he lay down and breathed slowly and evenly, the pain would subside. This time nothing relieved his torment. Falil opened his eyes and stared at the white ceiling. Shadows from the slatted window played across the smooth surface, intricate patterns of dark and light, intertwining in strange shapes. He concentrated on them, wondering in his pained state if they were real or imaginary.

Falil didn't know how long he lay there, praying silently for God to ease his pain. Many times he had asked the question whether the headaches were a punishment. Perhaps the work he was doing in the name of God wasn't enough, or his efforts left much to be desired. If that was so, and he had asked this before, all God had to do was send him a sign. Give him the words and the strength to do more. But nothing ever answered his questions, so he knew that he had to bear the pain. It was his burden, and he would carry it alone.

There were times when he considered that part of his life. The fact that by choice he was alone. Even in a crowded assembly of his followers he was solitary, unapproachable. It was self-inflicted. He had created the image of self-sufficiency as a way of showing his strength in his faith. When he was crowded by matters that filled his days it remained in the background. Yet there were times when he was on his own, self-imposed isolation his only companion, that he looked about him and wondered how it would be if there was someone at his side. Someone who would sit with him. To comfort him. And when, in that state of utter loneliness, stricken by the savage pain of his illness, he longed for a cooling hand to touch his burning flesh and soothe away the agony.

Faith in the eternal afterlife did little to aid his suffering in the here and now. As absolute as his sincerity was, he found himself ready to beg for relief from something other than a deity that couldn't, or wouldn't, help him in this world.

CHAPTER SIX

Kurdistan

Breakfast was a quick drink of coffee and a handful of warmed rice.

The chill of the night took a while to burn away, but now the sky was empty, cloudless and cold blue.

Badr and McCarter sat over the embers of the cook fire, nursing the last of their coffee.

"This place I want to show you is not the only one in the area," the Mossad agent said.

"There are others?"

"Information around here is sometimes slow to come together. What I get is made up from isolated reports, coming in by word of mouth. It isn't safe to use radio communications too much. The Iraqis have listening posts all over."

"And there are those of our people who take their money to spy on us," Hanif said bitterly. He was sitting across from McCarter and the Israeli. "If they find out we are going to make trouble for the Iraqi troops, they will send messages to the local commander. We have almost been caught a number of times because of these traitors." The Kurd warrior smiled. "But we too have our spies. The ones who betray us do not escape for long."

He pushed to his feet, tossing the dregs of his coffee into the fire, then strode away.

"What a bloody way to have to live," McCarter said.

"They have little choice," Badr replied. "They live on the edge, but they survive."

"I think it's time something was done for them."

Badr shrugged. "Our opinions are just that, my friend. Ours alone."

McCarter knew what the Mossad agent meant. Governments would follow their own agendas, regardless of the long term considerations, and the feelings of those in the field held little sway in the corridors of power.

"My information tells me there are a few of these caches scattered through the area. There have also been hints about similar ones around the Middle East. No confirmation yet. Our people are trying to pinpoint them. Until then all we have are the ones in this region."

"I'm ready when you are," McCarter said.

WHEN PHOENIX FORCE was ready to move, Hanif stood beside McCarter and Badr.

"You wish us to come with you?" the Kurd asked.

"It would be better if you remained behind to occupy the patrols. Draw them away from us," Badr said.

Hanif nodded, unfazed by his offer being declined. "It is what we do best."

"I will miss our fireside discussions," McCarter said.

Hanif studied him, not sure how to take the Briton's comment.

"English, you are a man of strange words, but for all that a good fighter. We may yet meet again before this is over. God be with you."

As far as McCarter was concerned, Hanif's words were praise indeed.

BADR AND the Stony Man commandos moved along unmarked trails, almost all of which were across solid rock where no mark was left behind. There were times when they crossed solid ground, some colored by yellow grass. On these high slopes vegetation was sparse and that which survived was hardy and brittle.

They traveled for hours. The terrain was tough, with lots of undulating, rocky slopes, crumbling, dusty strata, razorback ridges and dusty defiles. Sometimes they had to scale treacherous walls to maintain their forward movement, scrambling up sheer faces and over exposed peaks, then down into shadowed canyons where crisscross shadows plunged them into darkness and cold ravines denied any heat from the sun.

They paused a couple of times to take small amounts of water from their canteens, drinking sparingly, because any sudden intake of cold water in quantity could give them stomach cramps, curtailing swift movement if the need arose. They drank only enough to compensate for the loss of body moisture from their exertions. Once they rested for a full twenty minutes before tackling the next stage of their trek, and McCarter was pleased about that when he saw what they needed to do.

Badr had smiled at the look in McCarter's eyes. "Don't worry," he said. "Looks harder than it actually is."

"You're not bloody well fooling me with that one," McCarter said. "I can tell a bloody hard climb when I see it."

"Man needs to be part goat to live in this place," Manning commented.

"We going to sit here talking all day?" Encizo asked. "The sooner we get to the top of that the better I'm going to like it."

THE CLIMB TOOK them the better part of two hours. By the time they dragged themselves over the final ledge, sprawling on the rocky surface, they were panting, their lungs burning from the climb. Even though the commandos carried the minimum of equipment the climb had been hard.

Manning, slumped against a jutting slab of rock, sleeved sweat from his face.

"Remind me. Did I volunteer for this without a gun at my damned head?"

"Yeah," Encizo said. "Just like the rest of us."

"I'd forgotten."

"Few more miles," Badr told them. "We should be there before dark."

"That's a great comfort," McCarter said. "Next to stumbling around in the light, stumbling around in the bloody dark is my favorite pastime."

IN THE LATE AFTERNOON they settled themselves on a narrow ledge overlooking a deep ravine that snaked into the rock heart of the massive rock formation ahead of them.

"Down there where that stream runs into the ravine. Can you see?"

McCarter took his binoculars from his backpack and focused in on the spot Badr indicated. As the image sharpened, the Briton was able to make out the camp. He scanned the area, and what he saw surprised him. Apart from the number of people he saw, the sheer size of the cache was impressive.

"Bloody hell," McCarter said, "they are going to start World War III."

"That's what I'm worried about," Badr said. "That and the fact Israel is liable to be high on the target list."

Manning took the glasses and scanned the scene. "Most of the stuff is lightweight. The way they're handling it looks like it's being boxed for shipment."

"My sources tell me the stuff is coming and going all the time," Badr said. "I just wish I knew where."

Encizo raised his head, listening.

"Chopper coming in," Manning stated, having picked up the same sound.

"That way." Badr pointed.

"And another," Manning said, "from the east."

"Anybody else getting the bad feeling I am?" McCarter asked.

"They sound as if they're heading our way," Badr said.

The droning beat of rotors increased. The imperceptible dots in the empty sky began to take on form, growing with alarming speed as the pair of SA-330 Puma helicopters swooped down on the Stony Man team's position. They came in from opposite sides, hovering, fuselage doors open to expose machine guns aimed at the group below them.

"Ex-Iraqi military helicopters," Badr said. "But they still do the job."

The Pumas settled, rocking on their undercarriages. Armed figures cleared the cabin doors and spread in a half-circle.

"No resistance," McCarter snapped, then in an undertone added, "for now."

"Glad you said that," Manning muttered. "Thought for a minute you'd quit."

"My arse," McCarter said.

They laid their weapons on the ground and offered no resistance as the armed men searched them, removing all the weaponry they carried. The radio communication units were also removed, as well as the NVGs and the GPS. McCarter watched as the equipment was examined with interest before being dropped into a large canvas bag along with Phoenix Force's weapons. The bag was carried to one of the helicopters and placed inside.

Badr swore forcibly as he recognized a familiar face. "Dahoun!"

A dark-skinned man, clad in tan pants and shirt, wearing a pair of aviator glasses, stepped forward. He was smiling, as if he had just met an old, dear friend.

"Lev. So good to see you again."

"Now I know we have problems," the Mossad agent said. "I should have guessed you would be involved."

"You never change, Lev," Dahoun said. "Always seeing the worst in a person. Why can't you accept the inevitable. Your kind have had their day. Now we are going to take back our land and bury you Zionist pigs in the dirt where you belong.''

"It will never happen, you bastard!''

Ignoring the weapons trained on him, Badr pushed forward. Dahoun remained where he was. Only his head moved. A quick nod, and one of the armed men stepped forward to smash the butt of his Kalashnikov into the small of Badr's back. The Israeli stumbled, and his attacker moved in close, striking blow after blow at the agent's face and body with his weapon.

"You've proved your bloody point,'' McCarter yelled. "Leave the poor sod alone.''

Badr was on the ground, semiconscious, his face and head a shattered, bloody mess.

Dahoun turned in McCarter's direction. The smile still curled his thin lips.

"You will be the people the Americans sent to interfere. And by the way, what point is it I have proved?''

"That you're pretty tough when it comes to beating an unarmed man.''

"That goes without saying. The man with the gun doesn't have to prove anything. Let me guess now. You will be the one they call the English. You made quite an impression on those Kurdish criminals.''

Dahoun said something in his own tongue. Activity inside one of the helicopters drew McCarter's attention. A dusty figure clad in a shredded, bloody leather coat was held briefly in the opening before being thrown bodily to the ground.

Hanif.

He was dragged upright and maneuvered to the front of the group. He was barely able to stand unaided. His face had been battered to a bloody pulp, teeth smashed from the gums. His left eye was pulped. Matted blood soaked his beard and hair. He held his left hand close to his body, and McCarter saw that two fingers had been severed.

Dahoun saw the shock that registered in McCarter's eyes.

"Did you really think you could come here and not be found?"

Hanif spit blood at Dahoun's feet.

"Only because I had a traitor in my camp," he said slowly, the effort increasing his agony. "One who betrayed us all."

McCarter saw the man now. He recognized him as one of the *peshmerga* who had fought with them earlier. He was standing just behind Dahoun, and when McCarter spotted him the man lowered his gaze.

"They are all dead, English," Hanif said.

Dahoun moved with sudden urgency. He pulled an autopistol from his side and jammed the muzzle against the side of Hanif's head, pulling the trigger. The sharp sound of the shot was crisp in the clear air. Hanif's head snapped to one side, blood gouting from the exit wound. The Kurdish fighter was dead before he hit the ground.

"*Now* they are all dead," Dahoun said.

Encizo uttered a scream of rage. The Cuban moved with speed that defied interference. He slammed bodily into Dahoun, knocking the man off his feet and pounding him with his fists. Blood burst from Dahoun's split lip before Encizo was battered into submission by the armed terrorists.

"*Do not kill him!*" Dahoun roared, staggering to his feet. He pawed at the blood spilling down his chin, spattering the clean tan shirt he wore. "We need them alive for now."

Encizo and Badr were dragged to one of the helicopters and flung inside. McCarter and Manning were next. As he slumped on one of the seats, McCarter looked back. Hanif lay where he had fallen, his leather coat flapping in the rotor wash as the helicopters lifted off from the mountain slope.

The only consolation McCarter could see was that at least Hanif had died in his beloved mountains.

THE PUMA CARRYING Phoenix Force and Lev Badr touched down just beyond the main camp area. Encizo and Badr were dragged onto solid ground. The Israeli still couldn't stand without aid, so McCarter and Manning supported him. Encizo, hugging his hurt body, managed to walk on his own. The group was herded to an open lean-to and ordered to sit.

"I don't have time for you now," Dahoun said. He was still nursing his badly gashed lip. "I will later."

No one answered. Dahoun turned away, snapping orders that left two of the armed terrorists watching the captives.

"First one who says 'that was stupid' gets more of the same," Encizo warned.

"Jesus," Manning said, "after that display of temper I'm not saying a word."

McCarter took a long look around the camp. What he saw impressed him where the amount of equipment was concerned and pleased him when he realized that security around the place was pretty low. The terrorists, feeling safe and secure, didn't seem to be overly concerned about perimeter guards. That left some gaps in the setup, and maybe that would allow Phoenix Force an opportunity.

"David," Manning said, "Lev is in a pretty bad way."

The Israeli was barely conscious. The battering he had taken had left his face and head severely injured. Blood flowed from his ears and nose continuously.

"There isn't a thing we can do for him," Manning said, feeling the helplessness that came from the realization that Badr was dying.

"I know," McCarter said bitterly.

Manning sat with Badr resting against him. He held the Mossad agent for the next hour and refused to let go until McCarter explained that Badr was dead.

Dahoun showed up a short time later. He had changed his bloody shirt for a fresh one and paused as he passed the commandos.

"So I won't get a chance to speak to Lev? We would have had so much to discuss. I have to leave for a while. But I will be back and then we can have our talk, *English.*"

Dahoun crossed to where one of the Pumas was being warmed up ready for flight. Once he was onboard the helicopter took off and vanished into a sky that was rapidly darkening.

"Looks like we could be here a while," McCarter said.

"I hope not," Manning answered.

Stony Man Farm, Virginia

AKIRA TOKAIDO leaned across Kurtzman's workstation and placed a couple of printed sheets in front of him. Kurtzman examined them. Finally he grunted and looked up. "I'll be damned," he said. "You did it."

Akira didn't say anything. It was enough that he had actually cracked the encryption and got into the stored information.

"Only problem we have now is figuring out what the hell it means," Kurtzman said. Breaking the entry code was one thing. Making sense of the data was something else.

"Go take a break," Kurtzman said. "A long one, kid."

That coming from Kurtzman was high praise. He wasn't given to over-the-top expressions, so any sort of verbal thanks was something to be enjoyed.

As the young man left the Computer Room, Kurtzman called over Wethers and Delahunt. He showed them what Tokaido had come up with.

"He did it already?" Wethers said. "Aaron, we'll have to watch that kid. He's after our jobs."

"Damn right," Kurtzman said. "I'll fix it to have him disappear."

"Oh, cut it out, you guys," Delahunt chided. "Admit it, he worked a miracle."

"He did okay," Kurtzman grunted.

"Okay, let's see what we have," Wethers said as he picked up the printout Tokaido had placed on Kurtzman's desk, then wandered back to his own workstation. He dropped the printed data sheets on the desk in front of him, sat down and started to tap at his keyboard. Kurtzman and Delahunt followed suit, and the room fell silent as they concentrated on the puzzle before them.

Barbara Price stepped inside some time later and

from the grunted response she received when she spoke, she realized that the cyber team was busy with some problem requiring their full attention. She backed out and left them to it.

She saw Brognola approaching and waved him back.

"What are they up to?" he asked.

"I saw Akira a while back. He looked bushed. It seems he broke the lockout on the data from that laptop Able sent in. Aaron told him to go get some sleep. When I stuck my head in just now they were all slaving away. I guess they're trying to work out what all the data means."

They made their way to the tunnel and took the electric car to the farmhouse. Brognola followed Price to her office.

"Current update?" the big Fed asked as they settled in chairs.

"Able is following that lead they picked up from the FBI. Nothing from them yet. Katz and the guys are still in France with Ben Sharon."

"And what about our team in Kurdistan?"

Price shook her head.

"No word yet. The problem out there is communication. To be exact, the lack of communication. Once they get into those mountains there's no telling what might happen."

CHAPTER SEVEN

Nice, France

The maroon Mercedes followed Katz all the way to the hotel. The Israeli made no show that he had even noticed as he paid off the driver and made his way inside. As he had already informed the others, they were watching out for his arrival.

Sharon sat at a table in the hotel café, where he could see the drop-off point. Hawkins and James sat in a car in the hotel parking lot.

Katz walked into the hotel. The Mercedes dropped a man off, then found a slot and parked.

As Katz picked up his key and made for the elevator, his tail followed. As soon as the elevator doors closed, Sharon left his table and took the stairs. He knew which floor Katz would get off and sprinted up the steps. He was waiting when the elevator arrived. Two guests stepped out, followed by Katz, then his tail. Sharon let them pass before he eased out from the stairwell and followed some yards behind.

Pausing at his door, Katz put the key in the lock and turned the knob. The moment he did, his tail stepped up behind him, easing an autopistol from inside his jacket. Seeing this, Sharon did the very same thing, coming up hard behind the man and ramming the muzzle of his weapon into the man's side.

"Relax and it won't happen," the Mossad agent said, reaching around to relieve the man of his weapon.

Katz continued into the room, waited until Sharon and the tail had moved by, then closed the door.

"Neatly done, if a little close," Katz said.

"Are you losing faith?" Sharon asked.

After being thoroughly searched and his personal belongings placed on a table, the tall man was seated in a hardback chair. He was angry at being caught, but contained himself.

"You won't earn your money if this is an example of how you operate," Katz said to the man.

"Go to hell!"

"At least we know you understand English," Sharon said.

"Zionist pig!"

"And now we have established the level of your intelligence," Katz said. "This is going faster than I imagined."

"Does that mean I don't get to beat him senseless?" Sharon asked.

"I imagine we'll get to that sooner or later."

Katz took out his pistol and held it on the man in the chair.

"Tie him," Katz ordered. "If he tries to run, I'll have to kill him."

Sharon ripped the electrical cord from a table lamp and used it to secure the man's hands behind him. Then he stood back, examining the man's face.

"What is it?" Katz asked.

"I know him from somewhere," Sharon said. He studied the man for a time. Recognition shone in his eyes. *"Dahoun!"*

"His name is Dahoun?"

Sharon shook his head. "No. This one works for Dahoun."

Katz had been casually watching the captive's face. When the name Dahoun was mentioned he flinched slightly, then tried to cover his emotions.

"Tell me about him."

"Tricky character. Has connections, allegedly, with some of the Islamic resistance groups in Israel. Nothing proved yet, but we have had him under surveillance for the past few weeks. He runs a photographic studio in Haifa."

"So he could be tied in to these people we've been tangling with."

"Too much of a coincidence, one of his hired hands tailing you after what's been happening."

Katz wandered to the far end of the room and pulled out his sat-com unit. He spoke to Hawkins and told him and James to sit tight.

"If the car takes off, follow it. Find out where it comes from, then let me know."

"The guys in that Mercedes are starting to get restless," Hawkins reported. "They must be wondering what happened to their partner."

"Good. We'll just let them carry on wondering."

"If they decide to come inside, we'll be right behind them."

A cell phone started to ring. It was the one Sharon had confiscated when he had searched the tail man.

Katz saw the man struggle against his tethered wrists.

"If we let it ring," he said, "his partners are going to start worrying."

"HERE WE GO," Calvin James said.

He watched the maroon Mercedes back from its slot and drive out of the hotel parking lot, turning left as it hit the street. James followed at a discreet distance, able to keep the Mercedes in sight.

When Hawkins relayed the information to Katz the Israeli told them to stay with the earlier arrangements.

"You got it."

They followed the Mercedes out of town and east along the coast road. After a few miles the Mercedes turned off on a side road that led to a marina situated in a bay. James kept going until he was clear of the marina then pulled over.

"The car pulled in at a marina just along the coast," Hawkins reported to Katz.

"What's the name of the marina?"

Hawkins checked the sign at the entrance to the side road.

"The Shebin Bay Marina."

"YOU SOUND as if you know it," Katz said.

"I do. Or I at least know the owner. Kara Shebin. Israeli. Her late father was Dom Shebin."

"The shipping magnate?"

"That's right. Not just shipping. He had a wide range of business involvements. They all did, and still do, make a lot of money. He married late and had one child. Kara. Her mother died of cancer three years after the girl was born. Dom lived for the girl, gave her anything she wanted. When he died she inherited everything. The businesses are run by a trust. As well as the businesses, which bring in a fortune, Kara received a personal bequest of over two hundred million dollars.''

''Poor little rich girl?''

''Not exactly. Kara isn't stupid. She has a good head on her shoulders. She built the marina here and it's making money. That she got from her father. Her weakness is allying herself to what she calls worthy causes. Mainly environmental. She got into trouble with the authorities a number of times. We have met a few times. Her intentions are good. Just a little misdirected.''

''The question is, why are Dahoun's men going to her marina?''

''Could be entirely innocent. Dahoun may have a boat moored there for his trips between here and Israel.''

''Hey, wait,'' Sharon said. ''Kara has a motor launch she makes her trips in. Her father bought it for her just before he died. The *Kara II*. White painted with blue and gold stripes along the hull.''

Katz passed the information along to Hawkins.

''We'll check it out, boss,'' Hawkins said.

JAMES PARKED the car and stepped out, Hawkins following. The Mercedes was parked toward the end of the line of vehicles. The Phoenix Force commandos strolled along the path leading to the clubhouse and stepped inside. It was all polished wood and glass, very modern and expensive.

They found a bar and ordered drinks. The woman serving them smiled and conversed in English with an American accent.

"How long you worked here?" Hawkins asked.

"Almost two years. Haven't seen you around before."

"We're just visiting. Thought we'd look in and see about maybe doing some business."

"If you like sailing, this is the place. You have a boat?"

"Our company does. Uses it to take clients on trips."

"Who do we need to see?" James asked.

"Well, everything like that is handled by the owner, Kara Shebin. Only she isn't here at the moment. Her home is in Israel."

"Hey, there's a big motor launch moored at the jetty called the *Kara II*," James said.

"That belongs to her. I believe she loaned it to a friend. He's over there by the window."

"Any idea when she'll be back?" Hawkins asked pleasantly, finishing his drink.

"Next week, I believe."

"We'll call back," Hawkins said. "Thanks for the information."

"You're welcome."

Back in the car Hawkins called Katz and asked for Sharon to be put on the line.

"Describe Dahoun for me."

When Sharon had finished Hawkins said, "Fits the guy we saw talking to our friends from the Mercedes. They were in the bar at the marina. And here's the one for the main prize. It appears that Dahoun has borrowed Kara Shebin's motor launch. Don't that take the cherry pie?"

SHARON HANDED the transceiver to Katz. He glanced at the captive, who was looking very unsettled now.

Unable to hear all the conversation, the man had picked up enough to realize he was in trouble.

"Believe me when I say you're not walking away from this," Sharon said, crossing to where the man sat. "Dahoun is in way over his head on this one."

"I don't know what you are talking about."

Sharon leaned in close. "Oh, you do, my friend, and I'll see to it you don't see the light of day until you are an old man. Providing you stay alive. Lots of things can happen before you reach Israel."

"You think I'm afraid to die?"

"If you need to ask the question, I'd say yes," Katz told him.

"We are not playing games," Sharon said. "We already have enough information to deal with you."

"You have nothing."

"Nefu. Alexi. Both dead. They were negotiating the purchase of laptops for your principals. You see, we are not entirely stupid."

"And now we have you," Katz added. "Perhaps we need to take you somewhere private and quiet so we can really get to know you."

Sweat glistened on the man's face. He was no terrorist. No extremist ready to die for the cause. In reality he was nothing more than a petty criminal who had, because he worked for Dahoun, got himself in a position of high risk. His reaction to the posed threat would depend on how he valued his own life.

"Dahoun has just returned from the Middle East. He has a package to deliver."

"Where?"

"Haifa. He leaves tonight."

"On Kara Shebin's boat?"

The man nodded.

"How involved is Kara Shebin?" Sharon asked.

"Involved? She isn't involved. She believes she is helping Dahoun organize a protest against pollution. He dreamed it up just for her. He needed her boat to bring in explosives. The *Kara II* is so well-known around Haifa no one ever gives it a second glance."

"Somebody will get their knuckles rapped over that," Sharon promised.

Katz took Sharon aside. "Ben, I think we need to get to Israel. We need to see exactly what Dahoun is up to."

Ben Sharon arranged for the man he and Katz had taken prisoner to be collected by a local Mossad team and kept in isolation.

The following morning Katz, the men of Phoenix Force and Ben Sharon boarded a regular airline flight that would take them to Israel.

Israel

BRIGHT SUNLIGHT caught them as they crossed to the terminal. Once inside they pushed through the crowds, heading for the customs desk where Sharon had a word with one of the officers. Moments later they were being ushered to an office. As the door closed, a figure standing by the window turned to greet them.

"*Shalom,*" the man said, reaching out to take Ben Sharon's hand. "And these will be our friends from the U.S.A."

Sharon introduced Katz, Hawkins and James, using their cover names.

"This is Mordecai Bakul, my section chief. He's been briefed on the background to the affair."

Bakul held out a folder. "I had this compiled while you were on the way here. Everything we have on Dahoun and Kara Shebin. Are you sure she's involved with these people, Ben? I know she's been a damn nuisance over the years, but her protests have always been environmental rather than antigovernment."

"I think she's in over her head this time," Katz said. "Dahoun has told her a story she's swallowed, and she believes she's helping him make an issue over pollution."

"Kara's problem is she has too much money and nothing to do except spend it," Bakul said. He handed over the file. "Anything you need, Ben? I'm letting you run with this. Remember you have all the backing you want. A team has been briefed and they'll go on your word."

"Is the surveillance vehicle still in place?"

Bakul nodded. "Dahoun's studio is under twenty-four-hour watch."

"We'll get out there," Sharon said.

Katz nodded. "I could do with a shower and a bite to eat first."

"Rooms have been booked for you. Ben, there's a car waiting outside to take you to your hotel. Remember what I said. Anything you need, just give me a call."

THEY ATE in Katz's suite—fresh lobster, salad, bread baked in the hotel kitchen and fruit grown locally.

"Guys, I could get to like this place," Hawkins

said. He drained his wineglass. "Why is it when we get something good like this work has to be waiting around the corner?"

"One of life's unanswered questions," James replied.

Katz and Sharon were studying photographs of Dahoun's studio, which showed the building from all angles. There was also a street layout printed from a computer map, showing the position of Dahoun's building and the immediate area around it. "Stairs at the rear," Sharon said, "allow access to the upper floor where he has his office and living quarters."

"Where are the surveillance cameras?" Katz asked.

"There's one here on this telegraph pole, trained on the back stairs. Another here is watching the front of the studio. Two more show the street from both ends."

Hawkins and James had joined them, and they studied the details.

"Where's the surveillance vehicle?" Hawkins asked.

Sharon traced a line along Dahoun's street to a narrow side street on the map.

"Parked just around the corner of the street. Can't be seen from Dahoun's studio. He always comes in from this direction, so he never actually goes as far as the corner."

"Okay, guys, let's finish up here and go watch some TV," Katz suggested.

THEY WAITED inside the surveillance vehicle. Outside the afternoon was breathless and hot. Occasionally, dry wind blew in wisps of dust that peppered the side of the van. There was little activity at this time of the day. Only the distant sound of passing traffic disturbed the calm. The interior of the van was comfortable because Sharon had switched on the air-conditioning to relieve some of the heat.

When they had arrived to relieve the surveillance team the two men inside the van had taken the car, only too eager to change places.

The interior of the shabby van contained enough electronic equipment to outfit a small TV studio. The cameras Sharon had described earlier were linked to a control panel enabling the operator to change their position at will. It was also possible to alter the picture by using the zoom facility. As well as image capture, the van was fitted with digital sound surveillance. The TV cameras were fitted with powerful directional microphones so that conversations could also be monitored if there was a need. High-quality tape recorders listened in to captured sound while the TV images were recorded on videotape.

According to the log left by the departing team there was nothing to report. Dahoun's residence had remained deserted up to the present time. Sharon and the Stony Man team settled in, the Mossad agent briefing them all on the use of the surveillance equipment.

After the first hour conversation dried up. They sat and waited, because that was the nature of their business. The profession called for long periods of in-activity that were inevitably punctured by sudden and violent action. Every one of them was used to that. They took it in their stride, and each had his own way of dealing with the conditions placed on him.

Of them all, Ben Sharon had the monitor screens

to watch and this at least broke the monotony. The Mossad agent, leaning back on his swivel seat, kept a sharp lookout for any movement at the front and rear of Dahoun's studio. In the first two hours nothing happened. The studio remained deserted, but Sharon didn't worry. He had been on enough of these stakeouts to know that waiting could be an extremely long affair. A couple of hours now meant nothing. He had been on stakeouts that had run into days before anything happened. On this occasion Sharon had the feeling they wouldn't be kept waiting for too long. Just before 4:30 p.m. they got their break when a figure came into view on the camera at the rear of the studio. Sharon watched as Kara Shebin climbed the steps to the rear door and let herself in with a key.

"What do we have?" Katz asked when Sharon nudged him.

"Kara Shebin just went in through the back door."

They exited the van. Sharon and Katz took the rear while Hawkins and James watched the front of the studio.

Sharon found the rear door off the latch. Nodding to Katz, he drew his autopistol and gently eased the door open, wincing when it emitted a dry squeak. Luckily the sound wasn't loud. Slipping inside, Sharon waited until Katz was beside him.

They were in a bright kitchen that held the lingering aroma of ripe fruit. A bead curtain, still moving gently, covered the door that led to the main room. As Sharon eased through, he picked up sound off to his left. An open door at the far side of the living room led to a short passage. At the far end a flight of polished wood stairs led to the ground floor.

Sharon heard the sound again, coming from a room just along the passage. Nearing the open door Sharon picked up the sound of Kara Shebin's voice. From the way she was speaking she was using a telephone. Not wanting to alert anyone on the line, Sharon and Katz waited until the call had been terminated. Sharon heard the receiver being replaced and moved quickly. He stepped through the open door and confronted Shebin.

The young woman, dressed in expensive, casual clothing, was attractive, her black hair cut in a short cap. There was something in her look that told Katz, watching from just outside the door, that Kara Shebin could be a tough opponent.

Her beautiful face registered genuine shock. For a brief moment it looked as if she were going to make a break for the door. In an instant the panic was gone, replaced by professional calm.

"Ben, what are you doing here? Have you been following me? This is too much. I'll complain about this to—"

"Quick talking isn't going to get you out of this one, Kara," Sharon said.

At that moment Katz stepped into the room—it was set up as an office—and spoke to Sharon.

"I'll go and let the others in," he said.

"Are we going to be here for a long time?" Kara asked. "I have things to do."

Sharon shrugged. She frowned at his lack of words and sat on one of the office chairs. Crossing her legs, she turned her head so she was able to stare through the window at a patch of blue sky.

Katz was back in a short time, followed by Hawkins and James.

"Who the hell else do you have down there?" she demanded. "The Israeli army?"

"Maybe we'll just wait until Dahoun arrives," Sharon said.

"Leave him out of this," Shebin said. "Don't you realize what he's planning to do?"

"Kara, this is not personal. I'm only doing my job," Sharon told her.

"Is it your job to harass people? When all they want to do is make an innocent protest?"

"Miss Shebin," Katz said, "he's consorting with terrorists. Not protesters who want to keep the ocean clean. These people want to kill and destroy."

"Who is this man, Ben?"

"Someone who knows what he's talking about. A man I would trust with my life. And he is right, Kara. We have had Dahoun under surveillance for some time. He came back from the Middle East recently. He has been using your boat to smuggle in cargo for his terrorist friends."

"He befriended you, Miss Shebin," Katz said, "so he could use your boat, knowing it was unlikely to be stopped."

"No! No...that can't be true." Doubt had crept into her tone.

"Kara, I don't believe you are involved in what Dahoun is planning. What I do need is for you to tell me where he is."

Confusion took the beauty from Kara Shebin's face as she absorbed Sharon's words. Her eyes darted back and forth, from man to man, as if she were seeking reassurance that everything was going to be all right. She suddenly held up her hands, pushing at the air as though it might dissipate the terrible things Sharon had told her.

Katz moved to stand beside her. He rested his hand on the woman's shoulder.

"Listen to me, Kara. We haven't come here to terrorize you or to intimidate you. The things you have heard here are all true. Dahoun is a wanted man. The people he's in with are already responsible for a number of deaths. If we don't put a stop to their activities that number will rise. This city is probably one of their main targets. Kara, we have to find Dahoun."

"You say Dahoun is a terrorist. How do I know you're not lying to me?"

"Because we have no reason to lie."

"He told me he needed my help. That I would be doing something useful. Is this really true what you told me?" Shebin asked, staring at Katz in the hope he might tell her it was all a lie.

"I am afraid so, my dear. Dahoun is not interested in the environment."

"Was that Dahoun you were talking to on the phone?" James asked.

She nodded. "He asked me to come here and wait for him. He said he wanted to thank me for everything I had done to help him."

"Nice touch," Hawkins said.

"Dahoun's thank-you might have turned out to be something you might not have expected," Sharon stated.

"What do you mean?"

"Kara, he won't want witnesses around."

That really shocked her. The suggestion she might

have been in the position of being harmed. Even killed.

"Do you know where he is?" Katz asked.

Shebin took a moment to compose herself. She gazed around the room, almost without seeing.

"Yes, I think I do," she said, a faint self-mocking tone to her voice. "He asked me if I could find him a deserted place near the water where he could organize his protest banners. Somewhere isolated so he wouldn't be disturbed." Realization was hitting her now. "My God, he really did take me for a fool. My company owns some deserted land and property on the old docks. It's going to be redeveloped in a few months' time. I told him he could use it. Don't you see? If he used my boat he could unload any cargo directly onto the jetty where those buildings are."

"Kara, give us the location," Sharon said. "Then I'll get someone to take you home and keep watch over you until this is all over."

The young woman, her face pale with shock, stood. She sought out Katz.

"I really didn't know," she said. "You do believe me? I didn't know."

"It's all right, Kara," Katz said. "We understand. We'll have you looked after. You won't be involved any further."

THE AREA HAD SEEN better days. Shabby buildings with boarded windows. Trash drifting across the dusty ground.

Ben Sharon had parked the van a couple of streets away as there was little cover close to the buildings. They made their approach on foot until they stopped at the extreme corner of a building that offered the final piece of cover before the open ground between them and the object of their interest.

"No way we can cross that without being spotted," James observed. "Only option is to wait until dark."

"I agree in principle," Katz said. "Let's hope they don't decide to do anything before then."

Sharon scanned the area, shaking his head in frustration. He saw no alternative. "Even a rat would have a problem getting across unseen," he said.

Hawkins thought about that for a moment. "Not if it was underground," he said. "What about the drainage system, Ben?"

Sharon glanced at him "Explain."

"Let me take another look at those plans you brought along," Hawkins said.

Leaving Katz and James on watch, Hawkins and Sharon made their way back to the parked van. Inside Sharon took the chart and unrolled it, watching with interest as Hawkins studied it.

"There," Hawkins said. His finger traced the line indicated on the diagram. "According to this, the original storm drain overflow runs across this section and takes in those buildings."

"Should almost be under our feet right where we are," Sharon said.

"It's worth a look," Hawkins told him.

Sharon nodded.

"Go tell the others while I break out some gear," Hawkins said.

Returning to Katz and James, the Mossad agent told them what Hawkins had found.

"Are you going in?" Katz asked.

Sharon nodded. "It's the best chance we're going

to get. Either that or we wait until dark, and I don't think that's the best option.''

"You want me to stay here and keep watch?" Katz asked.

The Stony Man tactical adviser had already evaluated the requirements for taking to the storm drain. It would ask for a degree of agility and stamina he could have managed easily a few years previously. Though he was no frail geriatric, Katz knew and accepted his limitations. Above ground and handling a weapon he was still as formidable as ever. In the restrictive environment of the drainage tunnel he might very well become a liability to his partners, and Katz would never allow that to happen.

"That okay with you?" James asked.

"Somebody has to be on top to hold the fort," Katz said. "I've got my transceiver, so I can keep you informed if anything happens."

James nodded. He knew why Katz had volunteered, and he respected the man's decision.

BY THE TIME the others returned to the van Hawkins had most of the equipment ready. Each man took an Uzi, along with a couple of extra magazines that went into the combat harness they donned. Holsters for their autopistols were secured to the waist belts. Additional clips of ammo were taken for these, too. They were also equipped with smoke and fragmentation grenades. The transceivers were placed in pockets, and to the sets they attached the leads for the headsets they slipped on so they could talk without using their hands. Contact was made with Katz as a test that the link was working.

Sharon brought along a small TV scanner unit.

The compact equipment would allow them to use a minuscule camera contained in a flexible probe. It would let them check out areas without exposing themselves, ideal for their situation once they were inside the tunnel system.

A final check was made of the route they anticipated taking. Hawkins folded the chart and slipped it into the big pocket on the leg of his trousers, zipping it securely. They exited the van and checked out the road until they located the access cover shown on the chart. It turned out to be no more than a few yards from where they had parked. It took them a while to loosen the cover and raise it, but finally they were able to peer down the shaft.

Hawkins spotted the iron rungs embedded in the dusty concrete wall of the shaft. He switched on the flashlight fixed to the sleeve of his combat suit and swept the area.

"Here we go," he said, and started down. "Let's hope the weather stays dry. We get a flash flood, and we'll probably end up in the damn ocean."

Katz was able to pick up Hawkins's words, and he smiled to himself, not without a little envy, because he knew that his days as an active participant in such maneuvers were over.

"Take care, guys," he transmitted. "Don't get your feet wet."

THE TUNNEL WAS just about man height. They all needed to stoop slightly as they gathered at the bottom of the shaft. Being the last man down, Sharon had dragged the access cover back into place. The light from the opening vanished, and they were left in semidarkness. Only the beams from their three flashlights penetrated the gloom. The air was warm and dusty, and bore a stale smell.

"Everybody okay?" Hawkins asked.

"I guess so," James said. "Not exactly my chosen way of spending the afternoon, but what the hell."

They moved forward, checking the side tunnels and drain inlets as they traveled. They had committed the number of these to memory when they had been checking the chart, so as they counted them off they were able to assess how close they were to reaching the objective.

The floor of the tunnel was dry for the most part. Occasionally they stepped through pools of stagnant water, sometimes passing sections where the walls were wet and moisture dripped from the inlets. They soon discovered they weren't alone in the tunnel. The scratchy rattle of clawed feet indicated the presence of rats. Once or twice the beam from a flashlight would pick up the defiant glare from sharp red eyes watching them approach.

"What is it about rats that makes me shiver?" James asked.

"Maybe the fact they don't really give a damn about us. All they do is stare you out."

As they neared their objective they cut the talk, moving carefully so as not to create any sound that might advertise their presence.

Hawkins raised a hand to stop them. "I reckon this is the place," he said very softly.

They gathered together at the base of a shaft similar to the one they had used to get into the tunnel.

"According to the chart, the access cover is between two buildings. The one we want will be on our right when we come out."

Sharon activated the TV scanner and handed the probe to Hawkins. The Mossad agent asked for a test, and Hawkins moved the probe around the tunnel. The were able to see the image on the small monitor screen. Sharon adjusted the resolution, amplifying the brightness of the image. He glanced at Hawkins and nodded.

Hawkins slung his Uzi over his back and started up the iron rungs. Reaching the top, he peered through the grille of the cover. His angle of vision was restricted, but he was able to make out the upper section of a building on his right-hand side. He was unable to see anything else. For all he knew there might be an armed guard standing beyond his restricted vision.

Taking the camera probe, Hawkins slipped it through the grille and listened over his headphones as James relayed Sharon's instructions. As he moved the probe in a 360-degree arc, the camera displayed the exterior view on the monitor screen. The image showed the buildings and a parked panel truck that was standing between them. There were no guards in sight.

Hawkins maintained his watch for a couple more minutes. The site seemed secure for the time being. He knew full well that it could change at any moment, and quickly, too. He spoke into his microphone, discussing the situation with the others, and it was finally agreed that they had to make their move. The longer they waited the more likely conditions might alter.

He withdrew the probe and passed it down to Sharon.

Taking another step up the rungs, Hawkins put his

left shoulder to the cover and pushed. He felt the metal resist. Putting on more pressure, he heard a grating creak, then it moved. Hawkins kept lifting until he was able to get his hands under the cover and push it aside. He slid it clear of the opening. Reaching down, he pulled his Uzi free and brought his head and shoulders out into the open, with the SMG tracking ahead. He made a swift left-and-right scan of the immediate area and was inwardly relieved to see it was deserted. Hawkins pulled himself up and out of the shaft, moving to one side to provide cover for James and Sharon as they followed him up the shaft and onto firm ground. The access cover was replaced.

"We're above ground," James told Katz over the radio link. "We need to check things out first. If you hear shooting it's time to join us."

"Take care, guys," Katz replied.

Sharon had moved so he could check the license plate on the van.

"This has been parked outside the studio a number of times," he said. "We have it on video."

The sound of approaching footsteps from the enclosed area between the buildings alerted the trio. A man called to someone still inside the building.

"They're about to move the van," Sharon warned Hawkins and James.

The unexpected was the reason incursions into enemy territory went from soft to hard in a matter of seconds. The Stony Man commandos and Ben Sharon were in that fluid state, and the appearance of the opposition only confounded their fragile security. In scenarios such as the one they were in, decisions had to be made instantly. There was no time for discussion. No debating the right approach. It was a clear-cut matter of opportunities to be taken in order to stay alive.

As the figure of the man moving to take charge of the van appeared from around the front of the vehicle, Calvin James pushed upright from his crouching position. His right arm swept up and around, catching the unwary guy across the throat and taking him off his feet. He had no time to make a grab for the AK-74 slung from his left shoulder before he crashed to the ground with a jarring thump.

"Go, go, go," Sharon said, pushing Hawkins before him as they moved toward the rear of the van.

James was close on their heels. Although the takedown blow had been swift and silent, something had to have alerted the downed man's companions. A name was called, then repeated.

And then the clatter of hard boot soles on unseen steps reached their ears.

"So much for the silent approach," Hawkins muttered.

They flattened against the rear doors of the van, weapons up and ready. Sharon dropped to the ground and peered under the van.

"Three," he warned, "moving toward the front. One going to the left. No two. The third is staying put."

A screamed command reached their ears.

"They want us to come out and surrender," Sharon translated.

The pair moving to the left broke into a run, weapons rattling as they cocked them.

Hawkins dropped to the ground, then rolled to the side, exposing himself briefly before coming to rest on his stomach, the muzzle of his Uzi lifting. He fired two short bursts, catching both men in midstride. He stitched a burst across their bodies, spinning them off their feet.

James moved the instant Hawkins did, stepping out from the rear of the van and sprinting the length of the vehicle. He caught the third man as he was halfway through a turn that would have brought him face-to-face with his adversary. James fired twice, his Uzi on single shot, and took the guy out with 9 mm Parabellum rounds to the skull.

Hawkins and Sharon joined him.

"Steps over there," James said.

They cut across to the worn steps, taking brief cover at the bottom before James went up, covered by the others. He flattened against the wall to one side of the open door. A figure emerged, AK in his hands. James clouted him alongside the head with the Uzi. The guy lost his footing and pitched head-first down the steps. He sprawled across the ground, still clutching his weapon, and started to raise it. A single shot from Sharon's Uzi slammed him to the ground again.

James went through the door first. The room they entered was gloomy, lit only by light coming in through grimy windows. An open arch led to the main part of the building. There was a great deal of shouting from ahead. Raised voices. Anger mingled with surprise. The clatter of hurried movement.

Shadows moved along the passage ahead of James. The sudden chatter of an autoweapon hammered his ears. Bullets gouged and scored the dirty walls. Something tugged at one of James's sleeves. He returned fire, his stream of 9 mm slugs pushing the shooter back.

The end of the passage opened onto a large room with an elevated section at the far end. Hazy light filtered from the roof, which was dotted with glass frames.

James got a quick impression of wooden trestle tables stacked with cartons and equipment. It was the only view he got right then, because he was fighting for his life a fraction of a second later.

There were four, maybe five armed men in the workroom. They opened up with the autoweapons they carried, firing indiscriminately. Lines of slugs crisscrossed one another as the defenders fired. Plaster and wood splinters filled the air, peppering the backs of Sharon and the Stony Man commandos. They had dived to the floor the moment they cleared the end of the passage, and the volleys of shots passed over their heads.

Hawkins came to rest against the base of a wall. He pulled himself to a sitting position, his Uzi tracking ahead of him, and the moment he had a target in his sights he triggered a short burst. The target shuddered as 9 mm slugs cored into his chest. He fell back, knocking over a stack of cartons. James and Sharon found themselves in similar conflict with the defenders. They returned fire, the emphasis on accuracy rather than simply expending the bulk of their ammunition.

Each scored a hit.

The remaining defenders considered their position and decided on a retreat. While one gave covering fire the other used a heavy box to smash through the closest window. Still firing in the direction of Phoenix Force, the pair clambered over the sill and dropped to the open ground outside.

KATZ WAS CLOSING ON the building when he heard the window glass breaking. Moments later he saw two men hurl themselves out of the window. They hit the ground running, and within a couple of steps they spotted him.

The closest raised his AK-74, tracking the muzzle on Katz. The Israeli, who already had his autopistol in his hand, raised it and fired first. His bullet took the guy in the head, just above the left eye, and cored into his brain. The man arched over with a brief sound. The moment he had fired Katz sought his next target. He fired a split second after the remaining defender stroked his own trigger. The stream of slugs from the AK-74 chopped the earth inches to Katz's right. Unfazed by the closeness, Katz triggered his shot and put a bullet in the man's heart, stopping him in his tracks. The man went down hard and lay still.

DAHOUN WASN'T among the dead.

They checked out the building, starting with the room where they had encountered the terrorists. What they found there was a chilling reminder concerning the serious intent of the group. The amount of explosives stored would have been enough to construct a number of large car bombs. Diagrams, prepared for the terrorists, showed exactly how they would need to pack and prime the explosives.

"Someone has put in a lot of work making up these plans," Katz said as he ran his eyes over the diagrams. "The bombs are simple in design, but they would have created a massive amount of damage."

Sharon was already contacting the military to send in teams capable of removing the explosives.

"Damn these people," he said. "When are they ever going to quit?"

"I think you know that answer yourself," Katz said.

Sharon nodded. His face gave away his feelings as he slumped wearily against one of the worktables.

"There are times when I just want to pack it all in and find a nice, sunny beach somewhere. You know? A place where I can laze around and have a drink. Spend my time watching pretty girls run around in bikinis."

"Ben, you'd be bored to tears in a couple of days," James told him.

"You're probably right. But there has to be something better than all this."

"Sorry to break in," Katz said. "One thing I've noticed. All these bombs are activated by a simple device. Once activated, a button is depressed and held down. Take the pressure off, and the device detonates." He held up a tube-shaped plastic object and pressed the button on the top. Then he let go of the button. It popped up with a sharp click. "It means that the bomb is detonated from inside the car, and probably by the person driving it."

"Suicide bomb," Hawkins said. "No-win situation. Even if you shoot the driver of the car the bomb still goes off."

Katz glanced at Ben Sharon.

"This is the reason we carry on, Ben. To try and stop this kind of thing happening. And the only way is to do what we do. Behind the scenes. Going to all the dirty little corners where these people hide. It's too late once they get on the street. Driving a car loaded with a trunk full of high explosive they are going to take right into somewhere full of people. We have to stop them right here. Where they make the damn things. There is no other way.''

They stopped and listened and agreed. Because Katz was right. This was where it had to end. Here. Now. Not when they were driving into the front of a building, or into a town square full of families out for a stroll. The lines were drawn, and time was already starting to run out.

IN A SMALL ROOM at the top of the stairs they found electronic equipment—laptop computer, printer, a number of disks.

"This is all becoming very familiar," Katz said, bending over the laptop. "These people seem very involved with computers. The Iranians in Nice were eager to buy them. If they need so many, what does it suggest?"

"That they're going to use them for communication, passing data between the various cells." Hawkins paused, considering something else. "And e-mail. They could be receiving their instructions via the Internet. It's quick and easy to use."

"And you could use it to activate some grand plan by transmitting an e-mail to any number of people all at the same time," Katz said. "Anywhere in the world. All the person at the other end needs is a computer to receive the message."

"Like a laptop," Sharon said. "They're so common now no one even notices them. People use them all the time."

"Ideal for activating a terrorist cell."

"Press the Send button and blow the world to hell in one day," James observed.

Katz picked up the laptop and the disks. He was followed by James and Hawkins, who scooped up printed sheets scattered around the printer.

"I need to get these back to our people. Let them analyze any data they can extract."

"We'll stay on here and follow through with Ben," James said. "We still need to find Dahoun."

"I can organize a flight for you," Sharon said.

"Good," Katz said. "The sooner the better. This isn't over yet."

CHAPTER EIGHT

Canada

Able Team moved in on the farm, weapons up and ready. There were a number of bodies lying around the immediate area. Dead and dying. Blancanales skirted the smoking wreck of the panel truck that had exploded. The charred and blast-shredded corpse of the driver still remained, hunched over the wheel.

"Call Hal," Lyons said to Schwarz. "Put him in the picture and tell him to contact the Canadian authorities about this damn mess. Make sure he gets clearance for us. I don't want the cops coming in here with drawn guns."

Schwarz took out his sat-com unit and made the call.

As he closed in on the farm house, Carl Lyons detected movement behind one of the windows. He reacted instantly, dropping to the rain-soaked ground, and heard the sudden, vicious crackle of autofire. Slugs slapped the ground to his left. Lyons rolled, coming up against the side of a heavy-wheeled trailer. He pulled back behind the steel chassis.

Blancanales and Schwarz had responded to the outburst, taking cover.

"Hey, it's time to quit," Blancanales yelled. "It's all over."

"It will not be over until you are all dead."

Lyons snorted in frustration at the response. "Cut the crap talk, pal. You need to come out now. Hands in the air. Guns on the ground. This is no time for playing hard-asses."

"You think we are cowards? We will not negotiate. If you wish to stop us, then try."

Schwarz, still behind his cover, had Brognola on the line. He carefully explained their position and what had happened before.

"How many dead?"

"Hard to say," Schwarz told him. "We started taking shots before we could get to helping the casualties. Hal, get someone in here fast. If the wounded don't get help, there'll be more dead. And remember to tell the Mounties we're on their side."

An autoweapon opened up again. Slugs clanged off steel.

Lyons hated the rain and the wet ground. Water was dripping from the peak of his baseball cap, running down the back of his neck, and he didn't relish the idea of staying where he was for much longer.

He studied the farmhouse. It was a single-story building with a covered porch running the length of the structure. The exterior wall facing him had four windows set in the timber. The main door stood open, swinging slightly on its hinges. Lyons wondered why it was doing that. There was no breeze to speak of, and certainly not one strong enough to move a heavy timber door. The only reason it would move like that was if someone were standing behind it, maybe trying to peer through the gaps in the timber by edging the door back and forth.

Lyons wriggled under the trailer and moved to the end closest to the house. He rested the Uzi on a metal cross member and aimed at the door. He stroked off three short bursts, moving them up and across the door at body height. The door swung inward as splinters were chewed from the timber.

"Murderers!"

The raised voice was followed by a sustained burst of autofire from the same window as before. There was no care taken. The volley was sprayed back and forth across the yard, slugs striking indiscriminately.

Lyons only saw Blancanales as he raised up from his position to the far left of the window. His arm swung up and forward, then something round and dark slipped from his fingers. It described a perfect arc as it moved through the air and in through the window.

The blast from the grenade blew out part of the timber wall as well as the window frame. Splintered wood and the torn body of the shooter were hurled across the porch and onto the wet, muddy ground outside. Smoke curled from the gap in the wall, was caught by the rain and whipped away instantly.

They waited for a couple of minutes before making a break for the house. Blancanales covered Lyons as he went in first, then the positions were reversed so Blancanales could follow. The inside of the house had been partially wrecked by the fragmentation grenade Blancanales had thrown. Furniture had been overturned, possessions shattered.

Lyons found the body of the man he had shot

through the door. A number of his shots had found the man's chest and throat. He lay on his back, his fingers still curled around the grip of the H&K MP-5 he had been using. A heavy autopistol was tucked into the waistband of his dark trousers.

Lyons and Blancanales made a quick search of the house. No more of the enemy were inside. There was evidence of long-term occupation—bedding and possessions. One room had been turned into a prayer room. It had been carefully adorned with Islamic relics and prayer mats. Islamic scriptures were pinned to the walls, and an open copy of the Koran sat on a small table.

"What do you figure these say?" Blancanales asked.

He was staring at the scriptures pinned to the walls. Lyons shrugged.

"Bring them along. We can get them translated."

In the main room Blancanales noticed a laptop on the floor beside an overturned table. He picked it up and examined it.

"Looks exactly like the one we found in Ashar's apartment."

He tucked it under his arm and followed Lyons outside.

"Hey, Pol, you want to go check those police cruisers back there? Should be first-aid kits. We could use them."

Blancanales nodded and went to search the police vehicles parked in the trees behind the farm.

Lyons joined Schwarz and they did what they could for the wounded until Blancanales returned, medical kits hanging from straps over his shoulders.

ABLE TEAM WAS still tending to the wounded when the Canadian police and emergency vehicle convoy arrived. They gave all the information they could to the medics before they were summoned to face the man in charge.

His name was Glaser. He was a cop who had seen it all, but even he was stunned by the severity of the gun battle and the high casualty rate.

"I should be mad as hell with you people," he stormed, angry at the loss of life as well as the presence of fully armed, illicit intruders on Canadian soil. "But I guess you did a lot to help our guys, so I have to thank you for that. Now what the hell is all this about?"

Glaser had been instructed from levels of command high above him that Able Team, though unsanctioned, was now to be accepted as bona fide representatives of the U.S. government. Any lack of communication beforehand had been due to insufficient time and a need to investigate the situation at the Ghosh farm.

"At least it looks like your suspicions were correct," Glaser said. "Jesus, that's all we need. Terrorist cells on Canadian soil."

"Where did your people come from?" Schwarz asked.

Glaser ran a big hand through his hair. "Local cops. Seems they'd been keeping the place under observation for the last few days. Some local kids reported seeing armed men around the place. So the local chief decided to stage a raid. Probably figured it would look good in the headlines."

"Probably doesn't think that now," Blancanales said.

"I don't suppose he will," Glaser agreed. "He's one of the dead."

"This may not be any help," Lyons said, "but this group was only a part of something pretty big. The FBI gave us the background on this bunch. They were suspected of smuggling explosives into the U.S. We only got into it a few days ago ourselves. This visit was supposed to have been for recon only."

"How far down the line does it go?"

"We don't have all the numbers yet," Lyons explained, "but there are links to the Middle East."

Sirens began to wail as the ambulances pulled away from the farm and started to ferry the injured to hospitals.

"I probably don't need to mention this, but keep those terrorists under close watch," Lyons said. "If their people find out they've been taken alive, they might come after them."

Glaser allowed himself a tight smile. "Yeah? I hope the sons of bitches try."

"These people play rough."

"You don't say? Well, wait until they get me mad if you want to see rough." Glaser turned as his name was called. "Oh, by the way, hang around awhile. I need to talk to you before you leave."

"At least he didn't threaten to toss us in jail," Blancanales said.

"He isn't finished with us yet," Schwarz reminded him.

"Probably wants to shake our hands for what we did."

"What's it really like living on Fantasy Island?" Schwarz asked.

Glaser rejoined them a while later. Able Team was

sheltering by one of the big police trucks, drinking hot coffee supplied by one of the Canadian cops.

"The way our people see it, that panel truck must have been packed with explosives. They found traces in the wreckage. And some of these."

He handed a length of charred cable fitted with a pressure switch to Lyons.

"Now that is all we need," Lyons said. "This is one of those damn things that primes the charge when you press it down and doesn't make the connection until the button is released."

Glaser looked at the switch, then at the faces of the Stony Man commandos.

"You saying what I think you are?" Glaser asked.

Blancanales nodded. "This is one you don't walk away from," he said. "The guy who delivers a bomb attached to this goes down with the explosion."

"Time to call home and let them know," Lyons said.

Stony Man Farm, Virginia

"Not exactly the kind of news that makes you want to party," Brognola said.

He had just been speaking to Lyons, and had since informed the rest of the group.

"We talking suicide bombers here?" Akira Tokaido asked.

"It's one name for it," Hunt Wethers said.

"What is wrong with this world?" Delahunt asked. "Isn't there enough going on without this kind of thing? Why do these people hate us so much? Why can't we figure out a way to stop all the killing?"

"If we knew the answer to those questions, there wouldn't be a problem," Brognola said.

"Thanks, Hal, that helps a lot."

"Look, I wish had a solution, but I don't. Religion-based terrorism is the hardest to settle because it isn't a matter of saying this side has this piece of land, you have that. Or this faction brings in its own people to share the vote in an election. What we are dealing with isn't something you parcel up. It's dealing with what drives a person's life. Dictates how he acts and thinks, and the fact that what is ordinary to you or me is a terrible sin to the other guy. Look how easy it is to upset a whole religious society by simply writing a book like Salman Rushdie did. The guy didn't do it to betray religious law, but it did, and he had a price put on his head. Offend these people and they don't forgive, or forget. Our way is totally opposite to how they view life. And they feel we have offended them. Broken tradition, law, sacred rules. They refuse to sit down to discuss it. Instead they have decided we have to be punished. Plain and simple, with no way out."

Brognola sat down, feeling in his pocket for an antacid tablet.

"Big speech of the week," he said, smiling wearily. "Don't ask any more complicated questions, Carmen. You used up your quota."

"I guess I did."

"Okay, guys, discussion time over," Price said. "Let's get back to work. Able Team is on its way back in, bringing the computer they found at the farmhouse. It's our first real piece of evidence. See what you can get from it, Aaron. We need the whole team on this. Full-time."

CHAPTER NINE

Kurdistan

"How long is a while?" Manning asked.

The night had passed slowly. The darkness brought a severe temperature drop, leaving the Stony Man team exposed to the elements. Nothing was done to ease their discomfort. They were left in the open lean-to. The only consolation was that the terrorists guarding them were also obliged to remain in the open. The armed watchers carried AK-74s and patrolled back and forth in order to keep warm while the rest of the camp settled down for the night. The pair was relieved during the early hours.

Now the sky was starting to pale. Cold light was showing above the ridges. The Stony Man commandos had taken turns resting, one remaining awake at all times in case of any changes in their situation. With dawn coming, Manning had decided to ask the question.

"I think time's up," McCarter said.

He had been watching the two guards closely. Neither seemed as alert as they had a few hours ago. Having to constantly keep watch over the prisoners, stay awake and try to maintain some body heat had slackened their concentration to a degree. They were still moving around, but not as sharply. One had his Kalashnikov tucked under his arm as he rubbed his hands together to ward off the chill. His partner, some distance away, had his back to the lean-to as he took a moment to relieve himself.

It was a moment that wouldn't be repeated, McCarter knew, and it was about as good as they were going to get.

"Make or break, mates," McCarter said.

He had been flexing his arms and legs at every opportunity, getting the circulation going, working his fingers inside his combat suit to warm them up. As he finished speaking, McCarter burst into action, catapulting himself from beneath the lean-to. His long legs took him the couple of yards to the guard warming his hands.

As the terrorist raised his eyes, he saw the blur of movement as McCarter reached him. The Briton's left hand chopped in under the guard's jaw, the hard edge of his palm smashing into the terrorist's throat with force enough to shatter the windpipe. The choking guard offered no resistance when McCarter snatched the AK-74 from under his arm. The Phoenix Force leader reversed the weapon and slammed the butt into the guard's skull, dropping him to the ground.

The second guard heard the brief scuffle and turned, forgetting his activity, snatching at the rifle slung from his shoulder.

McCarter, down on one knee, had already raised his newly acquired weapon. He aimed and fired, knocking the guard down with a short burst.

Manning and Encizo went past McCarter as he snatched the autopistol from the man he had downed. He pushed to his feet and followed in Encizo's wake. Manning had grabbed the AK-74 dropped by the man McCarter had shot.

"Take this," the Briton said, pushing the autopistol in Encizo's direction. The Cuban took it, flicking off the safety and raising the weapon to trigger a single shot at a figure racing at them out of the shadows. The terrorist caught the slug in the chest and went down on his knees. The AK-74 in his hands went off, stitching the empty air with a volley of slugs.

"The chopper!" McCarter yelled as he led the way across the campsite, away from the bulk of the terrorists. Between the men of Phoenix Force and the resting helicopter were stacks of boxes containing the weapons waiting to be shipped out.

Manning positioned himself at the first stack of boxes, using his AK-74 to hold back the terrorists as they stumbled awake. The advantage was with the escapees due to the fact that the cover they were using consisted of boxed weapons and ammo. The terrorists were loath to fire in that direction in case they caused damage, or even an explosion.

Encizo dislodged an overhanging crate as he pushed himself around the stack, seeking cover. The crate hit the hard ground, the impact splitting the case open.

A number of handguns fell from the case, followed by thick cylinders. The autopistols were brand-new Beretta 92-F models, still in sealed plastic wraps. Alongside lay AAC M9-QD suppressers, the cylindrical tubes coated in an anodized matte black coating. Manning and Encizo took note of the large number of weapons.

"No expense spared," Manning said. Just before he moved on he scooped up one of the Berettas and a suppressor, tucking them inside his combat suit.

The Stony Man commandos moved away from the terrorists, using the arms dump as cover. The extent of the weaponry was brought to their attention as McCarter spotted crates marked U.S. and bearing the Mossberg imprint. The crates contained M-590 A1 compact 12-gauge pump shotguns.

"Supposed to be military supply only," he commented. "These blokes are well connected."

"Here's what we need," Encizo said, upending a crate and spilling a number of LAW-type launchers across the ground.

"Use the damn things," McCarter growled as he moved to the far end of the arms dump.

Peering around the edge, the Briton checked the distance to the helicopter. It stood on a raised section of ground with a clear area around it.

The only obstacle McCarter had to breach was the two-man machine-gun crew waiting at the base of the raised ground. Sensible thinking had posted guards on the helicopter.

The machine-gun crew, alerted by the shooting, was swinging the machine gun around to cover the area in front of them.

The terrorists were sharpening themselves up now, pushing back the effects of being awakened suddenly. Shouted orders were being passed back and forth. The rattle of weapons being cocked. Despite this, there was no shooting.

"Looks like we're safe as long as we stay here," Manning said.

"The hell with that," Encizo muttered.

He had one of the LAWs in his hands and was busy sliding out the fore and aft sections, readying the weapon for firing. He knelt beside the outer row of boxes, the LAW resting on his shoulder as he sighted along the tube. When he pressed the trigger the LAW gave a throaty growl and released its missile. The rocket struck toward the rear of the camp, near the rock face it butted up against. The sound of the explosion drowned the yells of anger and the screams of pain as the missile detonated.

"Keep them busy," McCarter said, and returned to check the machine-gun position.

He flicked the AK to single shot and raised it to his shoulder, sighting on the gunner, taking his time before he fired and put a slug through the man's left shoulder. The gunner half rose, a hand slapping his shattered shoulder. The moment he raised himself above the bulk of the machine gun McCarter hit him with a second shot, toppling the man.

The loader bent to push his partner aside, intending to man the gun himself.

McCarter sprinted in his direction, pausing only to loose a couple of rounds that drove the terrorist back.

At McCarter's rear Gary Manning saw dark shapes skirting the perimeter of the campsite, moving in a circle that would bring them to the helicopter. The Canadian crouched in the shadows of a stack of long boxes and put his Kalashnikov to his shoulder, sighting in on the moving figures.

Manning was the official sniper for Phoenix Force.

He would have preferred a more sophisticated weapon than a standard-issue AK-74, but there was little point in worrying over that. He tracked the lead figure moving on a course that would bring him to a face-off with McCarter.

Easing back on the trigger, Manning sent a single 5.45 mm slug at his target. He saw the terrorist falter and go down. The other men hesitated, giving Manning the space he needed for his second shot. This time he took his shot quickly, now having his range acquisition. Again he saw his man fall. The others turned and throwing caution to the wind began to fire in Manning's direction.

A second LAW banged off its projectile, the rocket streaking across the campsite, exploding among the gathered terrorists and decimating their number.

DAVID MCCARTER dropped to one knee, snapping the AK to his shoulder. The machine-gun loader had managed to grab the handles of the pivotal weapon and was hauling it around to line up on the lone figure. His finger was depressing the firing button when McCarter's shot cleaved its way through his upper chest. The terrorist yelled at the sheer agony engulfing his body, then slumped back. His fingers remained clamped around the firing handle, and his finger stiffened against the button. The machine gun began to rattle out its shots, spraying the area with random fire. McCarter dropped to the ground, cursing in a mixture of sheer alarm and anger.

A third LAW exploded, raining debris over the campsite, scattering more of the terrorists, who decided that holding back their own fire was pointless.

The crackle of autofire added to the general noise, slugs thumping into the crates around Encizo. He saw the wisdom in retreating and scooped up as many of the LAWs as he could before he backed away.

Flat on the ground, McCarter fired off a number of shots at the persistent loader, managing to hit the man and loosen his finger from the firing button. The machine gun fell silent, and McCarter pushed to his feet. He made a final run for the helicopter, throwing himself flat on his stomach under the rear of the aircraft.

Manning followed close on the Briton's heels, tossing aside his AK as he reached the machine gun. Dragging the barrel around, the Canadian began to fire in the direction of the terrorists who had tried to come in on the flank. The heavy fire from the machine gun pushed them back under cover.

Coming up on the blind side of the helicopter, McCarter opened the pilot's door and scrambled inside. He ran a quick eye over the instrument panel and the overhead switches, then began to switch on. The powering sequence seemed interminably slow, the long rotors sweeping the air lazily. McCarter coaxed the twin turbines with restrained impatience, muttering obscenities at them under his breath.

Encizo had caught up now. He slid open one of the main cabin doors, dumping his LAWs inside, then hauling himself onboard.

"Get me some time," McCarter yelled above the increasing whine of the turbines.

Encizo swung one of the swivel-mounted machine guns away from the inside of the cabin and aimed it across the campsite. The weapon was loaded and ready, so all Encizo had to do was press the trigger. The powerful gun began to fire, lacing the air with a stream of heavy bullets.

Manning's weapon locked as the belt of ammunition ran out. He snatched up his AK and turned for the helicopter, hauling himself in to one side of Encizo's thundering machine gun. Moving to the other side of the cabin, Manning dragged open the door and brought the machine gun on his side into play, adding it to Encizo's fire.

At the controls McCarter poured on the power, working the cyclic stick and the foot controls, feeling the Puma shudder as it tried to pull up off the ground. He corrected the machine as it swayed, added more revs and this time felt the helicopter respond with a positive feel. It lifted clear of the ground.

Terrorist weapons were turned on the helicopter with a vengeance, bullets clanging and thumping into the fuselage. McCarter flinched as something struck the Plexiglas canopy in front of him. The screen cracked but didn't shatter. He could feel the Puma vibrate as bullets pounded it, and he kept everything crossed mentally, hoping nothing important got hit. He swung the chopper around, giving Manning and Encizo a better field of fire. They raked the campsite from end to end, putting down a number of the terrorists and scattering the rest.

The Puma rose beyond the effective range of the autoweapons. McCarter leaned forward and checked the weapons' array. The Puma was equipped with cannon and rocket pods. He activated the firing mechanism and saw that the Puma was fully armed.

Manning leaned over his shoulder, eyeing the tactical-weapons setup.

"Nice target down there for you to practice on," he said.

"Just what I was thinking. Be a shame if we let all those guns fall into the wrong hands."

McCarter turned the Puma, angling the helicopter toward the campsite. In the clearing light he could see tiny figures running back and forth.

A sudden flash from below warned McCarter that someone had decided to use one of the LAW rockets. He swung the helicopter out of the missile's flight path, and it overshot by yards.

Targeting the bulky outline of the weapons dump, McCarter primed the rocket pod and fired off a salvo. The stream of missiles cut a blazing trail as they plunged to the ground. They struck the outer fringes of the stacked cases, detonating with powerful blasts that engulfed the munitions. A chain reaction set in, and the entire section of the campsite vanished in a series of crackling explosions that filled the air with flame and smoke and a considerable amount of debris. The blast expanded out as well as up, scattering men and equipment in all directions. A thick pall of smoke rose into the clear sky, staining the clean expanse of blue.

McCarter felt the control response turning heavy. He tried to overcome the sluggishness, but nothing happened.

"What is it?" Encizo asked. "We take a hit?"

"Maybe," McCarter replied. "Bloody lot of bullets were flying our way."

"We going to make it?" Manning asked. He

peered around as something caught his eye. "David, we're making smoke."

"Bugger it," McCarter said. "Pressure's dropping. Looks like an oil leak."

He used the Puma's remaining power to lift them over the looming rock face and away from the campsite.

"If those guys down there saw the smoke, they'll be coming after us."

"We'll go and see what we can take with us," Manning said.

He and Encizo made their way to the main cabin. There were gun racks against one of the bulkheads, holding a number of AKs. In storage compartments on the deck were magazines and a small number of Russian manufactured hand grenades.

Encizo discovered something that brought a smile to his lips. Pushed to the rear of the compartment was a bulky canvas bag. The Cuban recognized it as being similar to the one their gear had been collected in after their capture. Pulling open the top of the bag, Encizo saw their gear inside.

"Gary, look at this."

Manning joined him, and together they pulled out their weapons, radios and NVGs. The GPS unit was in with the other gear. Their satisfaction at regaining their weapons was nothing to what McCarter said when they handed him his beloved Hi-Power.

"Send in the bloody Republican Guard," the Briton said, holding up the Browning. "Even they couldn't stop me now."

Manning shook his head sadly. "Poor bastard believes it, as well."

"I heard that," McCarter said. "But it's bloody well true."

Dropping into the seat next to McCarter's, the Canadian produced the Beretta and suppresser he had picked up while they were on the ground.

"Pistols with silencers. Close-combat shotguns. What the hell are these guys up to, David? These have nothing to do with setting off bombs. Put a suppressor on a gun, it means you're about to do something sneaky."

McCarter nodded. "Been on my mind, too."

"More like covert ops."

"Assassinations maybe?"

They all felt the helicopter start to vibrate. The sound of the turbines began to falter. For a moment the sound surged as McCarter boosted the power, then it fell away again.

"Going down, mates," McCarter called. "Hang on to whatever you think valuable."

The Puma began to lose height with increasing speed, swinging a little as McCarter tried to keep it on an even course.

The engines began to power down, and McCarter struggled against the deadening pull of the controls.

"This might be a tad bumpy," he warned.

The rugged terrain appeared to rise up to meet them with alarming speed. McCarter, aware of the waning control remaining, held off until the last possible moment before he worked the stick and milked the fading turbines for a last few seconds of power. His maneuver pulled the helicopter back just short of the ground, so that there was a degree of resistance. They made ground zero with a little power, avoiding a deadweight landing. Even so the Puma hit hard, bouncing on its undercarriage. One tire burst, and the helicopter swung sharply, throwing Manning across the cabin.

McCarter hung onto the controls until the Puma settled, then cut all the power switches. He scrambled out of the seat and followed Manning to the main compartment. Encizo handed over their MP-5s and extra ammunition, then scooped up the additional LAWs he had brought along. Manning shouldered one of the AK-74s, as well. They cleared the smoking helicopter, heading for a dark mass of tumbled rock that would provide some cover while they decided on their next move.

Behind them the smoking helicopter showed flame. The fire spread along the turbine pods, creeping across the upper section.

"At least they won't be chasing us in that thing," McCarter said.

"Isn't that a comfort," Manning said. He was nursing a badly bruised shoulder received during the heavy landing.

"Fly it, no," Encizo pointed out. "But that smoke could be seen in Baghdad."

JAMAL SAYID GLANCED up from checking his weapons as he heard someone approaching.

"Well?"

"The helicopter went down no more than four miles away," the messenger said. He waited for a moment. "Jamal? Are we going after them?"

"I suppose we should."

The messenger, a lean, angry Lebanese, asked, "What else did you have in mind? Allow them to get away? If they reach safety, they can direct others here.''

"Yes? And what would they find? Have you looked around? There is nothing left."

The Lebanese frowned. "They must be stopped. Killed. If we allow them to walk away unpunished, what does it tell the world about our resolve? What Falil has decreed?"

"With respect, Falil is not here. Three Westerners have destroyed this place. Only three. Against how many? What does that tell the world about us, my friend?"

The Lebanese wouldn't be placated.

"It tells me to go after them. To kill them. They are the enemy, Jamal. Because we have suffered at their hands, do we give in before the real battle has commenced? Falil has told us to be prepared for a battle that will go on for a long time. He also said that we must expect some defeats, but not to let those defeats change our course. If we let this small setback scare us off, what happens when we suffer something larger?"

Sayid sighed. He knew he was hearing the truth. That they had to pursue the enemy commandos and make them pay for the destruction of the camp and the weapons cache. It had taken time and effort to gather everything in this remote spot. The men who had worked day and night on the creation of the site were entitled to settle the score. As leader in the absence of Dahoun, Sayid should be rallying them, not exhibiting a lack of resolve.

"Tell them we leave as soon as everyone has what he needs."

The Lebanese nodded. As he turned away he

paused. "Jamal, we need to settle something before we leave."

"What?"

"Haquim. The Kurd. The men do not like him around."

"I feel the same," Sayid said. "He betrayed his own for money. No doubt if the circumstances showed again he would sell us just as quickly."

"He is demanding his payment."

Sayid eased the heavy autopistol from the holster on his hip. He checked that the weapon was cocked and ready.

"Go and bring him," he said. "I'll pay him before we leave."

Sayid stood, his hands behind his back, the pistol cool in his grasp as he waited for the man called Haquim to come for his payment.

AN HOUR LATER they were on the trail of the three enemy commandos. They moved in single file across the empty slopes and ridges. Once they had reached the higher country beyond the camp it was possible to see the dark smoke that tainted the sky. The downed helicopter was still burning, marking the position where it had gone down. The reports from the advance party had indicated that the Puma hadn't been destroyed on landing. It had been left in one piece, suggesting that the three Westerners had survived and were probably now making their escape attempt.

The transceiver Sayid carried alerted him to an incoming message.

"Jamal, speak."

"We have seem them. All three. Moving toward the west."

"They will try to reach the border with Turkey. How far from them are you?"

"A few miles. They have made good time."

"You will need to intercept them. Stop them from traveling farther."

"Jamal, do we kill them?"

"I would prefer them alive. It would be profitable to have these men in our hands for a while before they died."

"If they resist?"

"Decide when you confront them. If taking them alive is going to cost us dear, then kill them."

"Understood."

THERE WERE FOUR in the advance party. They moved quickly, unhampered by additional equipment. Each man carried his AK-74, extra magazines and a knife, a small canteen of water, a transceiver and nothing else. Two were Iraqi, and they knew the mountainous area well. All were seasoned fighters, brought together by Falil's call to arms. One was Libyan. The fourth was a Pakistani.

All had come together as part of Falil's bonding of an Islamic collective, ready to endorse his campaign of restitution of the Islamic brotherhood through a relentless, ongoing conflict aimed at weakening the resolve and morale of the enemy by attrition. The intrusion of the Western invaders had only increased their determination to bring about Falil's prophecies of victory. The need to stop them before they returned to their base was fueled by the Islamics' sense of personal integrity. These foreigners, in the employ of their greatest enemy, had inflicted severe damage to the campsite and cache of weapons. It was an outrage that had to be redressed.

The transceiver carried by one of the Iraquis became active. He replied, acknowledging his caller.

"Our Russian friends are on their way to help you," Sayid informed him.

The Iraqi, Nadir, stared at the handset for a moment.

"Nadir? Did you hear what I said?"

"Of course. I was trying to understand why they are coming."

"It appears that these men were with the *peshmerga* who ambushed the oil convoy. Nadir, the loss of that oil cost us a great deal of money. The Russians, too."

"Why do we need these godless Russians? We can deal with our own problems."

"We have to be practical. The Russians have a helicopter. Also a number of land vehicles. Why not use them, allow them to assist us. Look at it from another view. If they are willing to put themselves in the line of fire, it seems a pity to deny them the privilege."

"How will Falil feel if we allow infidels to work with us?"

"I recall during one of his speeches he said something along the lines of use your enemies to defeat your enemies."

"As long as these Russians do not get in our way, send them in."

"Take care, my brother."

Nadir clicked off the transceiver. He saw the others watching him. They had most likely heard his side of the conversation and had to have understood what was happening.

"Let them do the donkey work for us," Nadir said.

"Russians. Donkeys. What's the difference?" asked one of his companions. "Let them go in first. They are as bad as our former prisoners. If we're lucky, they'll kill one another."

THE RUSSIANS FLEW IN with a liberated Mil Mi-17 Hip. The cargo helicopter, once belonging to a tactical squadron, still carried its 12.7 mm nose gun. The original paint job had been covered over with a dark blue color during its transition from military machine to smugglers' transport.

The pilot, Sergei Yentalov, was an ex-Soviet army pilot. Now he ran his thriving business from a base in Sevastopol. Despite the fact he was reasonably wealthy, Yentalov was unable to sit back and simply let his business run itself. He had to be involved. It was in his nature.

Beside him his partner, Mikhail Berkof, glanced at Yentalov

"Remind me again, Sergei. Just why are we doing this?"

"What happened the other day?"

"You know what happened. Those damned Kurdish idiots attacked the convoy."

"Correct. Because of that attack we lost valuable oil. Men. Vehicles. It has cost us a great deal of money. It also means we cannot deliver another shipment for at least two weeks. Customer dissatisfaction. That can be worse than losing the oil."

"So chasing all over these damned mountains is going to get all that back?"

Yentalov smiled. "Listen, Mikhail. The most important consideration. Nothing else matters. Delivery problems are ours. Not his. He doesn't care about reasons or excuses. All the man wants is what he ordered, delivered on time."

"I don't need a lesson in good trading practices."

"News of what happened to the convoy will get around quickly enough. We have to be seen dealing with it, otherwise our customers will start to believe we are weak. That is bad business practice. Let these Kurds and their American backers get away with it once, and before long our customer base will start to shrink."

"I suppose you're right."

Yentalov eased the Hip around in a banking curve that brought them in low across the undulating landscape. It was sparse, harsh country. He didn't like it, nor did he care for the people. They were too serious and wrapped up in their religious beliefs to see the real world. But Yentalov could forgive them that. He was here to make money for them and himself, and as long as that carried on he didn't give a damn how they wanted to run their affairs. It was their country.

Sayid had given him locations as best he could. Yentalov had seen the downed helicopter some time back, still smoking as it lay on the desolate mountain slope like some back-broken beetle. He had followed the direction of the pursuing Islamics and had passed them. Now he was tracing the expected route of the three Westerners as they made their run for freedom.

Sayid had said he wanted the fugitives alive. In the end that was up to them. They weren't going to give themselves up easily or without a fight. Yentalov had already realized that these weren't ordinary men. Not to have escaped from the Islamic camp, taking on Jamal's entire force and destroying the arms cache before flying off in the helicopter. The more he thought about it, the more Yentalov's admiration grew for them. They had delivered a big slap in the face to the elite terrorist force Falil was gathering. Three men against large odds, and they had gotten away with it.

"If these men were open to negotiation, I'd hire them myself," Yentalov said out loud. "I wish I could have seen Jamal's face when they shot their way out of his camp."

"And blew up his weapons dump, too," Berkof added, a slow smile edging across his lean face.

"I'm going to enjoy this," Yentalov said.

THEY FLEW ON for another half hour before Berkof yelled in triumph.

"I see them! There! Down there!"

He was pointing, jabbing a finger in the direction of the ground. Yentalov followed his finger and saw the three figures, pausing to stare at the approaching helicopter, then breaking into a run.

Yentalov grunted as he picked out the three small figures below. He worked the controls and sent the Hip in a shallow dive, leveling and then upping the revs to send the helicopter in the direction of the trio. His finger caressed the firing button for the 12.7 mm nose gun. He angled the chopper forward, raising the tail, then touched the trigger to send a crackling burst of fire from the nose gun. The line of slugs marched steadily across the brittle, dusty earth, kicking up debris that showered the three men as the Hip overflew them, banking as it gained height.

"TOO BLOODY CLOSE!" McCarter said as he scrambled back, to his feet.

He watched the dark blue Hip arc into the empty sky.

"Who the hell are they?" Manning asked. He was upright again, favoring the shoulder he'd injured.

"Whoever they are we obviously pissed them off," Encizo said, spitting dust out of his mouth.

They ran for cover, seeking the protection of rock formations that looked too far away. The illusion was created by the knowledge that the helicopter was turning for another run. Even as the rocks loomed larger, almost beckoning, the Hip dropped to a low altitude, skimming the ground as it laid out another vicious burst of fire.

The Phoenix Force trio separated, each taking a different avenue of escape as the chopper overshot.

Manning hauled himself to a stop, throwing up the H&K and firing a burst in the Hip's wake.

"Don't waste your ammo, Gary," McCarter yelled above the din of the helicopter.

Encizo reached the rock formation first, throwing himself into cover. As McCarter and Manning joined him, Encizo was priming one of his remaining LAW rocket launchers.

"Be a pity to destroy that thing," McCarter said. "Might be our way out of here."

"Maybe I should just try for the pilot," Encizo suggested. "You know. Just wing his shoulder."

McCarter glanced at the Cuban's deadpan expression.

"He's starting to get sarcastic," the Briton said.

"Wonder who he gets it from?" Manning asked.

THE HIP HAD dropped to a position some thirty feet from them, holding its position just ten feet off the ground, the rotor wash dragging dust and debris into the air. The nose gun was directed at the rock formation behind which Phoenix Force was crouched.

"Standoff," Manning said. "We try to break out, they shoot us down. We stay, those terrorists are going to show up."

Encizo had the LAW ready for firing.

"How do we do this?" he asked.

"Gary, how accurate is that thing?" McCarter asked, indicating the AK-74 Manning had brought along as backup to his H&K.

"Not exactly a sniper rifle, but fair. Why?"

"If Rafael got their attention with that launcher, there might be a chance for you to try for the pilot."

Manning checked out the spread of the rock formation.

"Let me get to the far end. It should get me a side shot through the cabin door."

The Canadian moved to the spot he'd chosen and settled himself at a point where he could see the side view of the Hip's cabin. The pilot's broad figure showed above the edge of the window frame. Manning checked the AK's load, making sure he had a full magazine. He flipped the selector to single shot. Catching McCarter's eye, he nodded.

McCarter tapped Encizo on the arm.

"Let them see you," the Briton said

"Easy for you to say," Encizo muttered as he slowly exposed himself above the rock formation, the

LAW already in position on his shoulder, aimed directly at the Hip's front canopy.

There was no immediate response from the Hip. The pilot had seen Encizo and also what he was wielding. The two men in the pilot's compartment had exchanged glances and would be considering their options. They were small. The helicopter wasn't fast enough to outrun something like the LAW rocket from its current position. Even if it was able to pull away at maximum speed, the LAW would reach it first.

"NOT SUCH a bright idea, after all," Berkof said.

His gaze was fixed on the slender tube being aimed directly at the helicopter canopy. Berkof had no doubts as to the intention of the man holding that tube. He also knew there was no way Yentalov could pull them out of range fast enough.

"I could shoot him." Yentalov suggested, his thumb hovering over the nose gun's firing button.

"Can you guarantee to hit him? The first time?"

Although the Hip was hovering, there was still a constant movement of the helicopter. Gentle swaying back and forth, slightly rising then falling. Not strong movement but enough to deny Yentalov one-hundred-percent accuracy. The man holding the LAW rocket launcher didn't need such precise targeting. Once he fired, the rocket couldn't fail to miss the bulk of the helicopter.

Frustration built rapidly. Yentalov didn't know what to do. It had seemed such an easy task when he had taken off earlier. Track down the enemy, kill or capture them. Three men against an armed helicopter. Now the tables had turned, and it was Yentalov who faced the moment of truth. Did he risk everything—including his life—in an attempt to get himself and Berkof out of this situation? If he survived, then nothing had been lost. If he failed, which was looking the more likely of the options, then his life and his dreams and his profits were lost. Yentalov looked at it that way because he was a practical man. Self-made. Never afraid of hard work or risk.

Perhaps, he thought, this was the way to see this moment. As a risk to be taken. Perhaps the biggest risk of his life. He usually had a better grip on the situation, had looked at and considered the chances he would be taking if he embarked on a particular venture. This time the options had been presented to him without prior consideration. And the time for working things out was quickly evaporating. Whichever way Yentalov turned, he was going to have to do it soon. Within seconds, not even minutes, because that LAW might explode at any moment, sending its fiery missile straight into his face.

"HE'S THINKING about it," Encizo said, "figuring whether he's fast enough to dodge this rocket."

"Let's hope he doesn't make up his mind too fast," McCarter replied. "Come on, Gary."

GARY MANNING HAD the pilot in his sights. The Canadian's finger held the trigger lightly, barely exerting any pressure. He was waiting until the Hip stopped rocking. The chopper's movement was slight but enough to make accurate shooting difficult, and Manning knew he would only get one chance. It would be the difference between walking out of the mountains or flying and possibly making contact via the chopper's radio with friends rather than enemies.

YENTALOV KEPT the Hip as level as he could. At the same time he began to ease the machine back. Only slightly, and keeping the movement as masked as possible from the man holding the LAW. The Russian had reached a decision concerning the Westerners. They would only destroy the Hip if there was no other way to resolve the stalemate, because, he realized, they needed the chopper in one piece. It would be their way out of the mountains. On foot, with no support, they might outrun the Islamic brothers for a time. But that wouldn't last for long. As good as they were, this was enemy territory. They had no friends here. They had escaped with very little in the way of equipment or supplies, so time wasn't on their side. If they could take command of a helicopter capable of flight, they could clear the area quickly and maybe even bring back reinforcements to strike at the Islamic group.

Yentalov was only surmising the scenario, but it seemed to fit. If the Westerners wanted him and his helicopter out of the game, why wait? They would have blown him out of the sky the moment he was in their sights. That hadn't happened, and Yentalov didn't believe it would. He smiled to himself as he eased the Hip back, gaining a few inches at a time, trying to gain a little distance and also widen his field of fire.

If he could only keep this up for a little while longer.

IT WAS Gary Manning's alternative view of the Hip that revealed to him the Russian pilot's tactical move. Head on, the gentle backward movement of the helicopter wouldn't be noticed.

Until it was too late.

"Clever," Manning said softly, "but not clever enough."

He took a breath and resighted, able to synchronize his aim with the gentle flow of the Hip as it reversed. The pilot's right shoulder and upper body held in Manning's sight for long enough. He stroked the trigger and felt the sharp backslap of the AK's butt as the weapon cracked.

YENTALOV FELT the impact even before he registered the splintering of the Plexiglas side window. The 5.45 mm slug cored deep into his shoulder, tumbling as it cleaved muscle and sinew, then struck his collarbone, fracturing it severely. Yentalov lost all control of his faculties as the trauma seized him. He turned in his seat, his eyes wide in shock, unable to even make a sound. His fingers slipped from the controls, his feet jerking over the pedals.

The Hip began to turn, losing height rapidly. The engine faltered as it lost power. The helicopter's weight took over, and it slid to the hard ground, bouncing heavily as the undercarriage groaned beneath the deadweight. The right-hand strut buckled, and the machine dipped.

Berkof tried to regain control. He was no pilot, having only recently started to learn under Yentalov's tutelage, and he was taken completely by surprise by what happened.

The Russian was still trying to stabilize the shuddering helicopter when he heard a tap on the side window. He turned to see one of the enemy aiming an AK-74 at him. The only thing that separated them was the Plexiglas window.

Berkof stared out the canopy and saw that the man with the LAW was approaching. He still had the weapon directed at the helicopter. A third man, carrying another Kalashnikov, was also heading toward the Hip.

The cabin door was yanked open.

"Out!" Manning snapped.

Berkof unbuckled his straps and slid from the cabin. He was shoved face-first against the side of the Hip, and someone searched him thoroughly, removing his weapons.

"Get your friend out," Manning said.

One of the other men had opened the door on Yentalov's side and had relieved him of his handgun. The same man helped Berkof to ease Yentalov out of the helicopter. They laid the semiconscious man on the ground. Yentalov was bleeding badly, groaning against the pain.

"You cannot leave us here," Berkof said.

"Why not?" McCarter asked sharply. "You were ready to mow us down with that bloody nose cannon."

"That was combat."

McCarter had to laugh at the sheer incongruity of the Russian's statement.

"Now we are your prisoners," Berkof said. "Prisoners have rights."

"Bloody nerve. Listen, mate, you seem to be forgetting something. This isn't a bleeding war we're in."

"No?" Berkof asked. "Is it not a war?"

Encizo had climbed into the back of the Hip and came out with a first-aid kit. He knelt beside Yentalov, who was unconscious, and stripped away the man's jacket and shirt. The bullet had chewed a messy hole going into the man's shoulder. The torn flesh was showing bone fragments.

"We could stow them in the back under guard," Manning suggested. "Hand them over once we reach friendly territory."

McCarter sighed. "You buggers are getting soft in your old age," he said. "Okay, I'm too bloody tired and hungry to argue. Get them onboard before I start crying."

TEN MINUTES LATER the Hip was back in the air, McCarter at the controls, taking the machine up steadily until he was certain that the forced landing hadn't done any damage. He felt a little better once he had reached satisfactory height and had the Hip on a steady course for the Turkish border.

Encizo and Manning had done what they could to make Yentalov comfortable. Once the Russian was settled Encizo remained with him and Berkof in the main cabin, while Manning joined McCarter in the pilot's section. As Manning dropped into the spare seat, McCarter glanced across at him.

"That was a bloody good shot," he said.

"I had to go when I did. That Russian was starting to back off. You probably couldn't see from where you were. I figure he was trying to widen his firing arc for the nose gun so he could make a try for you and Rafael."

"Sneaky bastard."

McCarter picked up a map he'd found among the pile of charts strewed around the cabin.

"We're somewhere here," he said. "Hand me that GPS unit, somebody." McCarter tapped in the coordinates from the map, and the GPS unit came up with their position as it connected with an orbiting satellite. "At least we know where we're going now."

McCarter picked up a set of headphones and put them on. He flicked on the radio and went through the wave bands, trying to pick up an incoming friendly signal. The reception wasn't all that good, and the Briton swore under his breath at the radio, which certainly couldn't be classed as state-of-the-art.

"My bloody electric razor has a better range than this thing!"

"Calm down and just fly," Manning said.

McCarter settled back to fly the Hip, still grumbling to himself about how it was no wonder the Soviet Empire had collapsed when it had to depend on such antiquated equipment.

"I could buy something better down the Portobello Road market in London."

"Yeah, yeah, we all know," Manning said. "And pie and peas and a pint of beer, wiv change out of a pound."

McCarter glared at him. "You bloody piss-taking poor excuse for a Canadian lumberjack."

"And so's your old man."

They ended up grinning like idiots at each other until a calm, measured voice with a distinct Texan accent came through the static emitting from the radio.

"Who the hell are you? And what are you doing on this restricted U.S. Air Force frequency?"

Stony Man Farm, Virginia

HAL BROGNOLA WAS en route to Stony Man when he was informed about Phoenix Force being picked up by the U.S. Air Force. By the time he touched down and made his way to the War Room, there was a full update waiting for him. Katz was there, as well, with all the data he had been able to pick up during his phase of the mission. So was Able Team. Brognola sat down at the conference table, gratefully accepting the fresh mug of coffee Barbara Price brought him.

He looked at the faces ringing the table, then glanced at Price.

"Let's have it, Barbara," he said.

CHAPTER TEN

"We'll have to wait until David and the others get in touch to hear their update," Brognola said.

"Knowing the way Phoenix operates, I can guess the tone," Price said.

"Are we being a touch cynical here?" Rosario Blancanales asked.

Price smiled. "I've been here before, remember?"

The door opened and Aaron Kurtzman rolled in, followed by Carmen Delahunt. They were carrying data files and computer disks. Delahunt placed the material on the table and took her place. Rolling his wheelchair to his usual position, Kurtzman activated a couple of the big monitor screens.

"Names first," Kurtzman said. "With photos if we have them."

He activated the first monitor, using a hand unit.

"Mustapha Ashar. His involvement with the people at the Nasram Ghosh farm in Ontario can only be guessed at. Go-between? U.S. organizer? Since the police action that wiped the place out we are going to need to watch Ashar closely. According to reports from our FBI liaison, Ashar has been staying put since the incident. Odd for a man who spent so much time visiting his relatives. Family loyalty seems to have been put on hold.

"Next up is our mystery man Joseph Haruni. Not so much of a mystery anymore. International cooperation has pinned him down as an active terrorist. And we have him at meetings with this guy, Mr. Fariq, a lawyer who seems to favor helping his Islamic brothers. Nothing wrong with that except when they turn out to be people like Ashar and Haruni. We have some more background on Fariq since last time. He's married and has three young children. Two boys. One girl. His wife is French. Met her in New York shortly after setting up his practice. She comes from a wealthy background and has legal expertise herself, so they're keeping it in the family."

"Until we have a clearer idea what's being planned," Brognola said, "we'll have to let these people run. If there are any covert cells in the background, they'll go to ground if we drag the high-profile players away."

"There could be a lot hanging on tracking this group down," Price said. "We have a two-front problem, here in the U.S. and a second group operating in the Middle East. We were dragged into this because there was a conceived threat from the so-called KHP. Okay, we were suckered to a point because that was nothing but a smoke screen set up by a genuine organization working a different agenda. But we're into this now, and there is a threat to interests both at home and abroad. All being run by the same group. Led by a guy known only as Falil. No ID yet. To be honest we don't have a great deal of information on this man."

"Mossad is trying to come up with something on

him," Katz said. "Ben Sharon is working all his sources. At the moment it's all vague. Whoever this Falil is, he doesn't go in for much in the way of publicity. No demands. No pronounced threats against anyone."

"What do you make of it?" Schwarz asked.

"I believe this man and his organization are planning some kind of coordinated attack. Here and in the Middle East. The lack of demands concerns me. It isn't as if they're asking for the return of land or the release of prisoners. If we hadn't become aware of them, I think they would have launched whatever they are planning and it would have hit hard."

Brognola shifted in his seat. "Katz, you above anyone in this room have a pretty good insight into the Middle East mind. Take one of your calculated guesses. What does this Falil want?"

The Israeli gathered his thoughts before he spoke, aware that his input might have a profound effect on how Stony Man might tackle the problem.

"If I've read the signs correctly, our mystery man and his group have a long-term objective. Not just a few isolated attacks on the U.S. and Middle East. There's more to this than token damage. I think Falil is looking at a protracted campaign. He's brought together Islamics from different countries. I believe we should be looking for extremists. Total, dedicated Muslims who, for whatever reason, have decided to band together and take on the enemies of Islam. The United States is considered the main defiler of Islam in every form. Right or wrong, that's the way they see it. They want to defeat us. To humiliate the U.S. and make its people pay for the policies of its government."

"What about the Middle East?" Lyons asked. "I can see where they're coming from with regard to Israel. Where does the rest of the region fit into this campaign?"

"Islamic purists would look at some Arab countries and condemn them as much as they do the U.S. Countries who are seen to have embraced Western culture to a degree. Those states where the strict observance of Islamic law has been eased to one side. Those countries who sell their oil to us and buy our goods. In the strict eye of Islamic law they are no longer pure."

"You know what you're saying, Katz?" Schwarz said. "That this group is willing to strike out against its own in the name of Islam. We could be looking at a total breakdown of the Middle East."

Katz nodded slowly. "An all-out war. Setting one group against the other with the intention of bringing the region back to unadulterated Islamic observance."

"This is one of two things," Blancanales said. "Totally crazy or downright frightening."

"Remember these are observations," Katz said. "Even I don't have all the answers on this one because we've been working against a group we don't have much background on."

"If I had to choose between the offerings of a strategy think tank and a Katz observation," Brognola said, "I know which one I'd pick."

Price turned to Kurtzman. "Aaron, before we go back to personalities, how about the data the teams brought back from the laptop, disks, cell phone?"

Kurtzman cleared his throat. Turning to his monitor screens, he brought a second one to life. "Laptops were high-specification models, capable of absorbing lots of data at fast speeds. They were all configured to receive and send e-mail. Fax messages. Okay, that's nothing new these days, but these babies were state-of-the-art. They would be expensive to buy. The ones we picked up here in the U.S. had come from a warehouse heist in New Jersey.

"The cell phone Katz brought back with him was another piece of high art. You can send e-mail messages to this model."

"Electronic communication seems to be something this group intends using big time," Price said. "It's a quick way to send out a message to distant points all at the same time."

"And a good way of keeping in touch without having to ID yourself," Katz pointed out. "As long as there's a phone line to connect to anywhere in the world, a person is able to receive instant information."

"Which is where we came in," Brognola said. "The Echelon listening system was where the messages were first logged. That gave us our way in. What we need now is contact with part of this group so we have a direction."

"Anything from the data on the computers?" Lyons asked.

"We're still working on it. Okay, Akira broke the lockouts and got us into the data. That's where it got hard. Damn things are all in some kind of code we haven't been able to break yet. Taking a guess, I'd say the information relates to dates and times and places. That's easy enough to figure. What we can't get is actual locations."

"What about the scriptures we pulled out of the farmhouse?" Blancanales asked.

"We're waiting for that to come back from our translators. Arabic script. You say you took it from an area set out for prayers?"

"Yeah."

"It could turn out to be nothing more than a passage from the Koran. Something those people used in their prayer sessions."

"Okay," Brognola said, "let's go with what we have. Any thoughts?"

"This guy Fariq, the lawyer," Schwarz said. "Do we assume he's in as deep as the others? He's been seen with Haruni and Ashar, but I'm wondering just how far he'd want to put his lifestyle and his standing at risk for them."

"Personal matters don't hold these people back when it comes to what they consider best for Islam," Price said.

"For some, maybe," Schwarz said. "But this Fariq doesn't strike me as a man on a short-term visit to this country. He's too well established. Look at his setup. Offices in New York and Canada. String of cars. He employs other lawyers, has staff and commitments. Hell, he's even married with a family behind him. Does that suggest a guy ready to hit the trenches?"

"So why has he been helping these people?" Blancanales asked. "Risking everything to bail them out of trouble?"

"Something we may have overlooked," Katz said. "What if Fariq is involved because he doesn't have any choice?"

"He's being forced to help? Is that what you mean?" Lyons asked. "Blackmail?"

"Wouldn't be the first time it's happened," Katz said. He sat back in his seat, watching the faces around the table as his words began to take hold. "Fariq has chosen America as his home and his workplace. If he became involved willingly with these people, he would have made a conscious decision to put family, home and profession at risk. That is a great deal. The majority of terrorists tend not to have such established lifestyles. The cause *is* their family, and they have little that can be used against them if they don't have filial attachments."

"It's worth looking at," Price said.

Lyons nodded. "Okay, we'll check it out."

"I hope we do a damn sight more than check it out," Schwarz said. "Look, guys, maybe I'm coming on strong here, but if this Falil and his terrorists are planning strikes here in the U.S. they have to be stopped. And I mean big time. If they decide to make the U.S. a target, we don't have time to sit back discussing niceties. How long do we wait before we get the message?"

"No argument from me," Brognola said. "I don't care what grievance these people have. If they bring the war to us, then they suffer the consequences."

Katz cleared his throat. "I'm sure I don't have to remind any of you about the dedication of these people. We don't have the hindsight to understand exactly what Falil may have told his organization. How he phrased his reasoning for this campaign. All I can say is this. The Islamic mind will be focused on one thing. The mission. Their interpretation of the facts and the way they go about implementing them will be totally alien to us. When they embark on the Jihad they will be single-minded. Direct in thought and deed. Almost like a human missile. They locate the target, they lock on and they never give in.''

"You can almost admire that kind of dedication," Blancanales said.

"Admire the devotion, but don't let that cloud your instincts. They believe they're fighting a just war. Doing it for God. From our perspective we need to be as dedicated, if not more, to maintaining *our* way of life. If you accept we are in the right then you face them as equals. You cannot afford to be sympathetic to their way of thinking. If you allow that to happen it will cloud your judgment, stay your finger on the trigger when you should be pulling it. If that happens, you are letting them win by default.''

"Let's move, people," Brognola said. "Carl, anything you need before you head out?"

"Only a ride to New York," Lyons said.

"You got it," Price said.

"NICE SPEECH," Brognola said as he and Katz left the War Room.

They were alone in the corridor, everyone else having gone their separate ways.

"I think it needed voicing," the Israeli said. "The Islamic mind-set is hard to understand sometimes. Their religion offers peace and tranquillity. Advocates it. But the laws governing the righting of perceived wrongs can be totally opposite to that. Islamic retribution, for want of a better word, is direct, without deviation. You do not talk to these people once they have their course set. All you can do is confront and defeat it. When it comes to facing such a threat, there is no place for sentiment. They die, or you die. For me the choice is simple. What I might need to do to achieve it will have to be done. I'll wrestle with my conscience and God afterward.''

A BELL JetRanger sat on the pad, its rotors turning slowly. The pilot was waiting on the concrete as Able Team, carrying its luggage, approached.

Jack Grimaldi, Stony Man's resident pilot, took one look at the trio of smartly dressed warriors and grinned from ear to ear. He dragged off his baseball cap and swept it across his body in a mock bow.

"If I'd known, I would have valeted the chopper, guys," he said.

Lyons ignored him. He threw his bags into the passenger compartment.

"Hey, I should be doing that, *sir*," Grimaldi said. He touched the sleeve of Blancanales's suit. "That is some class gear, Pol. You guys going to a convention?"

"Jack, you know where we are going," Lyons snapped. "How about getting us there?"

"Why sure, boss."

As the others settled in their seats, Grimaldi climbed into the pilot's seat and boosted the power. Humming to himself, he cleared the pad and took the JetRanger to altitude, setting a course that would take them to New York.

"Due to short notice we will not be having the normal in-flight service today."

"No little packets of salted peanuts?" Blancanales asked in a grieved tone.

"Sorry, no. Any complaints, take them up with the management."

"I might have one about the pilot," Lyons said.

"Touchy, touchy."

"He hasn't killed anyone today," Schwarz remarked.

"Feeling deprived, Carl?"

"Long time till midnight," Lyons threatened.

"I'm safe," Grimaldi said. "It's in my contract. Passengers are not allowed to harm the pilot while the aircraft is in flight."

Blancanales leaned forward to whisper, "Jack, you have to land some time."

New York City

"YOU WANT ME to wait around?" Grimaldi asked as they approached the city some time later.

"Yeah," Lyons said. "We may need to relocate once we've seen this Fariq character."

"No problem. Just call."

They touched down twenty minutes later. As they descended a heat haze could be seen hanging over the city. New York lay beneath a warm, blue sky. Barbara Price had arranged for a rental car to be waiting at the airfield. Grimaldi helped carry the bags across, and they were placed in the trunk of the big Lincoln.

"Jack, how's Jess?" Blancanales asked.

Jess Buchanan was a young woman Grimaldi had met during a previous mission when Able Team had been on Nassau. She ran a flying charter business on the island and had got caught up in Able Team's mission briefly. Grimaldi had pulled her out of trouble, and since then their relationship had grown.

"Saw her last week," Grimaldi said, slamming the

trunk lid shut. "She's fine. We're getting together soon."

"Tell her we said hello."

"Will do."

"Enough of the hearts and flowers," Lyons grumbled. "Can we go, guys?"

Blancanales grinned at Grimaldi as he climbed into the Lincoln. The pilot leaned in at Lyons's window.

"Take care, guys. And you, Carl."

"Yeah."

Grimaldi, chuckling to himself, wandered into the small office building. He located the vending machine and bought a coffee. As he emerged, he saw the Lincoln pulling out of the gate and making a right as it headed for the highway and New York.

"NICE RIDE," Schwarz observed as he sank back in the padded seat of the Lincoln.

"Pretty good," Blancanales agreed.

Lyons was driving. He remained silent, watching the road ahead and the traffic building.

"Carl, how do we play this?" Blancanales asked.

"Straight. What was said back at the Farm made sense. These terrorists have a hard-on for the U.S. If we've read things right and they figure to start hitting us, there's no sense pussyfooting around. Them or us. That seems to be the way it's being played."

"Fighting talk, my man," Blancanales said.

"Exactly what it is," Schwarz agreed.

Blancanales opened the briefcase he was carrying and passed over each man's handgun. Lyons laid his on the seat next to him.

There was an empty slot next to the building

where Fariq had his office in midtown. Lyons parked, checked his Python and slid it into the shoulder holster he was wearing beneath his dark suit.

They paused on the sidewalk as Lyons locked the Lincoln, then they walked inside the foyer of the building. The Able Team leader led the way to the bank of elevators. Fariq had his office suite on the fifth floor, and Blancanales keyed the button as they stepped inside an empty car. The elevator rose quickly, stopping with barely a jerk, and Able Team emerged onto the hushed fifth floor.

"Nice," Schwarz remarked as they walked to the glass doors bearing Fariq's name.

"Let's hope the guy is at home," Blancanales said, pushing through.

The reception area was plush, modern. Smoked glass and pale wood, a curving desk behind which sat a smiling young woman with impeccable features.

"Good afternoon, gentlemen," she said. "How may I help you?"

Lyons slid out his badge wallet and held it in front of the woman's face.

"Please inform Mr. Fariq we are here and that we need to see him urgently."

The woman pushed to her feet, ignoring the usual convention of phoning the boss. She crossed the thickly carpeted floor, giving Blancanales a moment to observe her shapely figure. He smiled, pleased. She tapped on a door, hesitated then pushed it open and went inside.

"I'll check to see if he has a side exit," Schwarz said, strolling casually across the reception area and around the corner.

The receptionist stepped out of the office and beckoned to Lyons.

"Would you step this way, gentlemen."

Schwarz rejoined them at that moment, and Able Team approached and were shown into Mr. Fariq's office.

The office was based on lines similar to the reception area. One wall was lined with books. The opposite one held a number of expensive paintings by contemporary artists, and glancing at them Blancanales assured himself they weren't reproductions.

Mr. Fariq sat behind a large desk, a number of folders and papers strewed across its surface. He was forty-three years old, with thick black hair just starting to gray at the sides. His clothing was expensive. He had the appearance of an extremely successful businessman.

But he had a problem.

Lyons saw it the moment he looked at the man. It showed in Fariq's eyes. The man was deeply concerned about something over which he had no control.

"So, what can I do to help you, gentlemen?" Fariq asked. He leaned forward to inspect the credentials being shown. "Please, sit down."

Lyons eased a chair around so he could look directly at Fariq.

"I think it's more what we can do for you, Mr. Fariq."

Fariq's smile failed to do anything except curl the edges of his mouth. In all other respects it was nothing more than a hollow gesture.

"Please?"

"Did you know that for some time you have been under FBI surveillance?"

"Why?" Now it was the experienced lawyer speaking. "Am I suspected of doing something illegal?"

"We can provide you with all the details," Schwarz said.

"Details? What details?"

Fariq was doing a fair impression of a man standing up for his personal integrity. Even now he was refusing to give anything away.

"Mr. Fariq," Lyons said, showing a little impatience, "can we stop playing this damn game? Time is something we don't have to spare, so do us the courtesy of not screwing around."

Fariq's eyes hardened as he swiveled his expensive seat to directly face Lyons.

"Then do the same, Mr. Kane, and tell me what the hell *you* want."

"Mustapha Ashar. Your association with this man."

"A client. I am representing him in a matter of—"

"Bullshit, Mr. Fariq," Schwarz snapped. "The man is involved up to his ass with a suspected terrorist group operating covertly within the United States. You know and we know he made regular visits to the Ghosh farm in Ontario. That same farm was the scene of a firefight between the occupants and the Canadian police. Evidence of high-explosive devices was found at the scene. It has been established the place was being used as a storage facility."

"Joseph Haruni," Lyons added. "Lebanese. He has been in contact with you. Visited your Canadian office. We have photographic evidence of the two of you together.''

''Another client?'' Schwarz asked. ''I hope not, Mr. Fariq.''

''Haruni is on the Most Wanted lists of a number of security agencies around the world,'' Blancanales said. ''A very dangerous man. A known terrorist with definite anti-U.S. feelings. So what's he doing here? Illegally, too. Did you arrange his entry into the country, by any chance? The way things are looking, Mr. Fariq, it might be a good idea to start saying goodbye to all this luxury.''

''The people Haruni is involved with are planning terrorist attacks here on American soil,'' Lyons said. ''I believe you took out American citizenship a few years ago, Mr. Fariq. So that means it's *your* soil, too. The country you swore the oath of allegiance to. Or was that part of your cover?''

Fariq's face darkened with rage. ''How dare you question my loyalty to this country? I *am* an American citizen.''

''So are we all, Mr. Fariq,'' Schwarz said. ''But don't use it as a shield if you are involved with people who want to attack us.''

Lyons took the moment to ask, ''How have they bought your cooperation, Mr. Fariq? Who have they threatened? Your wife? Children? Tell us so we can help before something happens we'll all regret.''

Fariq slumped back in his seat, despair etched across his face. His features had slackened as he let go and allowed pent-up emotions free.

Lyons glanced at his partners. They waited in silence, giving Fariq time to compose himself.

''Three months ago Ashar came to see me. He was

pleasant. Extremely well-informed about my life, my business and my family. All this came out as he discussed my feelings about America. How I justified my religion against my achievements. I wasn't sure what he wanted at first.

"Then he began to explain that if I refused to cooperate terrible things would happen to my family. We were being watched, he said. He showed me photographs of my wife and children. All taken recently, and he said it would have been so easy to have had a rifle trained on them instead of a camera. There were even shots of us inside the house taken through windows by a long-distance lens.

"Ashar said he needed me to act as an intermediary for a number of business transactions. He needed vehicles. Accommodation. I was to undertake all these things on behalf of his principals. I had to set up a dummy company so there were no ways of tracing things back to them. As I ran a legitimate business and had an excellent reputation, no one would suspect anything."

"Mr. Fariq, what was the extent of these dealings? Where was all the accommodation?"

"Across the country. In small towns and communities. Nothing in any of the large cities. Is that important?"

Lyons didn't answer because he didn't know.

"We will need details of every transaction you arranged for Ashar," Schwarz said. "And I mean everything. You understand?"

Fariq was a trapped man, caught between doing what he knew was right and protecting his threatened family.

"It's choice time, Mr. Fariq," Lyons said. "I

won't insult you by asking why you didn't inform the police or the FBI, because I can guess what Ashar told you would happen if you did.''

"Haruni was the one," Fariq said. "He came to me and told me that what Ashar had said about my family being watched was nothing to what he would do. He showed me photographs of women and children. They were families of people who had betrayed him." Fariq's voice broke, and he paused until he could speak again. "Haruni assured me that my family would suffer the same treatment. What could I do? Risk those things happening to my family? Too many times I have heard of people under protection being reached by their enemies. I'm not a fool. I understand real threats. I experience them as a lawyer. When I saw those terrible photographs of women and young children, saw the things they had done to them, I had no choice. Those photographs. Those children, some of them still alive and begging for it to end…''

Fariq stared across the room, his eyes mirroring the horror he had witnessed in the images shown to him. Then he looked directly at Lyons.

"Tell me, Mr. Kane. Be truthful. If you had been in my place, what would you have done?''

Lyons—truthfully—had no answer to that final question.

"WHAT ARE we going to do?" Ashar asked.

Haruni remained calm, refusing to allow Ashar's panic to unnerve him. He waited until Ashar had talked himself out.

"My brother, you are talking foolishness, looking at this through the eyes of a defeated man."

"What else should I do? The farm is lost. So are our people. The explosives have been destroyed, as well. If Falil orders us to begin our strikes against the Americans, what do we do? Throw sticks at them? Do you realize how long it took to bring all those explosives into Canada? I was arranging to have them shipped over the border next week."

"Then we will get more explosives," Haruni said. "Brother, you must stop concerning yourself about time. Have you forgotten Falil's words? We strike when we are sure all is ready. If it takes another month, so be it. Time is on our side. It works for us, not against us."

"But the Americans..."

Haruni smiled. "They see nothing. Look at this great city. So many people. So many buildings. Everyone going about their business content they are in a safe country. Ashar, one of the faithful could drive a truck loaded with explosives right into its heart and destroy it."

"That is not the plan!"

"Calm yourself, brother. I was saying how easy it would be. These Americans are not prepared for what we are about to bring them. When the day does come this nation will fall like a house of cards."

Ashar, who had lived in America for a great deal longer than Haruni, wasn't so convinced. He had seen the Americans up close, had talked to them, listened to them, and he had traveled outside New York. He understood the background of the country. How it had been forged from diverse cultures. How it had built itself from nothing to the richest, most powerful nation on Earth. That had to stand for something. The thin veneer that presented itself to the world as America covered a living, breathing entity with great reserves. In times of crisis, Ashar was sure, America would steel itself and fight back.

He said nothing. In truth Haruni frightened him. The man was of a different breed, an extreme, a man who lived only to avenge the wrongs perpetrated against Islam. Mustapha Ashar was a facilitator, a man who organized things. He had never killed in his life, and in truth the thought frightened him. Yet he had been seduced by the words of Falil. Understood the man's motives and wanted to help in his own way. Being in contact with Haruni hadn't been expected, as far as Ashar was concerned, and the more he had to work with the man the more cautious he became.

ASHAR RETURNED to his store and let himself inside. He went to the small office near the rear of the store and sat down. Through the glass partition he was able to see the whole store. No one had come into the place yet, so he boiled water and made himself a pot of strong, aromatic tea. Ashar became aware of the laptop sitting at the corner of his cluttered desk. It was his only contact with Falil. All his instructions came via the machine in the form of electronic mail. On an impulse he switched on the machine and waited until the screen lit. As the icons filled the screen, Ashar saw the Incoming Mail adviser flashing. He activated the program and watched the message bar appear. Ashar slid the pointer onto the bar and tapped the Open key. The message on-screen was brief: if we keep the faith nothing will be lost.

Ashar studied the message. He knew where it had come from. No doubt Haruni had been in touch with

Falil. This was the result. A faith-confirming message from Falil. A moment of comfort from the leader so far away in his sanctuary.

Reaching out, Ashar deleted the message and returned to the main menu. He stared at the screen. He didn't have Haruni's confidence in the success of the campaign. Things weren't as set as Falil might imagine. If the farm could be compromised so easily, what else might fall? What had the police learned from the farm in Canada? Names? Ashar had been the one to visit the place regularly. Had they connected him to any of the items found there?

Was he being watched now?

Pushing to his feet, Ashar went to the door. Even as he reached it he saw a large Lincoln pulled in against the curb. Three men stepped out of the vehicle and started toward the shop. For sure, Ashar thought, they weren't customers. The way they were dressed and the purposeful way they walked suggested police.

Ashar didn't waste any more time on speculation. He turned back into the store and ran to his office. He dragged open a drawer and pulled out the auto-pistol he had kept secreted in the cistern in the bathroom. Since the attack on the farm he had become nervous, and for the first time since being given the weapon Ashar had brought it with him to the store along with the laptop. He checked the weapon and eased off the safety.

As he emerged from the office the three men walked in through the front door.

"We want a word," one of them said. He was a tough-looking man with blond hair.

Ashar panicked, raised the pistol and pulled the

trigger. The bullet was wide of its mark, taking a chunk of plaster out of the wall. The moment he had fired Ashar regretted it. He was committed now. Fully. There was no way back. As Ashar turned to run deeper into the store a strange thought crossed his mind.

Had he, Mustapha Ashar, fired the first shot of Falil's war?

CARL LYONS DUCKED as plaster debris showered over him, and he pulled the Colt Python from his shoulder rig.

Close by, Blancanales and Schwarz had moved to cover.

"Pol, see if there's a back exit," Lyons snapped.

Blancanales slid out the open door and cut to the right where an alley ran down the side of the store. It reached a dead end after thirty feet. He found the side door near the end of the alley. It was a plain wood door that was designed to open outward. That didn't stop Blancanales. He rammed the door with his shoulder to test it and found it gave. He repeated the attack a few more times, and as the door began to splinter Blancanales heard more shooting from inside the store.

ASHAR FIRED a number of random shots, altering his aim with each pull of the trigger. He was edging to the rear of the store, his intention to leave by the back door if he could reach it. The three Americans had vanished from his view. They had taken cover and were waiting for him to make a foolish move and expose himself. Whatever else he might be, Ashar didn't consider himself a total idiot. There was no way he was about to step into the open.

He eased around some piled cartons containing new stock for the store. None of that mattered now. His priority was to get away from this place. Hide himself and contact Haruni. He would know what to do. Although he didn't particularly like Haruni, the man did have his uses.

Ashar stumbled as his foot caught the edge of a carton. The impact dislodged other cartons stacked on top, and they came crashing to the floor, spreading books across it. Ashar stepped over the mess and moved quickly to the rear exit.

He heard the thumping sound as the door came into view. The main panel was already splintered, and Ashar saw that it was being battered from the outside. Someone was trying to break in. He was caught between two forces.

Ashar fired two shots into the door. The battering ceased for a few seconds. He turned to look into the store and saw two suited figures weaving between the stocked shelves, moving in his direction

The battering commenced again, and the door bulged inward. One more powerful impact, and the door splintered, tumbling inside the store. A bulky man in a suit—one of those Ashar had seen crossing the street—stood in the opening. He had a raised autopistol in his hands, and it was aimed at Ashar.

The man yelled something that was lost on Ashar. He had already started to turn as the other two men came into view. They were armed, as well.

Mustapha Ashar had two choices: surrender to the brutal clutches of the Americans, or go out fighting.

If nothing else, he could at least die honorably for God.

He brought the autopistol to bear on one of the approaching figures.

Someone yelled for him to give himself up.

Ashar wished he could explain why that wasn't possible and began to pull the trigger, yelling his defiance and asking God for his blessing.

Ashar's pistol fired, the bullet slicing the sleeve of Lyons's jacket.

Lyons returned fire a split second after Blancanales triggered his gun. The first bullet caught Ashar in the back, high up, the impact twisting his body in a wrenching jerk. Blood spurted from the wound. Then Lyons's slug hit him dead center, taking out Ashar's heart in a burst of pain. The man stumbled, fell against a stack of cartons and crashed to the floor. He hit hard, the autopistol bouncing from his hand and spinning across the floor. Ashar sprawled face-down, dead before his gun came to a stop.

"Any one hurt?" Blancanales asked as he moved deeper into the store, kicking Ashar's weapon clear.

"We're fine," Schwarz said.

"Speak for yourself," Lyons muttered, fingering the gash in his sleeve.

Schwarz moved to close the store's front door.

Lyons took out his cell phone and keyed the speed dial for Stony Man.

"We're at the store Mustapha Ashar ran," he said. "The guy lost it when we walked in and started shooting. We're okay, but Ashar didn't make it. He didn't leave us any choice. Do me a favor. Contact Frank Delacort. We can let the FBI take over once we've done a search."

BLANCANALES HAD located the office and found the laptop Ashar had been using. He called in Lyons and Schwarz to take a look.

"You think this is the one we found in his apartment?" Schwarz asked.

"Same model," Lyons said. He picked it up and checked the serial number on the plate at the rear of the machine. "We can soon check it out."

Blancanales placed the laptop on the desk and began to scroll through the on-screen data.

"No problems accessing this one," he said. "The guy has a lot of information listed here, including Fariq's address and telephone numbers for his home and offices. Lot of other stuff, too. Problem is it doesn't mean a damn thing to me, guys."

"Anything for Haruni?"

Blancanales shrugged. "Telephone numbers. But they don't have names next to them."

"Maybe Stony Man can run them down."

The sound of police sirens reached their ears. Lyons pulled his badge wallet and headed for the door.

"Here we go again," Blancanales said.

CHAPTER ELEVEN

Sanctuary

Falil was troubled.

He maintained his outer calm, refusing to show his concern to those around him. The moment he allowed the mask to slip his followers would drift away and he would lose his control over them. He couldn't let that happen. Despite the escalation of setbacks Falil held fast to his will to succeed.

Incoming news told of the raid on the Haifa cell. The attack had left his team dead and the bomb-making facility dismantled by the Israeli military. This following the problems in France had been bad enough—yet there was more.

In Kurdistan a Western combat team had been allied to Kurdish rebels who had decimated one of the oil convoys that was providing much-needed money for Falil's campaign. The attackers had later eliminated all but a few of the group guarding one of the major arms caches. Although the men had been captured they had escaped. During that escape, they had laid waste to the arms dump before stealing the group's remaining helicopter. As a final insult, the commandos had later taken prisoner the Russians Yentalov and Berkof before making their final escape into Turkey. Too much seemed to be happening within a short space of time to be mere coincidence, Falil decided. The Americans, working alongside the Israelis, had better intel than he had imagined. It was unsettling to say the least. The U.S.A. had listening posts and informers everywhere, so it became easy for them to gain an insight into the working of any group once they identified it.

His own network of informers was finding it difficult to maintain up-to-date news due to the scare thrown into the situation by the recent events. The informers retreated, refusing to involve themselves while the present uncertainty remained. The American-sponsored team was obviously professional, and even Falil had to acknowledge its skill at overcoming odds.

Falil put his campaign on hold as a temporary safeguard while he considered how to combat the problem. He wasn't defeated. His resolve was the same. His long-term objectives remained fixed. However, he accepted there was need for a rethink. A way of getting around the nuisance of the Americans' team.

He shut himself away, denying access to his person. It allowed him time to consider the implications of the strikes against his people and the weapons caches. The double blow caused by the attack on the oil convoy, followed by the destruction of the supplies hidden in the mountains, was going to be hard to rectify.

Falil spent much of his lonely vigil in prayer, hoping that God might bless him with a vision or even a sign of what he needed to do. He resigned himself to having to solve the problem by his own guile, God denying him any solution. Falil took this as a divine way of testing his faith. God had challenged him to create his own miracle. Falil accepted the challenge, knowing that he had to make the correct decision. If he didn't make the right one, then many of his brothers would die. He had impressed on them that there would need to be sacrifices as the campaign got under way, and though they had accepted this edict during his speeches, now the moment was upon them there were those who seemed less than impressed at the unfortunate turn of events before the campaign proper had started.

The Iranians who had already expressed their displeasure were quick to point to the additional setbacks, and their unrest, Falil knew, might spread to others. He assured them there was no need to worry unduly. He promised them a victory. Something to show why they should keep the faith, and this was part of the reason he had closeted himself away. He wanted the time to decide how he could present them with a show of force that would both impress the doubters and at the same time strike a blow against the Americans.

His decision was easily reached, because in truth there was only one thing he could do in the short term, even though he had great reluctance in carrying out the operation.

Falil turned to his computer and began to compose the short e-mail that would set the event in motion.

New York

JOSEPH HARUNI STUDIED the message a number of times. He understood its meaning. It was clear and concise, leaving him in no doubt as to what he needed to do. The thing Haruni couldn't grasp was why. The use of the New York sleeper and his weapon had been a grand finale. A final strike at the end of the first phase of the attacks across America. Now Falil was demanding that device be used immediately. Haruni took his time considering the implications. He had to be sure that the message was genuine, that it had come from Falil. He had communicated with Falil recently, telling him about Ashar's nervousness, and Falil had given no indication of any change in the overall plan.

So why the change of heart now?

He turned from the computer screen and stood up, crossing the room to stare out the window. His view allowed him to see the city, spread out before him like a vision from hell. New York, the pinnacle of American vulgarity. It was a howling, godless place that never fell silent. Day and night its noise and smells, the garish lights and the mass of humanity bound within its walls, surged back and forth. An endless stream of avaricious people with little time for anything except their relentless pursuit of wealth and possessions.

Haruni had walked its dark, dirty streets at night, his senses assailed by the depravity and coarseness of its lowlife. He had watched these Americans attack one another for drugs and for money, had seen the misery they inflicted. And it was this loathsome disease they were sending out to the rest of the world, infecting every place they went. It was the reason for Falil's campaign, his holy war that would bring to America the suffering other nations felt every day of their lives. The complacency would fade once a number of American communities were touched by death and destruction. Only then would they become aware of the horrors of the real world.

Which was why Haruni couldn't fully understand why Falil seemed to be changing his agenda. The more he thought about it the more Haruni suspected something was wrong. He decided it was time he put his mind at rest.

Haruni picked up the telephone and dialed the number of Mustapha Ashar's bookstore. He would start with the people he had contact with in America to see if they had any knowledge. If nothing came from that, he would telephone Falil himself to get his confirmation.

Ashar's phone rang and continued ringing for a while. No one answered. Haruni was ready to put down the phone when the answering machine cut in and informed him Ashar was out and that a message could be left. Normally Haruni wouldn't have bothered with the machine, but he needed some answers, so he left a brief message for Ashar and asked him to call back as soon as possible.

FRANK DELACORT WAS almost through the door when one of his colleagues called him back.

"Our tap just picked up a call to Ashar's store. The guy left a message. He spoke in English and seemed a little anxious about something. He wanted Ashar to call him back."

"He leave any ID?" Delacort asked.

The agent smiled. "Called himself Joseph."

"Did he now." Delacort picked up one of the field office phones and called the number Carl Lyons had left him. When Lyons answered Delacort repeated what he had been told.

"You been able to rundown the location of the phone Joseph used?"

"Just coming through now," Delacort said.

"THANKS FOR THAT," Lyons said. He broke the connection on his cell phone. "That was Frank Delacort. The FBI put a tap on Ashar's phone after they took over from us. They just picked up a caller leaving a message on Ashar's answering machine. The guy needed to talk to Ashar. Called himself Joseph."

"As in Joseph Haruni?" Blancanales asked.

"It's the only Joseph we know having any connection with Ashar," Lyons said. "The FBI traced the call to an address in Queens."

"We going?" Schwarz asked.

"I think so," Lyons said. He opened his cell phone and called Stony Man. Once connected to Kurtzman he gave him the phone number and asked him to check it out against numbers they had picked up from Ashar. Within a couple of minutes the number had been located in the data Able Team had found. Lyons thanked Kurtzman. "Number confirmed. It was one Ashar used regularly."

WHEN ASHAR HADN'T returned his call Haruni called twice more. Each time he was connected to Ashar's answering machine. Haruni tried Ashar's home number. No answer. He became concerned. Never before had he failed to get through to Ashar, whether at home or at the store. Something had to be wrong, he decided.

Haruni left his rooming house and called a taxi. He was dropped off a block away from the store and walked until he was across the street from it.

The store was obviously closed, and FBI tape was fixed across the door, denying anyone access to the building. He drew back into an alley, turning quickly, and walked to the far end. When he emerged on the far side he moved along the sidewalk, losing himself in the crowd. His mind was racing as he thought ahead. Was this why Falil was asking for the New York sleeper to be activated? Did he already know something had taken place at the store? Perhaps Ashar was dead, killed by the FBI. Had they stumbled on some connection that had led them to Ashar?

Haruni remained calm. If the truth was that Ashar had been taken by the FBI, had his name been mentioned? He was aware that he was a wanted man, on the lists of a number of countries, but he had no worries about that. He accepted the problem as part of his profession. It made him a marked man, but it also bestowed upon him a degree of respect within the terrorist community. And despite it he had entered and was able to walk the streets of America untouched. He didn't fool himself into thinking he was totally untouchable. He was as vulnerable as the next man. At the moment his luck was running well. Now that there seemed the chance that Ashar had been compromised in some way, then Haruni's position might well be in danger. If that was so, he needed to be on his guard.

He entered a diner and located a pay phone. He called Fariq's office, intending to check with the lawyer. He was told that the man wasn't available in either the New York or the Canadian office. When he asked when the lawyer would be available the woman suggested he speak to one of Fariq's associates. Haruni hung up immediately. Leaving the diner, he merged with the crowds on the sidewalk, walking without purpose while he decided what to do.

The facts told their own story.

He had been unable to contact Ashar. That had never happened before. Fariq also seemed to be unavailable; another unusual situation. Since the implied threats against his family, the lawyer had proved a reliable contact. Suddenly he was out of reach. One contact broken was acceptable. Two weren't.

Haruni located another pay phone and dialed the number that would connect him with his people watching over Fariq's family. The voice on the other end of the phone held a note of anxiety.

"Tell me what has happened," Haruni said.

"They came early this morning," the man said. "Many cars. Many armed men. FBI. They surrounded the house. They took Fariq's family away. There was even a helicopter overhead."

"And now?"

"Some stayed behind. Inside the house. Others guard the grounds."

Haruni digested the information. "There is no point in staying. Leave the area. Return to the house and wait for me there."

He walked again, moving in the general direction of the rooming house. Acceptance of the organization being badly compromised was building within him. He didn't like the thought of all the planning and organization going to waste, but sense had to prevail over pride. Haruni saw now that Falil's decision had some strong reasoning. If the main plan needed to be abandoned for the foreseeable future, then at least they could strike a significant blow with the sleeper and his prearranged mission. If it had to be so, then let it be now while at least some of them were free and clear.

It took him some time to make his way back to his rooming house. In his room he made himself a drink, then sat down and picked up the telephone. The number sprang into his mind the moment his fingers reached for the buttons. He heard the soft pulse of sound as the digits were registered, and then he heard the phone start to ring.

Haruni glanced out the window at the busy city street. Soon, he thought. Soon it would all change.

HE HAD ALWAYS KNOWN the day would come. Even though time had pushed it to the back of his mind he had known it would come. There were days when he forgot completely why he was in America, when his everyday activities filled his mind and he went about his tasks as if nothing else mattered. But there was always something to snap his wandering mind back on track. A small item in a newspaper. Or a report on television that would present him with images from his past and bring him to reality.

His life was ordered, regular. He existed quietly, holding down a steady, undemanding job as an insurance broker. It was a nine-to-five job, five days a week. He lived alone in a small apartment that was situated on the third floor of a converted building on the fringes of Brooklyn. His street was unremarkable, reasonably peaceful, and he had no problems with his neighborhood or the people who inhabited it.

On the last Saturday of each month he would drive his four-year-old Toyota to another part of the city, where he maintained a small lockup. The lockup was in a small business complex near the river, in the shadow of one of New York's many bridges. Here he faithfully maintained the machine of destruction under his command, the means by which, if the call ever came, he would be able to unleash terror and death upon New York. Now the city was as familiar to him as the place of his birth many thousands of miles away.

In his lockup he spent his one Saturday each month checking and rechecking the silent, cold machine. Like him, it waited with infinite patience for the call that would bring it to life. Unlike him, it bore its solitude with little distress, untainted by temptation. Without distraction. Lacking the human frailties, the machine required nothing. Even his diligent cleaning and inspection meant nothing to it. It existed in a soulless void. Waiting obediently, and always ready...

On that weekend he had planned a brief excursion from the city following his visit to the lockup. He had, for the first time, actually missed the previous visit, and his conscience had driven him back to the place, where he had spent the entire day filling the hours with repeated checks and rechecks, even though he knew there was no need. On the Sunday morning he had risen early, completed his prayers and set off. Driving from the city, he had taken to the open country, following the winding highway that brought him to a green, forested area. Parking his car, he had simply sat taking in the solitude. He couldn't deny the beauty of America. It had breath-taking vistas. Endless timbered forests that stretched for miles. Green and full of lush vegetation. He had seen farms nestling in rolling hills, contended herds of healthy cattle.

In his work and during his daily life he came into contact with many Americans. For the most part he found them pleasant, gregarious people. Always ready to share and to give, and it was this contrast that made him consider his actions in coming to this country.

The problem lay in his view of the people and the place. There had been a slow, almost imperceptible change in his attitude toward the country he been sent to create chaos out of calm, on the express orders of his masters. On his arrival he had been fired with the enthusiasm of religious fervor, fully indoctrinated into the blinkered view of the fanatic. With the gradual exposure to everyday American life, and contact with the people, those views had shifted ever so slightly, yet enough to make him step back and rethink his values.

His instructors had told him that America was a barren wasteland of evil, a vast place populated by a vapid, godless people who existed only to take all that was good from the world and make it their own. They were corrupt, ignorant and without pity. Their cities were nothing more than violent war zones where the inhabitants were slowly killing one another.

He had seen and read of terrible things that frightened him. Yet he had also been on the receiving end of great generosity. The city itself, like any great conurbation, had its darker side. This had to be coupled with great beauty and sights that still took his breath.

In the nearly two years he had been in New York, making his life among these people, he had started to question the reasons for his presence. At first they had been nagging little uncertainties. There one moment and gone the next, yet always a fragment was lodged deep in his mind. Each time it recurred it left a stronger trace, and all the while he was steeping himself in the fabric of the society he had come to harm.

Try as he might, he found he was unable to rid himself of that pale shadow of doubt. It clung to him, unobtrusive, yet always there. Chafing at his resolve. Nibbling away at his convictions. He wrestled with his changing heart, aware that if he turned away from his holy mission he would be forever damned. God, as forgiving as He was, could always turn His other face.

To his horror at first admission, he realized that his faith had become a matter for his conscience. He argued with himself, deliberately immersing himself in his faith. Yet as time drifted by and no call came, his deliberations toward his reasons for being in America became less clear. His focus had shifted, almost without his knowing. He no longer accepted at face value what he had been taught. What his instructors had drilled into him during long, relentless sessions.

He could see them clearly in his mind. The bearded clerics who had intoned the evil of the great Satan. The dead nation that called itself America. Over and over they had harangued and castigated the

U.S.A. and all its allies. The West, they told him, was an open pit of hell, a decaying society choking in the foul stench of its excesses. A terrible sickness that needed to be cleansed. To be expunged from the world, leaving a cleaner place for the rising tide of Islam. The coming battle would end the cancer of the West, plunging those decadent nations into desolation.

And there had been others. Men from the West itself who had joined the Islamic brethren. Men who advised, told him all about the customs and the vices of America. He had listened, though sometimes he had wondered about the reasoning of these men. They had turned their backs on their own countries and were now advising others on the evil of those very nations.

He had learned not to ask too many questions. Especially anything to do with the advisers. In his heart he felt their motives were ruled more by cash payments than by any ideological motives. So he listened and nodded and made his notes, taking everything they said under consideration.

He had arrived in America armed with a valid passport and papers, all provided by the security department back home. He had been met at the airport by a man from his own hometown, who had been in America for a long time, and who arranged for incoming nationals to be eased into American society without too much hardship. Within a week he had his job and his apartment. The Toyota he received after three months.

Since then his life had developed steadily, and although he had tried to remain isolated, the natural friendliness of his American associates had slowly drawn him into their circle. Aware that if he remained too insular he might attract unwanted attention, he had allowed them to introduce him to innocent pleasures. Once a week he went bowling with a small group. On occasion he went out for a meal with his friends, and over the months his association with these Americans began to crumble his reserve. He studied them closely, as he had been taught, but did it with a different agenda than the one demanded by his instructors.

These Americans didn't resemble in any way the evil monsters he had been told about. They were just ordinary people. They had their ambitions. Their dreams. What permeated most often was the simple desire to have a good life. To be content. To have families. There was little of the desire to conquer the world. To dominate and destroy Islam. He found, actually, that the average American had few desires that extended beyond the shores of their nation. He began to realize that because the country was so large and self-contained, his American friends were sometimes totally unaware of the world outside.

He often returned to his apartment at night and sat staring at the blank screen of his television set, trying to come to terms with the two images of America he had.

One was the America he had been told about by his instructors. The America of hate and violence and seething masses intent on the subjugation of Islam.

The other was represented by his daily experience, with his colleagues and friends, and his own experience of the American reality. Of a vast nation, rich in material wealth and populated by a great amalgam of nationalities, religions, politics. That they existed together in relative harmony had to say something about the American philosophy. He knew that if he looked hard enough he would find someone who hated Islam, as there would be someone who hated other racial religious groups, but he was wise enough to understand that wherever he went—in any country—he would find *some* intolerance. What he had not, could not, find, was a country ranting and raving and planning the total destruction of his people.

His confusion was only manifested when he realized one day that he hadn't thought about his mission to America for almost a month. His initial guilt created a strong reaction, and he spent that Saturday in his lockup, checking and rechecking his machine. Making certain it was in pristine condition. There had been a driving pressure behind the long hours, and he had worked until he had sweated, his mood frantic, intense, going home exhausted and racked with a guilt feeling that he found hard to dismiss.

On *that* Sunday morning he had risen early, showered, dressed, and had driven his car out of the city, searching for some isolated spot where he could sit and consider his future.

His cell phone rang, and he wondered who would be calling him on a Sunday. Picking it up, he keyed the answer button and listened to the cool, measured tones of the man he hadn't heard from for almost three years. It was a voice he had almost forgotten, issuing the command that was intended to set in motion his mission. He listened, his heart pounding and his stomach churning with a sickness born of desolation.

''Do you understand?''

Without knowing how he managed to speak, he mumbled his acknowledgment.

"Very shortly you will receive your final instructions. Keep this telephone with you twenty-four hours a day. Understand?"

"I understand."

"Be sure you do."

The line fell silent.

He was alone again, staring at the same landscape but seeing nothing. One short telephone call had destroyed his future. In the space of a few seconds his life had been radically altered. Life, which had seemed promising only a little while back, now stretched before him shrouded in a gray mist.

And there was nothing he could do about it.

The fingers of his left hand tapped against the rim of the steering wheel as he tried to alter what had just taken place. He couldn't. It was written. Carved in stone. Whether it was destiny, or simply pure misfortune, he was irrevocably caught up in a grim game that had one ending.

Death and suffering for thousands, maybe even millions. And there was nothing he could do to prevent it.

He considered that.

Perhaps there was something he could do. Or not do, to be exact. Leaning forward, he switched on the engine and turned the Toyota around. Driving slowly, he returned to the city and his apartment, which suddenly took on a bleak appearance. He made himself a mug of coffee and sat down, staring at the blank television screen. He drank and thought, considering the options open to him.

It was late when he finally moved. He had made

his choice, and however it turned out, there was no going back.

Of one thing he was certain—he would not carry through his appointed mission.

CHAPTER TWELVE

Israel

David McCarter stepped out of the interrogation room and crossed to the window, staring out across the compound of the Israeli military base. The day was hot, with a dry wind blowing fine dust around the area. He could hear it rattling against the bleached wooden sides of the building. Over a period of time the abrasive action would wear away the surface of the wood, exposing the underside. Something akin to wearing down the resistance of a captive under questioning. Both required time. Plenty of time.

Which was something McCarter didn't have in abundance. He needed his answers now. Not later. Unfortunately, his source was proving stubborn to the extreme degree.

Mikhail Berkof was refusing to say a thing. His resistance did him credit, or would have done if McCarter had been awarding such things. As far as the Briton was concerned, Berkof was just being a pain in the ass.

It wasn't a difficult question McCarter was asking. Just the location of the man called Falil. His base.

Headquarters. Even his local corner store. Berkof refused to say anything. He had been refusing for the past twenty-four hours, and even McCarter's patience was wearing thin.

The door at the end of the passage opened and Calvin James stepped through. He was looking cool and rested, and by some miracle he was carrying a chilled can of Classic Coca-Cola in his hand. He handed it to McCarter who took a long swallow.

"That, my old mate, was bloody marvelous. There any more around this sweatbox?"

James waggled one hand. "Maybe, my man. Depends on my powers of persuasion with the guy who operates the PX."

"Well, persuade away, Cal, because I have a feeling this is going to run and run."

"No progress?"

"Berkof must think he's back in the damned military. Won't give anything but his name."

"What is it? Loyalty? Or is he scared of this Falil?"

"Not sure. The loyalty is a bit off the wall. These Russians are in it for the money, clear and simple. I don't see staying faithful as an option. Somebody comes up with a better deal tomorrow they'd be there with both hands held out. If I had to choose, I'd go for his being scared. He doesn't want to do anything that might bring this Falil down on his head. We all know how long an arm these terrorists have. And especially the Islamics. They have long memories and they don't give up easily. If they heard Berkof had pointed the finger at Falil, there'd be a *Fatwa* on CNN news the next day with his name on it."

James nodded. He turned away and paced up and down the passage for a minute, then turned and jabbed a finger at McCarter.

"Damn right," he said. "Damn right, David!"

McCarter waited for more, and when it didn't come he decided to drain the can of Coke.

James was suddenly smiling, as if he had told himself a funny story.

"Tell me what you're grinning at," McCarter said. "I hate it when you do that."

A FULL MOON hung over the desert. Pale light filtered down into the compound, and near silence enveloped the area. Somewhere within the sprawl of buildings a radio played music. An occasional raised voice broke the peace.

The first explosion shattered the silence with brutal suddenness, then came the chatter of autofire. Someone yelled in pain. More explosions followed. Dirt rattled against the sides of buildings.

The window on the far side of Mikhail Berkof's room shattered. The Russian sat up, staring around the semidark room. He heard movement outside the window. Dark-clad figures armed with Kalashnikov autorifles scrambled through to surround him, weapons directed at his chest. Every man wore a black outfit, even down to the ski masks covering their faces.

"Berkof?"

"Yes. Who are you?"

The reply was in Russian. "Friends. Come to get you out of here before the Israelis kill you. Or Falil's men get their hands on you for betraying them."

"Betray? What do you—"

"No time for talk now. If we don't leave, we will be outnumbered once the Israelis radio for help. Move, man!"

Berkof was roughly dragged from his bed. Manhandled to the window. He could hear more shooting. The dull thump of grenades. Bullets slapped against the wall of the hut. Someone hauled Berkof over the windowsill and dumped him outside where more hands caught hold of him and half-ran, half-dragged him across the compound.

One of the black-clad figures gave a cry and went down.

"Move him! Move him!" the Russian speaker screamed.

Berkof, dazed by the frantic motion, his eyes stinging from dust and drifting smoke, saw the black shape of a helicopter hovering just inside the base perimeter fence. A number of black-clad figures was protecting the machine, firing at the distant figures of Israeli defenders.

Men went down on both sides.

Berkof was thrown inside the open door of the hovering chopper. His liberators followed, and the machine began to rise, quickly swinging over the fence and into the darkness beyond.

Below the firefight continued. Detonations crackled and smoke billowed into the night sky.

"What about the wounded?" Berkof asked.

"If they fall they pay the price," someone said. "We were contracted to get you and Yentalov out. That's all."

"Who set this up?"

"Friends of Yentalov. We were always on standby when he was out doing something risky. He said it was insurance for the pair of you if you ever got into trouble. Sounds like you have a good friend there."

"Pity it didn't go as planned," someone said.

"At least we got one of them."

"I suppose so."

Berkof glanced up, concerned. "Where is Sergei?"

"The Muslims reached him first," he was told. "Took him from the hospital. Left the place looking like a slaughterhouse."

One of the men laughed harshly. "There were more dead than alive in the place after they left. They must have wanted him very badly."

"This man Falil is after blood. Yours as well as Yentalov's."

Berkof leaned against the side of the cabin. "I don't understand. Why is Falil angry at us?"

"He has learned that you sold out to the Kurds. That you let them attack the oil convoy."

"No!" Berkof yelled. "That is not true. Why would we do that?"

"Because you made a secret deal with the Kurds to sell them the oil. The money will buy them better weapons and supplies so they can fight the Iraqi military."

"This is stupid," Berkof said. "Sergei and I would never do that. Who spread that story?"

"How the hell are we supposed to know? You have probably made enemies out here. You know what these Arabs are like. If you upset them, they pay you back big time."

"Dammit, we didn't make any fucking deal!"

"Well, it's of no consequence now. Yentalov will

have to suffer for you both when they get him to Falil's base.''

''No! You can't leave—''

''Telling us our job now? If you're so damn clever, explain how we rescue Yentalov when we don't even know where this base is? It was easy finding you because we have friends in the area. It's different with the Muslims. They are very close-mouthed. If we knew where to find this base, we could mount a raid quickly. But we don't so we only take you home. Life stinks, eh?''

The man turned away to speak with his partners, leaving Berkof alone with his thoughts, huddled against the side of the helicopter as it pushed on through the darkness.

He was thinking about Yentalov. Of the times they had struggled through adversity, lean and hard times, only to emerge on the other side secure and wealthy. Now all that could be ended if Yentalov fell into the hands of Falil. Berkof had always been struck by Falil's cold attitude. His total dedication to his cause. The Russian didn't like the man, but as Yentalov was fond of saying, ''Like a man or not, business is business. Despise him if you want, only remember that his money is the same as the next man's.''

The helicopter lurched as it struck an air pocket. The jolt brought Berkof to his senses. He reached out to touch the main man on the shoulder.

''Could you get him out?''

''You think the Muslims would be worse than those fucking Israelis we left back there? Of course we could get him out—if we knew where he was!''

''Get me a chart,'' Berkof said.

He opened up the sheet when it was passed to him. Someone used a flashlight to illuminate the chart.

"Where are we?" Berkof asked.

A finger jabbed the chart. "Israeli base. We're heading north at the present. Meeting a ship off the coast."

Berkof traced his finger across the map and left Israel behind as he picked up the Egyptian coastline and followed it—to Libya.

"Here. Inland from the Gulf of Sirte. Heading south, about thirty miles in."

It was desolate country, bordering on desert, with little to sustain life.

"What are we looking for?"

"A small settlement. White buildings in a walled enclosure, with a fountained garden in the center."

"Defended?"

"Falil puts on a show of being a man of peace, but he has armed guards. A helicopter pad. Much electronic equipment inside."

"What about the Libyans?"

"Falil pays them well for the base. It used to be a summer house. Belonging to some military commander who fell out of favor. As long as Falil pays his rent the Libyans leave him alone. But he can call on them for assistance if he needs it."

"Well, we wouldn't want that happening," a voice said in very clear, pronounced English.

Berkof, confused, looked around. In the dim light from the overhead lamp one of the Russians pulled off his ski mask. He was smiling as he leaned in closer to Berkof.

"He sang like a bloody canary," David McCarter said.

"Good idea, or what?" Calvin James asked as he removed his mask.

One by one Berkof's rescuers revealed themselves. They comprised the American combat team and a number of Israelis, including the Russian-speaking man who had conversed with Berkof.

Ben Sharon leaned into the pilot's cabin and tapped the man on the shoulder. "We can go back now."

Berkof felt the chopper bank and slide as it turned. He was beginning to feel sick in his stomach. Only it wasn't from the flight. He had been well and truly duped, fooled into believing he had been freed by Russian mercenaries when all along it had been nothing but an elaborate ruse concocted by his captors in order to locate Falil's base. If he hadn't felt so disgusted with himself at being taken in, Berkof might have seen the funny side to the situation. As it was, he decided to save the memory for a better time.

Stony Man Farm, Virginia

KURTZMAN EASED his wheelchair away from the workstation. He rolled silently across the smooth, antistatic floor covering to where his renowned coffeepot bubbled on its stand and helped himself to a fresh mug. He sat drinking, aware of the solitude inside the Computer Room.

To an outsider the place might have appeared dead, with little apparent activity. In truth it was entirely the opposite. As far as Kurtzman was concerned, the room was alive. At this late hour it was devoid of any human presence save that of Kurtzman himself. But the machines were talking, humming away with their usual quiet efficiency, gathering data, displaying information. Collating facts and figures that would be analyzed and dissected by the cyber team when they reported for duty.

Monitor screens glowed with images gathered from around the globe. Larger wall screens displayed magnified maps showing current political and military status from a dozen potential hot spots. Columns of figures and text constantly altered as new information came in from numerous agency data banks, keeping Stony Man informed of changes within governments and regimes. Updated detail on the status of terrorist groups. Their activities and current locations. The gathered data separated information that was known from that which was designated as predicted.

Satellite images downloaded from the electronic information gathering allowed detailed examination of activity spanning the globe. The images flickered on and off at regular intervals, being replaced as and when updates were fed in. The cyber team could call up any image from a particular orbiting bird and could access and utilize the satellites for Stony Man's urgent requirements. At the flick of a key the team could lock on practically any area on a global scale, providing the accessed satellite's orbit was in the right position to provide a keyhole. To benefit from those time scales the cyber team had constant screen readouts that told them the position of every satellite in orbit and where it would be located at any given time. It wasn't the ideal setup, but until technology allowed greater control and access it was the best available.

During access time, it was possible to zoom in, magnify and sharpen an image to startling clarity. With the speedy advances of equipment the parameters of satellite surveillance were widening at an alarming rate. Digital imagery was allowing them greater control over what they saw, and Kurtzman was sometimes impressed at the results they were able to produce.

Clutching his coffee mug, he rolled his chair to his workstation. Touching a switch, he activated one of the blank TV screens. The twenty-four-hour CNN news channel flared into life. Kurtzman eased up the volume and followed a news report coming in from some distant Asian trouble spot. He watched it for a while, then flicked through a range of channels, picking up sports action, movies, a rerun of an old Western series in black and white, and smiled as he recalled watching the show every week when he was much younger.

Kurtzman was wide awake for some reason. Too alert to sleep. His mind was buzzing with the current mission, chafing at the need to be involved, and he knew he wouldn't rest until he contrived some input for the teams in the field.

He had finished his coffee and was considering a second mug when the door burst open and Barbara Price hurried in.

"Call just came through from Phoenix Force," she said. "They have a location for Falil's HQ in Libya."

Kurtzman reached for the sheet she held out to

him. He scanned the information, then turned to his keyboard.

"Barbara, get the team in. Everybody. No exceptions. We've got work to do."

He turned to his station, already immersed in the intricacies of linking to one of the orbiting satellites. His monitor told him which bird would be available first, and Kurtzman lost no time as he logged himself on and began the sequence that would put the satellite under his command for the time it would take to locate and scan the Libyan base.

Kurtzman would make a broad sweep first, allowing the satellite to pinpoint the exact position of the base. Then he would take a closer look, utilizing digital cameras for images, following up by using thermal imagery to pick out heat sources that would show where power generators were situated. Phoenix Force was going to need the information as quickly as possible, and Kurtzman would bend every rule in the book to provide it.

Within minutes the full complement of the cyber team was assembled and given their particular tasks. Hal Brognola joined them soon after so that he could be brought up-to-date with the data the team had collated earlier from the information provided by Able Team, as well as being in on the satellite scan Kurtzman was setting up.

"Be another thirty minutes before I get a bird lined up," Kurtzman said. "I had to do a little queue jumping. Hal, those military types get real snotty if they get shunted around."

"Hey, why don't we get our own satellite in orbit?" Tokaido asked. "Save a lot of time."

Brognola had to smile. "Great idea," he said.

"You want to start the collection with the change in your pocket?"

"We could have it deducted from his salary," Delahunt suggested.

"Yeah. You wouldn't feel it so much," Wethers added.

"Be nice, though," Delahunt said. "Stony Bird One."

"Bunch of comics," Tokaido said. "That's the last time I make a suggestion."

"Aaron, don't these people have enough work?" Brognola asked.

"Heads up, guys," Kurtzman said. "Let's give the man what he wants."

"We called you in to give you an update on the data the guys brought in," Barbara Price said to Brognola.

"Took us some hard time but I think we've made sense of all those figures," Kurtzman said. "What we have from those computers are locations, times, dates. We had to have a lot of the stuff translated because whoever devised it used a lot of Arabic script. Had us confused for a time until we figured the way it had been developed."

"Hal, we need to go for all these locations pretty fast," Price said, spreading printout sheets for Brognola to see.

The big Fed studied the data. The way Kurtzman and his team had laid it out meant he was able to grasp the content quickly. What he read brought a chill to his spine.

The overall plan had locations in more than two dozen communities spread across the U.S.A. Medium and small towns. Places no one would expect a terrorist attack because the locations were isolated from the mainstream. Once the designated explosive devices, all carefully detailed, had been set off, there would have been disaster. The devices were designed to be placed in strategic spots, causing the most injury and damage. Small-town America would have been left with its emergency services stretched. Hospitals and law-enforcement agencies would have found it difficult to cope in such places. Apart from the physical damage there would have been the aftermath of shock and panic. Communities far removed from terrorism would have been left reeling. People killed and injured, property and services devastated. A campaign along the lines Falil had planned would have struck a terrible chord in the hearts and minds of innocent Americans who suddenly found themselves in a war zone. Brognola saw it as the opening shots in a new, terrifying terrorist war against the ordinary citizens of America. Those who lived in the isolated, rural areas of the nation. It would have brought a dark time to America, and knowing the mind of the terrorist community, Brognola realized it would have only been a start. There would have been more to come.

"There were similar attacks planned for Israel and the UK," Price said. "Falil must have his people in place, waiting for his signal once they have their weaponry in place."

"The explosives that were detonated at the Ghosh farm must have been part of the material intended for the U.S.," Kurtzman said. "We might have places and names here, but we don't know how many of them are supplied and ready."

"Aaron, I need copies of these sheets. We need

them sent to all the state authorities where the locations are. Those places need to be hit now. Get the explosives and the people off the streets. Shut them down. Same goes for the locations overseas. Let them all know. I want this done fast before anyone gets hurt.''

''Already under way,'' Kurtzman said.

''One thing worries me,'' Price said. ''Joseph Haruni is still on the loose. He won't give up easily. Able Team is going to have a fight on their hands when they tangle with him.''

Brognola read the printed information, guided by Wethers, who pointed out the main areas of concern. He was still looking through the material when Kurtzman's satellite keyhole came online.

''Time to rock and roll,'' Kurtzman said.

He put the image up on one of the big wall screens so everyone could watch the satellite sweep. Using his keyboard, Kurtzman tapped in the coordinates, and the satellite arced in its orbit, beginning the precise scan that would lock on to Kurtzman's commands.

The image came into focus, showing the featureless terrain of the Libyan landscape. Under Kurtzman's skilled control the orbiting satellite located the base. At first it was a high shot, with the base in the center of the screen. While Kurtzman concentrated on clarifying the image, Wethers, working from his own station, was compiling a series of photographs using the onboard digital camera. Every shot was saved and identified with date and time. With each successive repositioning of the image Wethers enhanced the picture, isolating and photographing any area that showed significant detail. Kurtzman eventually had the image almost at ground level, and the watchers were able to see figures moving around the base. They saw parked cars. A helicopter resting on a pad outside the walled house. The detail was startling. Clear and precise. It was hard to believe it was coming from a piece of hardware floating in space above Earth.

"Don't those look like machine-gun posts?" Wethers said, indicating two positions outside the north wall.

Kurtzman locked on to the sections of the image and zoomed in, clicking his way to close-ups of the areas. He enhanced and sharpened the images.

"Damn right," he said. "Get shots of those."

When the emplacements had been logged Kurtzman keyed in the command for the thermal scan. The picture image changed from reality to the subdued colors transmitted by the thermal camera. Kurtzman made a slow pass over the base from one end to the other. The computer noted and compiled the incoming data, downloading it into the Stony Man information database.

They had just finished the final scan when the satellite began to move out of range and the picture started to break. Kurtzman ended the contact, returning the satellite to its standard orbit.

"Okay, people," he said. "Go through everything we picked up. I want a tidy package we can send out. I want this done fast. Phoenix Force is going to need all the information we can give them before they go in."

As the team moved to analyze and decipher the information Kurtzman wheeled himself to the coffeepot.

"Sharp as ever," Brognola said, joining the computer expert and pouring himself a mug of the steaming brew. "That was impressive."

"Be even better when we get that hardware update you've been promising," Kurtzman said gruffly.

"Yeah, don't push it, pal. If we get a good result from this mission, maybe I can bend the President's arm a little."

Kurtzman raised his mug.

"I'll remember you said that."

Brognola smiled. "Don't hold your breath."

CHAPTER THIRTEEN

New York

Blancanales and Schwarz were out of the car before it stopped moving. They hit the steps of the rooming house at a run and went through the entrance lobby and up the stairs, weapons out and ready. Kurtzman had checked the phone billing database and had pulled the room number assigned for the phone he had traced. It was number seven, one flight up.

Blancanales pointed to the door as he and Schwarz crossed the landing. Coming up close behind his partner, Schwarz saw Blancanales lift his foot and kick the door open. It slammed back against the wall, sagging where the top hinge had broken.

Blancanales went in fast, ducking and breaking left. Behind him Schwarz covered his back. The room was empty, untidy, and containing the bare essentials. There was a small bathroom to one side. It showed signs that someone had been using it recently. Soap in the basin was still moist, and a towel draped from the door handle was damp.

"Damn!" Schwarz said, jamming his pistol into his holster. "We missed him."

Lyons appeared in the doorway, waving his badge wallet in the faces of interested spectators.

"Nothing?"

"Nada!" Blancanales said.

Lyons prowled the room. He checked the bathroom, reaching up to touch the light bulb hanging from the ceiling.

"He hasn't been gone long."

"Maybe he clued in that things were starting to fall apart and took a powder," Schwarz said.

Lyons shook his head. "I don't think so. This son of a bitch is too much of a professional to cut and run. I'd say he's got the message, but he won't go without leaving us something to remember him by."

"You figure he's got a surprise for us?"

"Damned right he has. Some backup plan. A surprise that won't be sweet and sugary. Bet your life on that."

"So where is he?" Blancanales asked.

Lyons pulled out his cell phone. He speed dialed Stony Man and asked for Kurtzman.

"We're at Haruni's rooming house. He's gone. I'm playing a hunch here. About the only one we might have. Check the call list from this number. Look for a new number. One Haruni has called in the last day or so. Forget all the others. This one will only have been contacted a couple of times."

"You going to tell us?" Schwarz asked.

Lyons ignored him, waiting for Kurtzman's response.

"Strong, silent type," Blancanales said.

"Pain in the ass," Schwarz added.

Blancanales thought about it. "Same thing."

"Okay. Name? Kerim Habib. Give me a rundown."

Kurtzman was scrolling data from his monitor and relaying it to Lyons, who listened in silence. Finally he thanked Kurtzman and hung up.

"Let's go," he said, and headed out of the room.

They were in the car, Schwarz driving and following Lyons's directions, when Blancanales exploded.

"Come on, Carl, do we have to ask in writing?"

Lyons glanced at him as if he didn't know him, then grinned.

"Yeah, sorry. Look, I got to thinking about the situation. Here we have Haruni looking to make a big exit. Now he hasn't been around long enough to get anything in place for the job. We agreed on that?"

"I guess so."

"Okay. Let's assume that Falil, when he was organizing this campaign, figures that he needs a backup plan in case things fall flat. What does he do? Wait until the last minute? I don't think so. Falil must have been working on this for a while. Maybe a few years. He'd want his fail-safe in place. Established. Ready to be used if the time came. To do that he needs a guy around to work it. So he plants one, a guy who fits in and goes around like a regular joe. Just waiting for the call."

"A sleeper," Schwarz said.

"I knew that," Blancanales admitted.

"Kerim Habib arrived in the U.S. three years ago. His papers were in order. Everything by the book. Had a job in the city. Lives here, too. Lives a nice quiet life. No convictions. No untoward political views. Very average nice guy. You probably wouldn't notice him on an empty street.''

''But he's been called by Haruni?'' Schwarz asked.

''Twice in the last couple of days. In fact the latest call was earlier this morning.''

''If Habib is the sleeper, Haruni must be his control.''

''And the only reason a controller calls a sleeper is to activate him,'' Blancanales said.

''All fits,'' Lyons said.

''Let's hope so,'' Blancanales said. ''We're going to look stupid if he's only called to sell him insurance.''

''Well, if that's all it is I'll buy a damn policy myself,'' Schwarz said.

''YOU WAIT HERE,'' Haruni instructed his backup crew. ''Once I have what I need from this idiot Habib, we can set this operation into motion.''

''Will we have time to leave the city before it starts?'' one of the men asked.

Haruni smiled. ''Do I detect a lack of faith?''

''I don't care what you call it,'' the man said. ''I will reach paradise in a time of my own choosing.''

''That I can understand. My own feeling exactly. There is plenty to do here before traveling to the afterlife.

''Rest assured, my brothers. The device will be delivered to its site and a timer set. Before it activates we will have boarded a waiting jet and be on our way.''

Haruni left the car and crossed the quiet street. He made his way into the building and climbed the stairs to Habib's floor. Before he rang the bell he took out his heavy autopistol and held it out of sight behind his back.

He rang the bell and heard it sound inside the apartment. After a few moments he detected movement behind the door. He rang the bell a second time.

"Who is there?"

"It is Haruni. We need to talk, Kerim."

"No!"

"My brother, at least allow me to speak face-to-face. I respect your decision, but I must discuss this with you before I leave the country. Extend me this courtesy at least."

There was a silence. Haruni waited, allowing Habib the chance to consider his request.

"Please, my brother."

The chain was released slowly, as if Habib still hadn't fully made his choice. The lock clicked free and the door opened a few inches. Kerim Habib's face showed half in shadow as he studied his visitor

Haruni made no move. He stood still. He wasn't about to startle Habib at this stage and have the door slammed shut in his face.

"I am alone, Kerim Habib. All I wish for is to talk and part company on good terms."

Still hesitation. Habib glanced over Habib's shoulder, checking the passage. Haruni eased to one side to refrain from blocking Habib's vision. He stood passively silent, his hands clasped behind his back.

The metal of the autopistol had warmed to his skin temperature. It felt solid and reassuring in Haruni's hands.

Habib opened the door fully to allow his visitor to step inside. Haruni moved by him, turning as he did to avoid showing the autopistol in his hands.

"I am grateful for your time," Haruni said, maintaining his guise as the polite guest.

Habib closed the door. The lock clicked into position and Habib turned, raising a hand to invite his guest into his apartment. His eyes met those of Haruni.

The smile had gone. Haruni's expression showed the contempt he felt for Habib.

Habib realized the mistake he had made.

Too late.

Haruni's hand came into view, the large autopistol sweeping up in a blur. The cold, hard steel crunched against Habib's nose, breaking it with a soft sound. Blood spurted immediately, gushing over Habib's mouth and dribbling down his white shirt. Stunned by the impact, Habib stepped back. Pain and confusion dulled his judgment, and he failed to avoid the second blow. It smacked against his mouth, loosening teeth and splitting his gums. Habib slumped against the wall, his eyes darting back and forth as his numbed senses tried to reassert themselves.

Moving in close, Haruni hit Habib a number of times, then caught hold of Habib's hair and dragged him into the center of the room. Haruni swung his victim around, smashing the gun across the back of Habib's skull, pitching him facedown on the carpet.

He stood and watched as Habib fumbled on the floor. Disoriented from the brutal blows, burning with pain and indifferent to anything but his own survival, Habib, in a moment of clarity, wondered how long he had left to live. He was under no illusion. Haruni would have little use for him once their business was concluded.

He wouldn't want to leave anyone behind who could betray him.

He would also feel it his duty to punish Habib for his crime in refusing to carry out his mission. Even now Habib realized he had made the foolish error of telling Haruni, the second time he called, that he wasn't going to go through with the mission. That he refused to do the one thing that would bring death and suffering to Americans he now felt were his friends. He had begged forgiveness, trying to explain to Haruni that he was unable to do what was asked of him. Oddly, Haruni had remained calm. He had been pleasant enough, telling Habib not to worry. That he had nothing to regret.

After the call Habib had paced his apartment, wondering how he could clear himself of the nagging doubt in his mind concerning Haruni. Could he trust the man? Would Haruni move on and forget what Habib had refused to do? Or would he return to demand the mission be carried through?

Whatever the outcome Habib felt that he had justified himself. In truth he had become part of America. He had friends. Had established himself among the locals. How could he in all conscience bring suffering and death to these people? To the women and children he saw every day? To his colleagues at work? This place was his home now. No matter what his original purpose, his attitude had changed and so had his purpose in America. This was no longer the place of his enemies. It was the home of his friends.

HARUNI BENT OVER the bleeding figure. He caught hold of Habib's shirt and turned him on his back.

"Brother, you have little time left. Don't waste it. Give me what I want and I will end it quickly."

"I will not help—"

"You will, brother, you will," Haruni said.

He pulled a slim knife from a sheath inside his jacket, using his left hand to guide it quickly. The blade had an edge like a scalpel and it cut flesh deeply. Blood bubbled and ran freely. Terrible pain engulfed Habib. The blade flashed again. More pain, more shivering agony that tore a wrenching scream from Habib's lips.

"Tell me quickly and it stops, brother."

Habib shook his head, blood spraying red droplets across the carpet.

Again the knife did its cold work, cutting, severing. Habib tried to scream again, but his mouth was wet and bloody from the cruel cuts. Soft flaps of moist flesh hung loosely, exposed nerves white-hot with agony.

"They do say that the eye is sensitive to pain," Haruni whispered.

Habib flailed with his hands, desperate to push aside the knife. The sharp blade slashed his fingers, slicing them open, almost severing one. And then it arced down at his face, the needle tip piercing the left eye, pushing in deep.

It was only a little time after that Habib gave the information Haruni needed. The final cut ended Habib's agony and his life.

"LEFT HERE," Lyons said.

Schwarz took the corner and they rolled onto the quiet street. Lyons checked off the buildings. He left it to Blancanales to look for any possible threats.

"That's it," Lyons instructed.

Schwarz swung the car into a space right outside the building and cut the engine. They sat for a moment checking out the area.

"I hate these setups," Lyons said. "All looks clear until you step out and a guy opens up from a window or off a rooftop."

"Yeah, well, you want to live forever?" Blancanales asked, pushing open his door.

He eased out of the car, one hand inside his jacket, his fingers closed around the butt of his autopistol. The Able Team pro might have looked casual, but his instincts were on full alert, his eyes skimming the area for any sudden movement. No situation as fluid as the one they were in could be guaranteed totally risk free. In the end it came down to making the move that might carry it forward or invite trouble. Risk was part of their profession, and if they were to gain any ground it had to be taken.

Out the corner of his eye Blancanales saw his partners emerge from the car, each taking a section of the street as they stood upright. Lyons moved up the steps of the building and stopped just inside the door, covering his partners as they joined him.

"That was fun," Blancanales said. Despite his outer cool he had a cold spot running down his spine. It happened every time. The day it didn't Blancanales would know it was time he quit.

"Let's go," Lyons said, and they climbed the stairs to the floor where Kerim Habib lived.

THE DOOR WAS closed and locked. Carl Lyons drew back, then launched a hard kick just below the lock.

The door crashed open and Able Team went in fast, weapons out and tracking ahead of them.

Silence.

Blancanales closed the door.

Ahead of the others Lyons advanced into the main room, searching.

It was hard not to miss the spread-eagled body on the floor. Or the pooled blood soaking the carpet under and around it. Lyons closed on the body. He didn't need to get too close to know that the man was dead. The savagely slit throat had done it. If not, the amount of blood that had come from the terrible mutilations would have eventually led to the same thing.

"Jesus," Schwarz said softly.

Blancanales's response was similar to Schwarz's when he saw the body.

"We assume this is Habib?" Schwarz asked.

"So why is he dead?" Blancanales countered. "And why cut him up like this?"

"Somebody wanted something. Habib wouldn't give it. So he was persuaded." Lyons cast around the room. "Maybe Habib had a change of heart and didn't want to carry through with what he'd been sent here for. Haruni did, only he didn't know where Habib kept the package."

"You want to bet he does now?" Blancanales asked.

"Great," Schwarz said. "All we have to do is figure out where."

As if by some silent agreement, they began to search the apartment, looking for anything that might tell them where Haruni had gone.

They pulled out drawers, emptied cupboards, checked under chairs, the bed, went through every pocket of every item of clothing Habib had owned.

"What the hell are we looking for, anyway?" Blancanales asked.

"Listen, guys," Schwarz said. "We have to assume whatever Habib's device was he wouldn't risk keeping it here in the apartment. So he has to have it stored somewhere else. So maybe there's an address for a locker. A storage facility. This thing has been waiting for some time. He would have needed to keep it somewhere long-term."

"And if he did he would have had to pay rent," Lyons said.

"Did he have a bank account? Maybe we can get a statement of payments."

"Not if he used a false name," Blancanales said.

"I don't think he would risk anything like that. Banks want too much information and they keep records," Lyons said.

Schwarz had pulled out a drawer full of papers. He went through them one by one, patiently examining them.

"Look at this," he said.

He held up a thin wad of papers held together by a paper clip.

"Payments to a company here in Brooklyn. They rent out lockups. Receipts here go back a year and a half. All made out to a Mr. Aman. Monthly cash payments for a lockup unit."

"Where?"

Schwarz turned the wad over, checking it carefully.

"Doesn't say."

"Those things have a telephone number?" Lyons asked.

Schwarz handed him the wad, and Lyons took out his cell phone and dialed.

"I would like to speak to whoever is in charge," Lyons said. "You can tell him it is Agent Kane, Justice Department. I need to speak to him right away." There was a pause, and Lyons smiled. "Well, Mr. Panelli, let me put it this way. I don't have time to waste pretending to be who I am. You want proof I can give you truckloads. I can also have a car full of agents from the local field office descend on you like the wrath of God if you do not stop wasting my time. Now, if you think you have impressed your office staff enough playing the big man, just answer me a simple question. I have in my hand a receipt for a lockup you rent to a Mr. Aman. Rental agreement number 744225. All I want is your cooperation in confirming where that lockup is located." There was another pause while the office behind Mr. Panelli erupted into frantic action. "Unit 23. East Dock Avenue. Near the Brooklyn Bridge? Thank you, Mr. Panelli. Your help is greatly appreciated."

Lyons shut off his phone, then dialed again.

"Frank?" he said when Delacort came on the line. "We could use your help on this. You want to join us?" He gave Delacort the address of Habib's building. "See you shortly."

"How come?" Blancanales asked.

"He's local. We may need surveillance to track Haruni. The FBI and NYPD have the facilities for that. This could turn out to be something we need to work on fast. Come on, guys, I'm improvising.''

Blancanales nodded. ''I'm impressed,'' he said. ''Improvising is such a big word.''

CHAPTER FOURTEEN

Israel

"According to what we've pulled from the data stored in the computers taken from Falil's people, he's got a hell of a master plan set up. Specific targets here in the U.S., with his people in place just waiting for the word," Brognola explained.

"Are you closing them down?" McCarter asked.

"All under way. The FBI is coordinating with the local enforcement agencies in each area. They're setting everything up to go at the same time. Take each cell down fast so they don't have time to get the word out."

"What about the situation over this way?"

"The details are coming through shortly," Brognola said. "The site Katz hit in Haifa looks like it was one of the main centers in Israel. Distribution point, I guess. There are a few more locations to be checked. Latest info to come off the printer details four sites in London with a few more around the UK. We're passing these along to the UK authorities so they can deal with them."

"Middle East sites?" McCarter asked.

There was a pause while Brognola selected more printout sheets, then he came back on the line. "Little more involved. These aren't sites as such. Seem to be more concerned with personalities involved in pro-Western regimes. Looks like more of a hit list. We figure Falil's intent is to take out people and upset the apple cart big time."

"He doesn't care who he upsets," McCarter said. "Could explain the silenced Berettas and the up-close shotguns we found at that cache. Just the kind of weapons they'd need for an assassination attempt."

"How are things shaping for your trip?"

"Okay. We go in tonight. High-altitude drop. The Israelis are pulling out all the stops. We should have everything we need."

"Data from our satellite scan is being processed right now," the big Fed said. "Soon as it breaks it'll be coming through to in-flight. Should help you plan your strike."

Kurtzman's input via the satellite imaging would furnish them with valuable data.

"What about Falil's neighbors?" McCarter asked, referring to the Libyan presence.

"According to the satellite sweep, there's nothing close by. Our boy Falil chose his spot well. It's away from normal patrol areas. We estimate it would take anything up to an hour, hour and a half before help could arrive."

"If we're not out under that time, we won't be leaving at all," McCarter said.

"Hell, you'd better be out," Brognola told him, "No one gave you permission for an extended stay."

"Bloody hell, you're a hard man."

"Take care. Same for the rest of the guys."

McCarter cut the connection and pushed his chair away from the desk. He left the small office and rejoined the others as they checked and rechecked their weapons and gear.

They were keeping it down to the minimum. No heavy packs. Just weapons, explosives and grenades. Calvin James would have a small medical pack with him. Gary Manning, the Phoenix Force sniper, was in his element because Ben Sharon had located a Barnett crossbow for him, along with a supply of cyanide-shafted bolts. The Mossad, with their wide experience of covert work, had an impressive array of arms. They had handed out extra 9 mm ammunition for the team's H&K MP-5s and their autopistols. Sharon, who was accompanying Phoenix Force, had given them a briefing on their insertion procedure.

"We'll leave on a C-130. By the time we hit Libyan airspace we'll be at twenty-three thousand feet. We depressurize as we approach and do a HALO drop. Weather tonight is reported as calm with little wind, so there shouldn't be drift. The idea is to come down within ten miles of the objective. From there we walk in."

"How about extraction?" James asked.

"We have one of our Black Hawk choppers on board a recovery ship that will be stationed off the coast. When we're ready to go we transmit a signal and the chopper will be with us in less than an hour."

Sharon made room for McCarter to take over.

"Okay, we know how we get in and out. Before we go in there should be satellite pictures coming through that should give us the layout of this base.

Intel isn't as detailed as we would like, but choice isn't always what we get on these deals. As far as our mission brief, we have two things to deal with.

"First is to locate and destroy any and all computer equipment we find. This Falil character seems to favor cyber space as his means of communication. So we deny him that. Secondly we disable as much as we can of his superstructure. This base is on our hit list, and if anyone gets in our way that is their problem.

"We understand enough about Falil's plans to know he intends to create a bloody great deal of harm and injury to anyone within one of his targets. I don't care whether that's in the U.S., Israel, London or downtown Beirut. This bloke is intent on stirring up trouble if we let him. If he succeeds, we could have war zones popping up everywhere. So we stop him."

"We still haven't been able to find Dahoun," Sharon said. "Since we took out the cell in Haifa, he's vanished. No one seems to know where he is. Could be he's jumped to Libya, staying with Falil while they decide which way to go. I hope he is there. I want to deal with him. He's been pretty busy here in Israel. As far as Mossad is concerned, we don't want him back."

"Okay, guys," McCarter said. "We have about an hour before the aircraft will be ready to go. Time to grab something to eat. I'm famished, personally."

"There's a surprise," James said.

"Insubordination in the ranks there," McCarter said. "Stand up, man."

James uncoiled his lean form, hands resting on his hips. McCarter looked him up and down. "Mmm," he said. "Quite tall, isn't he."

Grinning, James trailed after the Briton as the men went in search of their preflight meal.

THE C-130 bristled with exterior antenna and radar dishes. Inside it had been fitted with full-spec communication and surveillance equipment, much of it courtesy of the U.S. Much of the Israeli agency information gathering had a connection with U.S. interest in the Middle East, so the input of American technology had a price. Not that Mossad had any complaints. The information highway ran in both directions. Cooperation, though not always running smoothly, was necessary. At this moment in time it was vital.

Once the Stony Man team and Ben Sharon were onboard, the aircraft taxied out to the runway and gathered speed as the tower gave the all clear. The four massive turboprop engines pushed the aircraft to takeoff speed, and it was in the air with surprising speed.

Sharon led the way to the communications deck. Flat-screen monitors showed map schematics of the area, pinpointing their position. There were ever-changing data banks, feeding in information on weather conditions, the deployment of unfriendly craft both in the air and on the ocean. Satellite uplinks fed in current military and civilian scans.

There was a separate cell that monitored radar, another handling radio communications. A constant, muted chatter of sound came from the built-in speakers, coming through in a number of languages.

"Ben, I'm impressed," Gary Manning said.

"Looks like you have everything you need except a McDonald's." Hawkins grinned.

"We'll commission one if it's kosher," Sharon said.

He threaded his way to a vacant workstation.

"All yours."

The connection had already been made, and when the final keystroke was made Kurtzman's voice came through strong and clear. Once the men of Phoenix Force were in position, Kurtzman sent his package of data on the Libyan base.

The first monitor showed the digital images as seen by the satellite on its first scan.

"This should give you an idea of the layout," Kurtzman said. "Looks like quite a setup. This is no log cabin."

The team studied the images as Kurtzman went through them slowly, backing up whenever anyone queried anything or asked for a longer look.

"Next images are from the thermal imagery. We picked up a major heat source here and figure it comes from a generator running the power supply."

Kurtzman had boxed the section. The monitor clicked as it showed enhanced shots of the isolated area. "We picked up other heat signatures inside the buildings. See the way they're moving around? These are your terrorists. Now here we got a stronger source. Concentrated in this section. At a guess I'd say this could be your central control room. Heat coming from computers, probably."

McCarter turned to a second monitor that was showing more of the digital images.

"What's this outside the north wall? One at each corner. Looks like gun emplacements to me. Anyone agree?"

James peered at the screen, nodding.

"I'd say so."

"You're right," Kurtzman said. "We got close-ups."

The image clicked its way through the enhancement process, closing down on the images until the men were able to clearly identify the machine-gun emplacements.

"FN-MAGs," Manning said. "We'll need to take them out before we go over the wall."

Kurtzman continued his delivery of the facts, even as Manning and Hawkins were discussing the merits of the 7.62 mm machine gun.

"To the far right we have a helicopter pad," Kurtzman said. "Chopper was in place at the time we were looking."

He led them through the entire package, answering all the questions the team came up with until they were satisfied there was nothing else they could gain from the images.

"Tell everyone thanks," McCarter said. "Great job."

Using the precise monitoring of the satellite, McCarter was able to connect the GPS unit and extract the data he needed to store in the memory. He was able to lock on to the exact position of Falil's base.

"Save us wandering around the bloody desert all night," he said.

With the connection to Stony Man ended the team went over the details of the package Kurtzman had sent them. They were able to obtain printouts of the images.

Hawkins and Manning were still talking about the

machine-gun emplacements and the threat they presented.

"No contest," the Canadian said. "We have to take them out before we move in."

"Ground is pretty open right up to them," Hawkins commented.

"It can be done," Manning said.

"It'll leave that area clear," Hawkins pointed out, indicating the terrain covered by the machine guns.

"Both facing north," Sharon said. "In the direction of the sea."

"They wouldn't be expecting any attack to come from inland," Encizo said. "Most likely any assault *would* come from the seaward side."

"As long as the damn things aren't pointing up in the air we're all right," James remarked. "Dropping in by parachute leaves me feeling vulnerable."

"Here, take a look at this one," Hawkins said.

"The generator?" McCarter said. "If they're running computers, they're going to need a constant power supply. I don't know how dependable the local supply is, but Falil couldn't risk a sudden blackout. We'll keep that in mind. Locate and shut down the power source. We hit and he loses control of his computer set-up and his light source. Gives us the advantage."

"Disable the generator and they lose their light," Hawkins agreed, "but most laptops have a built-in power source. If you keep them charged from a regular supply, there'll still be a few hours stored in the computer."

"Point taken. We still go for the generator. Computers will have to be handled separately."

"Do we collect any data? Or do we destroy it

all?'' Manning asked. "There might be information stored we could use.''

"We're not going to have time to check every machine they might have," Sharon said. "Why not grab a couple and demolish the rest?''

"Pick up as many disks as we can," Manning said. "That's where they'll have everything backed up.''

"We'll do that," McCarter replied. "Listen up. I don't want anyone holding back just because he figures he's got time for a few more disks. We go in, do the job and get the bloody hell out of the place.''

"Pity that satellite can't tell us how many we're going up against," Encizo said.

"You want everything done for you?" Hawkins asked.

"TEN MINUTES to drop zone," the pilot announced.

The warning light came on, and they all donned their oxygen masks so the cargo area could be depressurized. Helmets were donned and secured. Night-vision goggles were locked into place. The crewman acting as jump master oversaw the procedure, checking off the time.

McCarter led the way to where the ramp had powered open. The pilot called that they were right on course, following the computerized navigation instructions.

"Wait! Wait!" the Israeli crewman said. Then his hand clapped down on McCarter's shoulder. "Go!"

McCarter didn't hesitate. He moved quickly to the edge of the ramp and flung himself into the black abyss. One by one the rest of the team followed suit. As the last man cleared the ramp, the crewman hit the button. The ramp began to close even as the huge aircraft began its slow turn, heading back to Israel.

THE NIGHT WAS black and the air cold. Wind whistled by the six men as they plummeted toward the Libyan desert. Clothing was snapped taut against their bodies as they dropped.

It was only as the chutes opened that they were able to take stock of their situation and start to observe the lie of the land they were floating down to.

McCarter checked the GPS unit. The readout showed him they were well within the computerized location. He had operated in the field long before navigation had become such a sophisticated art, and he was pretty confident that any of the team could do the same. He sometimes wondered whether they were becoming far too dependent on the capricious whims of electronic machines. There would always be the time when machines weren't available, for one reason or another, and those were the times when the men stood out from the boys. The true survivor was the man who was stranded in the wilderness with nothing but the clothes he wore and who walked out six weeks later still capable of telling you what time of day it was. There was nothing wrong with using the creations of the electronic age as long as the basics were still remembered the day somebody pulled the plug.

McCarter landed hard, calling himself a bloody idiot for not concentrating. He unfastened his helmet and dumped it, pulling on the black woolen cap he carried. He gathered his chute and harness and scooped out a hole in the sandy earth to bury them. The others were doing the same. They gathered around and established their position. Sharon was familiar with the area and pointed the way. After a weapon and equipment check, they unlimbered their Uzi SMGs, and with McCarter in the lead set off.

The Briton referred to the GPS every so often, checking to make sure they were on course.

They traveled steadily for close to an hour. As they neared the base, McCarter sent Encizo ahead to make a visual confirmation of their position. The GPS could guide them in, but it was unable to assess the actual situation.

"About a quarter mile ahead. A little to the east. But it's there."

"How close did you get?" McCarter asked.

Encizo squatted in the dust, opening his canteen to wet his lips and spit before taking a small sip of water.

"Close enough to see both those machine-gun posts. One at each corner of the compound."

"Wall height?"

"Eight feet. This place wasn't built as a fortress, remember. I did spot lights at the corners of the walls, so security has been looked at."

McCarter nodded.

"All right, lads, let's go. Nice steady stroll should get us there."

Stony Man Farm, Virginia

THE COMPUTER ROOM was hushed, only the hum of the electronic machines intruding into the silence. Most of the lights were out as the team gathered in front of one of the wall screens.

Kurtzman tapped at his keyboard, bringing the satellite on-line. The wall screen cleared itself as the bird's orbit brought it to the coordinates Kurtzman had tapped in. He enhanced the image, seeking a low scan, and then switched to thermal imaging.

The cold, multilayered image filled the screen. The edge of the screen showed a data stream, numbers and symbols indicating the range and magnification. Under Kurtzman's skilled guidance the satellite's cameras located and locked on to Falil's base, the flickering outline of the house and surrounding wall standing out clearly. Within the perimeter they could see the heat signatures of people, hot spots in and around the sprawling residence, the shape of the generator, pulsing with heat.

"Any time now," Barbara Price said, her tone soft. It was as if she dare not speak too loudly in case she disturbed the subdued mood. Kurtzman eased the image to the north end of the perimeter, where the two machine-gun emplacements were situated.

"They'll deal with those first," Katz said.

Time passed with infinite slowness. No one said anything, nor moved. They were witnessing a real-time event unfolding before their eyes, a joining of Stony Man with one of the combat teams thousands of miles away on the other side of the world. All courtesy of the electronic machines that made the facility function. The gathering of data. The unraveling of cyber codes and intrusive eavesdropping. That was how Stony Man operated on a daily basis. Now, though, they were about to became involved in the living reality of the culmination of all their endeavors.

Combat by proxy.

They were bystanders about to see the event, not just read a report after the strike.

"Hey, I see something."

It was Tokaido. He was pointing to the far edge of the screen, to an area beyond the north wall.

Six moving shapes. Human figures, advancing from the desert beyond, and closing rapidly with the base.

Sanctuary

DAHOUN FOUND Falil standing at an upper floor balcony. The robed figure remained staring across the soft desert night as Dahoun crossed to stand beside him.

"Disturbing news from America," Dahoun said.

"We will survive it," Falil replied. "As you have survived the trouble in Haifa. Time will pass, and we will gather our strength, learn from our mistakes and return."

"Your resilience amazes me," Dahoun said. "How do you reconcile each disaster?"

Falil glanced at him. He smiled, even though it took a great effort. There were dark circles beneath his eyes that others took as a result of the enormous pressure he was under. None of them knew about the terrible pain he was forced to live with, and which this very evening was crushing him.

"How else can I see it? What should I do? Surrender and let the infidels win without having fired a single shot at them? No, my brother, better to let them have their small moment believing they have defeated us, and then strike as we will in New York. While they occupy themselves with the aftermath we withdraw into the shadows and build again. Only this time we do not make the same mistakes.''

''What can I do?''

''Make checks on all your people. See how far the Mossad has broken up your organization. Find out if any of the stockpiles are untouched. Take care. The Mossad may have left them intact, but there could be agents watching, waiting to arrest anyone who approaches the cache.''

''I'll be careful.''

''What about the woman you used. The one with the boat.''

''Kara Shebin?'' Dahoun laughed. ''Forget about her. She knows nothing except what I told her. The authorities will have questioned her by now. What can she tell them? Only that I made a fool out of her. Which was not difficult.''

''Be careful if you return to Israel. Mossad has a long memory, and they use many people to spy for them. And this woman may harbor revenge in her heart.''

''My photographic studio will have to be abandoned. I'll find somewhere else to make my base once I decide where to go.''

''If you require finance be sure to let me know,'' Falil said.

''I will. May I stay here for a while? Until things quieten down.''

''You are welcome, brother. Take time. Let this place renew your faith. Rest yourself and then we can set our plans for the future.''

Falil talked a little while longer with Dahoun and then excused himself. He made his way to his room and closed the door. He crossed to the small bathroom and bent over the basin, sluicing cold water over his head. He wet a small towel and pressed it to his burning flesh, making silent prayers in the hope he could rid himself of the headache. The pain had come again quickly, and he realized that the time between each attack became shorter. Lying on his narrow bed, his eyes aching from the pressure, Falil begged God to allow him enough time to exact his revenge on the infidels of the West and the traitors within his own people. If he was to die, he wanted to achieve this one victory, or at least set it in motion so that his followers could maintain the momentum.

He lay in silent agony, his body turning this way and that as he tried to relieve the agony, even though he knew nothing would stop it. The attack would diminish in its own time. He could do nothing but endure it.

If he had been a vain man, Falil would have asked why he had been punished so much. First his family destroyed by the land mine, he himself left crippled by that same blast. The disappointment of his carefully arranged campaign against the infidels going astray. And the suffering he was forced to endure from the pains inside his head. Surely it was more than enough for one man, especially one who had devoted his life to the service of God in the hope he might avenge the wrongs done to Islam.

If Falil had been a vain man, he might have posed that question. In his troubled mind he had formed it but that was as far as it got. There was little to be gained from self-pity, from the inglorious need to understand his own weaknesses when all around him others were suffering far greater deprivations.

So the questions remained as nothing more than misty curiosities within Falil's subconscious.

He lay in the silent darkness of his bare room, enduring his private pain, looking ahead to when he might be able to gather his followers and start to build once again.

THE BASE LAY no more than thirty feet in front of them, pale white in the soft night. It was almost midnight. To their right they could make out the bulk of the helicopter parked on its circled pad. It was far enough away from the walled enclosure to keep its lone sentry out of earshot of any small noise.

The lights mounted on the corners of the wall, above the bunkers, threw beams of light at wide angles to either side of the compound. McCarter studied them for a time, deciding they weren't about to cause them any problems. Once the generator was shut down the lights would go, too.

Gary Manning was setting up his crossbow. He had a number of the wooden shafts lying in the sand beside him ready for use. One was already in position, the crossbow locked and ready for firing.

"We need those guns out of action before we move in," McCarter said. "I don't want us coming back out and running into those bloody things."

Manning was studying the machine-gun positions and calculating distance. Each weapon had a gunner and a loader. He decided the best way would be to eliminate the gunner, then the loader.

The rest of the team left the Canadian alone as he made his preparations. Manning was singularly skilled at this tactical operation. This particular takedown was difficult. Manning had to take out both members of each gun crew.

Only when he was ready did Manning turn and signal James to his side. He handed the man three of the wooden bolts.

"Soon as I fire the first give me another," he instructed. "I'm going for the crew on the left first. If I do it without alerting the other team, we go for them next."

James nodded. He took the solid, heavy shafts and held them ready.

Slipping his night-vision goggles into place, Manning waited until his eyes adjusted to the green illumination. He stretched himself out in the sand, the crossbow against his shoulder, and took aim, taking his time until he had the range and angle set in his mind. He was able to study the two-man crew. The men were in full view and not exactly on full alert. The long night had probably slowed their reaction time, and that would be to Manning's advantage.

He settled his sights on the gunner. Holding the shot, Manning settled himself, then gently stroked the crossbow's trigger. He felt the soft jolt as the bolt was released and heard the faint whoosh of its passage.

He pulled back on the cocking mechanism, heard it click into place, then held out his hand for the second bolt. James placed it in the Canadian's grasp. Manning slid the bolt into place, put the sights on the loader, who was staring at his partner's slumping form. The man turned to look out beyond the perimeter, presenting Manning with a larger target. The bolt snapped through his neck, releasing the cyanide, and the man fell facedown over his already dead partner.

James held out the third bolt and Manning dropped it in place. He arced the crossbow in the direction of the second gun crew. Neither of them appeared to have noticed what had happened to the first crew.

Manning's shot struck the gunner between the shoulders, throwing him against the edge of the bunker. The man's partner reached out to support him, unsure what was wrong until he saw the feathered shaft protruding from his partner's back. He turned, snatching up the AK-74 leaning against the side of the bunker.

The fourth bolt left the Barnett crossbow, covering the distance to its target in a split second. The shaft buried itself in the target's chest, the wood core shattering on impact and releasing its load of cyanide. The sentry stiffened, falling back out of sight as the poison spread swiftly through his system.

Observing the dispatch of the fourth man, Mc-Carter gave the word and the rest of the force moved to join Manning and James.

"Nicely done," McCarter said. "Let's move up to the wall. Disable those damn machine guns first."

"What about the guy guarding the chopper?" Encizo asked.

"I'll deal with him," Manning said.

They headed for the bunkers, slipping over the low concrete wall. Easing the bodies aside, Hawkins and Encizo went to work on the heavy machine gun while McCarter stood watch. Ben Sharon went with Manning and James to deal with the second gun and the remaining sentry.

Minutes later they regrouped.

"You three stay together," McCarter said to Manning, James and Sharon. "Take the west side of the compound. We'll cover the east. Remember our objectives. Communications capability via computer. Any data we can pick up. This place has to be shut down. We need to break the lines of contact between Falil and his cells. And let's not forget the generator. Whoever locates it first puts it out of action."

Each man put on his headset and activated his transceiver. They were checked out and found to be working.

"Call signs are Fox one for us," McCarter said. "Fox two for you blokes. Anyone gets in bad trouble just yell. I want to leave here with the same number that went in."

Weapons were given a final check before the two three-man teams moved out.

Scaling the compound wall wasn't difficult, delayed only as long as it took the first up to confirm the absence of any sensor alarms topping it. The others followed quickly, dropping inside the compound and remaining concealed behind thick shrubbery while the way ahead was checked and plans of action formulated.

SOMETHING MADE HIM sit up. The pain in his head was severe. Despite the agony, Falil was aware of a disturbance. He didn't understand what had alerted him. He only knew there was danger close by.

He got to his feet and moved very slowly to the balcony. Each step sent waves of dull, nagging pain rolling through his skull. He stood in the open, resting one hand against the cool wall, steadying himself. He felt weak, dizzy, and he remained where he was

for a time. Sweat glistened on his face and ran into
his eyes, stinging them. He took a few steps forward.
Reaching the walled edge of the balcony, he gazed
across the compound. Soft lights, coming from the
various interiors of the structure, threw a crisscross
design of black shadow and pale illumination across
the flagged courtyard in the center of the area.
Though it was late there were a number of his followers still awake. He heard the low murmur of
voices, a faint trickle of music from a radio. The cool
night air held the scent of flowers from the carefully
tended gardens within the compound.

To the casual observer the atmosphere was one of
tranquil calm. Falil sensed something different,
something off balance. A threat.

His eyes caught what he imagined was a flicker of
movement at the far end of the compound, close to
the north wall where a wide tract of shrubbery grew.
Falil looked again. His eyes were having problems
focusing because of the pain from his headache, yet
he insisted to himself that he had seen movement
there. He cautioned himself against overreaction. The
movement, if it had existed, could have been nothing
more than the shrubbery moving in the night breeze.

He considered that, then rejected it.

The night was particularly still. There was no
breeze. Nothing to disturb the shrubbery. Nothing
natural. But something concealed within the undergrowth might brush against it and cause it to move.

And that something could be hostile intruders.
Falil found more credence in that thought than any
other.

Perhaps the Mossad had located the base. Or even
the interfering Americans who had already caused

his organization so much aggravation. Had they tracked him down? Were they even now inside the walls of his sanctuary? He paused for a moment. Was he allowing his feelings of anger against the Americans to lead him into flights of fancy? Was he imagining their presence? The effects of the continuing pain from his crippling headache might be producing imaginary fears.

Falil turned away from the balcony and returned to his room. He refused to accept he was hearing and even seeing things that didn't exist. In the darkness of his room he stood with his head bowed, hands clasped to his skull, pressing against the very bone as if he were trying to squeeze out the hurt.

If he had been imagining it all, why had he suddenly woken with a premonition of something being wrong? He reached for the internal telephone on the wall beside the door and was connected to the security detail.

"Is everything secure?"

"Yes, sir. Why do you ask?"

"A feeling. Have the grounds thoroughly checked. Start at the north wall. Let me know when you have completed your patrol."

"Very well. I will have it done immediately."

"Good. Thank you."

It made no difference whether anything was found or not. He would be justified either way. For his diligence if he was proved right. And for his thoroughness in maintaining a secure base if nothing was found.

Falil managed a thin smile. At least on this occasion he could feel confident that he had done the right thing.

Making his way to the bathroom, he ran cold water and soaked his towel again so he could hold it against his head and face. The water felt good against his hot flesh, and he spent a few minutes bent over the basin. With the soaked cloth in his hand Falil made a slow return to the bedroom. He sat on the edge of the bed, slowly rocking as he held the cloth to his skin.

He was still there minutes later when he heard someone shouting from the courtyard below his room. He recognized the voice as belonging to one of his security guards. The man shouted again. Falil was unable to decipher the words, but he registered the agitation in the man's tone.

Footsteps rattled across the courtyard.

And then Falil heard the thing he feared the most—the shattering rattle of automatic gunfire.

He hadn't been imagining things. There were intruders inside his compound, disturbing the peace of his sanctuary.

It seemed Falil's war had come home—with a vengeance.

CHAPTER FIFTEEN

"Heads up," McCarter said over the com unit. "Don't ask how, but I have a feeling we've been detected."

He was watching a group of five or six figures moving across the wide compound in the general direction of the north wall section. There was no mistaking the serious intent of the newcomers, especially when the rattle of their weapons could be heard clearly.

Commands were snapped out in Arabic, the group splitting. To the left of McCarter's position a door was flung open, bright light spilling out across the compound. Armed figures emerged.

"Not good," James whispered.

McCarter eased back his H&K's cocking bolt.

"Okay," he said. "Let's get this show on the road."

The moment McCarter, Hawkins and Encizo moved someone opened fire. The sharp crack of an AK-74 preceded a full volley of shots in and around the shrubbery. The Phoenix Force trio had wisely flattened out, so the shots went over their heads. Shredded leaves and twigs showered across their prone bodies.

Hawkins plucked a grenade from his webbing, pulled the pin and lobbed the projectile across the compound. It detonated with a loud blast, scattering men and putting a couple down on the ground, bodies punctured and bleeding. In the few seconds of confusion, while the attacking force was regrouping, Fox 1 gathered themselves and made for the closest cover offered by the main building. They flattened against the wall, trading shots with those defenders who had seen their move.

Bullets slapped against the white stucco covering the wall, tearing deep gouges in the structure. Splinters of stone misted the air, peppering the black combat suits of McCarter and his partners.

"Door back here," Encizo said and moved to investigate.

McCarter and Hawkins offered covering fire for the Cuban to kick open the door and check inside. Encizo saw a narrow, enclosed flight of stone steps leading to an upper floor. He chose a stun grenade, primed it and threw it to the upper landing. Then he dodged back outside.

"Stun grenade," he warned.

The muffled explosion and smoke engulfed the stairwell for a few seconds. As the noise died down, Encizo went inside, the others following on his heels, still holding back the defenders with their deadly autofire. McCarter brought up the rear, delivering short bursts from his SMG, shell casings rattling sharply as they fell to the flagged courtyard.

Encizo went up the stairs and flattened against the wall on the landing. He peered around the corner and saw an enclosed passage running forty feet to the right. There were no doorways except one at the far end of the passage.

There was one man on his knees, shaking his head from the concussion blast of the grenade Encizo had thrown. As the Cuban set eyes on him, the man closed his fingers around the AK-74 he had dropped. He pushed to his knees, the Kalashnikov rising as he picked up the sound of the approaching trio. He opened fire without taking direct aim, his burst raking the walls high up. Wiping his watering eyes with his sleeves, the man lowered the muzzle of his weapon to man height.

Hawkins triggered his MP-5 and put a burst into the man's chest, knocking him off his knees. The man fell to the floor, his finger jerking the trigger and sending a final burst into the ceiling, showering Fox 1 with white plaster dust.

McCarter, still bringing up the rear, turned as he heard noise behind him and realized that the defenders from the courtyard were following up the steps. The Briton freed a fragmentation grenade, primed it and threw it back along the passage. He curved it in toward the wall directly opposite the landing. The grenade bounced against the wall, then rolled out and vanished through the opening. When it exploded the force of the blast sent shock waves down the passage. McCarter saw the rolling cloud of smoke and dust coming from the landing and picked up the sound of voices raised in pain and anger.

Hawkins stood with his back to the wall, his H&K trained on the closed door as Encizo tried the handle. The door wasn't locked. Encizo glanced at Hawkins, who nodded. The Cuban freed the catch, then used his boot to shove the door open. Hawkins scanned the room on the other side, his H&K moving from side to side, up and down, as he covered every angle he could see. Encizo dropped to one knee, peering around the frame of the door. He caught a glimpse of a large room with a number of desks and chairs, some of the desks holding computers.

The crackle of autofire told them the room wasn't empty. The firing came from Encizo's right, out of his line of vision. He pulled his head back as the slugs chewed at the door frame. Wood splinters lashed at his cheek, gouging the flesh.

"Bastard!" Encizo muttered, clutching his face and coming away with his hand bloody.

The unseen shooter fired again, shredding more wood from the door frame.

Hawkins, watching the angle of the shots from his better position, took a breath, ducked low and lunged across the floor, landing on his shoulder and rolling behind one of the desks. The shooter picked up on Hawkins's move and altered his line of fire, raking the area with a murderous volley. Chairs bounced under the impact, debris filling the air.

From where he crouched Encizo could see Hawkins scrambling deeper into the room ahead of the shooter, who was unable to see him clearly because of the clutter of furniture. The Cuban watched the trail of shots snaking across the floor, chewing at the covering, splintering the wood of desks and chairs.

Pushing to his feet, Encizo glanced at McCarter.

"Cover me."

McCarter nodded.

Encizo eased to the edge of the door frame, then quickly stepped around it and into the room. He turned immediately to his right and spotted the shooter standing on the far side of the room. The man was intent on tracking Hawkins's moving form, so he missed Encizo's appearance for a scant second. Then his peripheral vision registered the Cuban's presence, and the shooter arced his weapon round, anger blazing in his eyes.

Encizo fired first, placing a solid burst in the guy's chest, spinning him off his feet. The man went down hard, his weapon still firing into the air as he fell on his face, blood spraying in spidery fingers across the floor.

Hawkins got to his feet, shaking wood splinters off his clothing. He moved to the far side of the room and placed himself where he could watch the door.

McCarter stepped in behind Encizo. The Briton slammed the door they had just used. There were securing bolts at top and bottom, and he slammed these home, then turned his attention to the room, running his eyes across the computer equipment.

"This doesn't look like the main computer setup," Hawkins said.

"Most of them aren't fully connected," Encizo agreed.

"Trash them any way," McCarter said.

MANNING AND HIS TEAM had skirted the end of the main building where it stopped short of the north wall. It brought them out on the far side of the structure in a service area, where doors led into the extensive kitchen. Farther along they could see a stone building from which they could hear the solid pulse of the diesel engine that powered the generator. As they moved along the wall, scanning the area for movement, they were able to see more detail. Standing some twenty feet to one side of the generator housing was a large fuel tank on metal legs.

"Fox one from Fox two," Manning said into his microphone. "We found the generator. Soon as possible we'll disable, so stand by. Fox two out."

"On your left," Sharon called, turning to meet the armed figures coming out of the shadows.

Muzzle-flashes lit up the darkness. The howl of autofire was followed by the sound of slugs impacting with the wall and ground close to where Fox 2 had been standing.

Manning, James and Sharon had split at the Israeli's call, and now they returned fire with fire.

James caught his first target as the distant shooter, clad in tan shirt and pants and wearing a kaffiyeh, made the mistake of stepping into a pool of light close by one of the fuel tank's supporting legs. Spun by the burst from James's weapon, the man fell against the steel support, clinging to it until loss of blood weakened him and he slid to the ground.

By this time James had moved on, stalking another defender, driving two short bursts into the man and flinging him to the ground.

Sharon had dealt with his first opponent, firing calmly and ignoring the frantic volley of shots from the other that were going wild.

Gary Manning had worked his way closer to the generator housing, engaging the enemy as he went, using the shadows as cover. Once he had reached the flat wall that formed one end of the housing the Canadian activated his transceiver.

"I need some covering fire, guys. Give me time to get inside this housing, and I'll plant an explosive pack."

"You got it," James came back.

"Acknowledged," Sharon replied.

Seconds later Manning heard the increased fire coming from his partners. The sustained bursts drove the defenders undercover, giving Manning the opportunity to move along the side wall of the enclosure until he found the entrance. There was no door, simply an opening. Manning pushed to his feet and began to step inside. That was when he caught a moving shadow and realized he wasn't alone.

Manning didn't hesitate, not wanting to alert the person waiting that he had been spotted. The big Canadian continued inside the enclosure but took two sharp steps to the left as he rounded the edge of the opening.

In the pale glare from a utility light set in the wall of the enclosure Manning saw a dark figure lunge forward, the blade of a knife shining in the light. Manning's would-be killer faltered as the Phoenix Force pro easily avoided the thrust of the blade. A grunt of exertion burst from the man's lips as he twisted, attempting to bring himself in line for a second thrust, but by this time Manning had already countered. The Canadian swung around sharply, coming up almost behind the knife man. He kicked against the back of the man's knees, dropping him to the ground. Manning slammed the point of his elbow into the base of the man's neck, pitching him facedown on the ground. Standing over the downed man Manning drove the sole of his boot into the back of the man's skull, ramming his face into the concrete.

Moving quickly to the large generator, Manning took a pair of the compact explosive packs from his small satchel. He planted one on the generator section and the second on the diesel engine providing the power to drive it. Manning set the timers for two minutes. Snatching his H&K the big Canadian left the enclosure, skirted the wall and took a crouching run to the large fuel tank. He placed two more packs, setting the timers for one minute thirty.

"Packages in place," he said into his microphone. "One minute thirty."

"LIGHTS OUT in one minute thirty," McCarter informed Hawkins and Encizo."

"We're set here," Encizo said.

He had set an explosive charge in the room capable of rendering all the equipment useless.

"Could be it's time we got the hell out of here, then," Hawkins suggested.

They gathered around the door, and Encizo eased it open. Beyond was a wide landing with stairs leading up to the next floor and down to the ground floor. They slipped through and closed the door behind them.

"Do we flip a coin?" Hawkins asked.

"Who brings money on a trip like this?" Encizo asked.

"I never go anywhere without my American Express," Hawkins said.

McCarter grunted. "Remind me to check your bloody expenses from now on. Now I suggest we move away from this door unless you want your arses separating from the rest of you."

They stepped away from the door and along the landing, aware of the crackle of gunfire coming from outside the building.

A raised voice alerted them and the thump of boots on the stairs as figures rushed up to confront them.

McCarter glanced at his watch.

"Time's about up," he said.

A closed door on their left afforded some possible cover. They turned, and Encizo booted the door open. As they stepped inside, weapons ready in case of meeting someone, McCarter turned and kicked the door shut behind them. The room they had entered was empty, holding nothing more exciting than stacked furniture. McCarter waved his partners to move aside, away from the door. Encizo and Hawkins had barely done that when the thunder of autofire sounded and bullets penetrated the door.

"Any second now," McCarter said.

The explosion was louder than any of them had expected. The blast was strong enough to tear off the door of the room they had vacated. The force rattled the walls.

The rumble of the blast hadn't died when an even louder explosion sounded outside the building. Manning's explosives, set around the generator, had blown. The blast shattered windows and shook the building. It was closely followed by an even heavier explosion as the fuel tank blew, lighting up the night with a scorching mushroom of fire, the blast sending burning fuel raining down around the compound. Immediately the lights went out. The only illumination came from the blazing fuel tank and the numerous small fires the burning fuel had started.

McCarter peered out the window, his face gleaming in the orange glare from the fire outside.

"Someone is going to be well pissed now."

He ejected the magazine in his H&K, snapped in

a fresh one and cocked the weapon. "Let's go, chums."

The door opened onto a landing that was strewed with debris and a number of bodies. The room they had planted the explosive in was a total wreck. Smoke still drifted across their path.

"Down to proper business," McCarter muttered, adjusting his night-vision goggles. "Let's find this bloody control center."

"AND HOW DO WE get out of this?" the Iranian delegate asked, his features darkened with anger.

"How we deal with any threat?" Falil said. "We face it and defeat it."

"I begin to wonder whether your promises are worth anything."

"Now wait a minute," Dahoun said. He would have gone for the Iranian if Falil hadn't put out a hand to stop him.

"Don't you see? This is exactly how our enemies will win. If we always fall back to the old ways, when our nations argued between themselves over every little matter. Divided we are weak. If we stand together, we can defeat all those who come against us."

The Iranian turned to his delegation.

"Decide for yourselves. But listen to what I say. Stay with this one and you will die. That is the only certainty."

"What are you going to do?"

The Iranian glanced at his companion. "Me? I'm getting out of here before this damn place burns to the ground."

Dahoun caught the man's sleeve.

"If you try to leave, they'll kill you."

The Iranian reached inside his robe and pulled out an autopistol. "They can try," he said. "It won't be the first time."

He walked out of the room, followed by his delegation.

"Let them go," Falil said gently. "It is their decision. There are enough of us to deal with this."

Beyond the room they were in the sound of gunfire rattled on. The battle was joined in earnest now, and even Falil—deep in his heart—knew that before this night was over his campaign would be decided one way or another.

"What do we do?" Dahoun asked.

"I'll move to the control room. There are messages I have to send before anything else happens to prevent it."

"I'll go see if I can help the others. These damned Americans have to be stopped."

Dahoun snatched up the Kalashnikov he had brought in with him and left the room.

THEY CRASHED through one of the doors leading into the kitchen area. Pots of food simmered on stone ovens. The aroma of rich coffee hung in the air. Through the night-vision goggles the kitchen was bathed in a ghostly, green-tinged light.

As Manning led the way, pounding feet sounded close by. The Fox 2 team separated and took cover behind whatever they could find.

Four armed men clattered into the kitchen, weapons up, arguing vehemently between themselves in Arabic.

James located a clear target first and took out the

closest of the men with a short burst from his H&K. The moment he fired, Manning and Sharon stepped into view, cutting loose as they appeared. The remaining three went down with their weapons silent.

"Somebody's coming from outside," Sharon warned. They turned and saw shadowed figures approaching the kitchen area. Someone opened up, then others, and autofire raked the kitchen, shattering pottery and sending utensils flying. Slugs cored into the clay pots on the ovens, blowing them apart and scattering their contents in all directions. On his knees behind one of the ovens Manning unlimbered a grenade, pulled the pin and exposed himself just long enough to hurl the grenade out one of the kitchen windows. The subsequent blast took out two of the opposition and scattered the rest in disarray.

Before they moved out of the kitchen both James and Sharon took the pins from grenades and rolled the bombs across the kitchen floor. Then they followed Manning and emerged from the empty kitchen in advance of the twin blasts.

Fox 2 stood with their backs to a wall, waiting out the last few seconds before the grenades went off, sending smoke out of the kitchen, through the door.

A tiled, wide room spread before them. It had a high, domed ceiling fitted with ornately painted glass panels. Chairs and rugs covered the floor. In the center of the room a plain stone fountain splashed with water.

Shadows moved on the far side of the room. They would have been unseen if the men of Fox 2 hadn't been wearing their night-vision gear. They were, however, able to see their opponents.

Spreading in a line, Manning and his partners

opened fire on the enemy and cut them down. A couple returned fire, aiming in the direction of the muzzle-flashes. Fox 2 had the advantage of being able to track its targets, avoiding a waste of ammunition.

"Let's check out any rooms down here," Manning said into his microphone.

"You got it."

They moved around the darkened floor, kicking open doors and engaging any of the enemy who resisted. The attack launched by Phoenix Force seemed to have created a great deal of confusion. Falil's people seemed to have discarded any form of concentrated resistance. They scattered before the solid fire of the Stony Man team, offering token fire but with a lack of coordination. There didn't appear to be anyone leading them, pushing them forward to organize into fighting groups. Each pocket of resistance seemed to be operating on its own.

A door caved in under Manning's boot.

Light met them. A number of battery-powered storm lanterns had been lit to provide a degree of illumination.

A figure turned as they burst in, autopistol clutched in his hand. The weapon settled on target and fired. Ben Sharon slumped back against the door frame, blood starting to stain his left shoulder.

James and Manning fired as one, the force of their combined shots lifting the figure over a table as blood soaked his chest. He crashed down on the far side, moaning but still resisting. Turning on his back, he fired from under the table, his bullet skinning James's left thigh, drawing a gasp of pain from the black warrior.

"Sneaky son of a bitch!" James said. He lowered the muzzle of his MP-5 and fired under the table. His shots battered the shooter's skull, snapping his head back in a rush of bloody brain and skull debris.

Manning caught a second figure trying to make a break for an open window. His shots hit the man in the left side, shoving him forward into the wall where his nose was crushed. The man went to the floor in a ragged heap, bloody and stilled.

Despite his injury, Sharon stood guard at the door as Manning and James checked out the room. On the tables were explosive devices—blocks of plastique, detonators, timers.

"Busy little bomb factory," James said. "Why don't we see if these things work?"

"Good idea," Manning said.

He took one of the devices and set the timer for forty minutes. He placed the device among all the others.

"We need to be out of here in thirty," Manning informed McCarter and the others over the com unit.

Sharon was leaning against the wall. His face was pale, sheened with sweat. His shoulder was bloody, and so was the hand held over the wound.

"We need to move," James said. "Get Ben somewhere so I can deal with this."

"I'm fine."

"Believe me when I say you're not. Shock could kick in any time. You could go down, and then we'd need to carry you."

"Then do it now," Manning said. "Here is as good as anywhere in this place."

James opened his medi-pack and took out what he needed. He exposed Sharon's shoulder and made a quick examination of the wound. The bullet had gone through the soft tissue, lodging to one side of the shoulder bone. James did what he could to clean the cavity.

"You want me to give you a shot? Ease the pain?"

"Feeling the pain is going to keep me awake," Sharon said.

"Ben, you'd fit into this team no trouble," James muttered. "Man, you are just as stubborn as the rest."

"I'll take that as a compliment."

James placed a pressure pad over the wound, then quickly fashioned a bandage. As he pulled Sharon's jumpsuit back in place, James said, "This is where I tell you not to get involved in too much exercise."

"Sure, Doc, I understand."

"Okay, you guys, can we move on?" Manning said impatiently. "Falil and his people aren't going to leave us alone for long."

The Canadian's words turned out to be prophetic.

As they emerged from the large room, they heard movement. Someone was issuing orders in a loud voice, and armed figures began to move into Fox 2's night vision. They were slipping into the section of the building from a number of points, having adjusted to the sudden darkness. Some were carrying flashlights, the beams probing the gloom.

Gunfire still crackled intermittently from elsewhere within the house and compound. It appeared Fox 1 was still on the move.

One of the defenders whirled and fired into the blackness. The volley was nowhere near Fox 2.

"Nervous or what?" James asked softly.

"How would you feel being dragged out of bed and thrown into a firefight?"

"Best time to hit them," Sharon replied, "is right now."

He opened up with his Uzi, despite his injured shoulder, and knocked two of the advancing men off their feet. Someone returned fire, bullets striking the wall close by.

Manning and James triggered their MP-5s, and the darkness was suddenly crisscrossed by muzzle-flashes from both sides.

Fox 2 still had the advantage of their night-vision capability. It enabled them to alter position quickly and regularly, still keeping the enemy in sight. Falil's defenders found themselves outgunned, not by superior numbers, but by an opposing force who had mobility on their side, allowing them to stay out of range of the enemy weapons.

Manning caught a robed, bearded figure spinning from left to right, firing at will, his slugs chipping walls and floor but little else. The Canadian drove a short blast at the figure and saw him fall.

The clash lasted no more than a minute or so, Falil's people withdrawing in confusion, leaving a number of their group on the floor.

FALIL SAT before the main monitor, making the line connection so he could transmit e-mail. The screen flickered, the Internet browser's logo appearing, and he leaned forward, narrowing his eyes against yet another headache. The image blurred, then sharpened. Falil waited with growing impatience for the connection to be fully established, knowing at the back of his mind that time was running out. The attack force that had breached the walls of the compound was now rampaging through the house and grounds. Already the attackers had destroyed the generator, blowing up the fuel supply. He realized that one of the reasons for the power cutoff would have been aimed at blanking out Falil's computer systems, shutting him off from his cells, which were only sitting waiting for his command to activate them. They had only partially succeeded, due to Falil's foresight in placing a backup system within the cyber control room. On the roof, directly overhead, was a smaller generator. It had its own fuel supply, and the power it created was used exclusively by the computer room—light, air-conditioning and powering the computers themselves.

Access to the room was through a solid door, the only exit via the roof. Falil had sealed off all the original windows with steel shutters. The entry door was guarded twenty-four hours a day, and no one came or went without his approval.

Little of that concerned him, or even mattered. Falil waited for his cyber connection to be made so he could issue his final orders via his network of cells. He needed to pass on his instructions, to inform his people to stand down and withdraw. There was no opportunity now for the whole of the operation to continue. Not until he had time to regroup, build his armament again. Until then his people would go back to their normal occupations, carrying on as if nothing had disturbed their lives.

The only strike he was initiating against America would be carried out via his sleeper in New York. The man had already been contacted by Haruni, who was his control, and the plan should be well into its final phase.

The screen flipped to the main Internet message window, and Falil began to compose his message. He kept it simple, telling his people to stand down and await further orders. Falil saw no reason to go into detail. That part of the operation had nothing to do with the cells. They were there to carry out his commands, not question his decisions. It had been the same with the creation of the false Kurdish rebel group, his ruse to distract the Americans and their allies while he went about formulating his greater plan.

It had been unfortunate that the Americans had been able to see through the deception so quickly. It had brought them to Kurdistan and contact with the *peshmerga* leader—Hanif. From there the Americans had gone from strength to strength, overcoming any obstacles placed in their way.

Now it appeared they were here in his own sanctuary.

Falil tapped out the last of the message, keying the command that would simultaneously send the e-mail to every one of his cells scattered throughout America and the Middle East. Many of his followers would be bitterly disappointed at his decision, but given time they would realize the wisdom there. He waited as the message was transmitted, watching the screen as each recipient would be logged, showing that the message had gone through.

He leaned back in his seat, rubbing the back of his head where the pain was building its tight grip on his skull. The ripple of pain had begun to extend along the sides of his head, terminating above his eyes. This was when the pain was at its height, burrowing deep into his skull and seeming to tear at his very being. This wasn't a time when he needed to be distracted by the pain in his head. Clear, precise thinking was his priority.

Falil leaned forward, briefly forgetting the pain, as messages began to flicker on screen. Messages that were telling him most of his cells in America had rejected the e-mail. That there was no access to the recipients' Internet site. Falil watched the numbers go up. Now there were similar ones coming from the UK and Israel.

What was happening?

Falil didn't panic. He ran a check on the e-mail sites he could access and found they had been shut down. Not just the computer on standby, but the whole of the built-in hardware disabled. The implications were clear. There was no reason his own people would do such a thing. Their contact with the sanctuary and Falil himself came through the computer systems. Without them the connection was lost.

So if his people hadn't closed down the sites, then who? In Falil's mind there was only one possibility.

The Americans.

Who else would it be? Perhaps Mossad. The Israeli force was persistent, and they were extremely capable. Falil wondered if the Americans and Mossad had joined forces, pooling their knowledge. Whoever and whatever had happened only meant that they had comprised a skilled group capable of locating and attacking Falil's stronghold.

He exhausted his checks and counterchecks. The truth was there on the monitor. *No access.* If the cells had shut down communication, had it happened because they had been compromised? Had the Americans gained enough knowledge to be able to locate and move on his cells? The possibilities seemed endless, and Falil accepted there was some serious cause for the shutdown.

He reached for the transceiver lying on the desk and put out a call for Jamal Sayid. The man had arrived from Kurdistan earlier in the day, having completed his assignment to check on the arms caches scattered around the region. His news hadn't been encouraging. A number of the caches had been raided by local security forces and destroyed. In running battles with these attackers a half dozen of Falil's followers had been killed. They had died as martyrs rather than allow themselves to fall into the hands of their sworn enemies.

Sayid, eager and still willing to accept Falil's decision, would no doubt be leading the resistance against the raiding party. Above everything, the man was a born fighter.

Through the heavy walls Falil was able to hear the gunfire and the occasional detonation of a grenade.

"Jamal here. Do you need me?"

"I have not been able to contact our people in the U.S.A. There are shutdowns in the system."

"Then what do we do?"

"I believe we should leave, my brother. Join me and we will use the helicopter."

"I understand."

As Sayid went off-line, Falil pushed away from the desk. Limping, he reached the far end of the room. He pulled on a rope dangling from the ceiling. The action released the mechanism whereby an extensible ladder was lowered, opening the trapdoor that gave access to the roof.

Returning to the desk, Falil tried one last time to access the e-mail recipients. Nothing.

Falil was denied contact with his people. He was unable to tell how they were, what had happened to them. However much he regretted that, it was inescapable.

He had to face it. His intricate plan, with its distant participants, which had been intended to leave the mark of Islam indelibly stamped on the faces of their enemies—all had slipped away from his control. It wasn't the time to analyze why. That would have to come later. Falil, if he still wanted an opportunity to make his strike, needed to move on. To abandon his sanctuary. He needed time to reorganize, to find some quiet corner of the world where he could begin to salvage what he might from the wreckage.

Submitting to the savage burn of pain in his skull, Falil leaned his head in his hands. The pain had increased. Now it pulsed with monotonous regularity, savage in its intensity. He closed his eyes for a moment, but even that small process hurt.

He felt something warm in the palms of his hands, and when he inspected them he saw blood. It was coming from his nose, trickling over his mouth and dripping from his chin. Falil sat upright. Pushing back his chair and crossing the room, he shouldered open the door to the small washroom. He crossed to the wash basin and peered into the mirror. Blood was streaming from his nose. It had already stained the front of his robe. He turned on the water and rinsed his face, then used one of the white towels to staunch the blood flow. The flow continued. Falil returned to the com room. He saw the light flashing above the entry door. He crossed to the door and released the internal lock.

Jamal Sayid stood there, wild-eyed, brandishing a Kalashnikov. He wore a shoulder holster carrying a heavy autopistol. The moment the door opened he shouldered his way inside and strode across the room to stare at the waiting ladder.

"The ones down there. They are same Westerners who were with those stinking Kurd bandits. They are killing everyone they find."

Falil locked the door. He crossed to his desk and opened a drawer. From it he took an automatic pistol. He tucked it in the belt around his robed waist. Then he knelt beside his desk, opened the safe set in the solid floor, took out the master disks and pushed them inside his robe.

"What is wrong with your face?" Sayid asked. "Have you been hit?"

"It is nothing. Just a nosebleed. I get them sometimes."

Falil hadn't noticed that the towel he was holding was red with blood, the cloth sodden. He became aware of the dripping blood and returned to the bathroom where he tossed aside the soaked towel and took a fresh one after rinsing his face again. Peering in the mirror, he saw the darkness beneath his eyes. His head was still heavy with pain.

"Where is Dahoun?" Jamal asked.

"Facing the enemy," Falil said. "I have not been able to contact him."

"We should go. Get you away from here."

Falil glanced around the room. Once it had been

the center of his ambition. Now it resembled nothing more than a deserted office.

"Falil!"

He turned at the sound of Sayid's voice, aware that he should go. If he died here, this night, then all of his plans would die with him. If he moved on, there would always be another chance to start over again.

Falil climbed the ladder and dragged himself onto the roof of the building. He stood in the cool night air, swaying as a wave of nausea swept over him. He felt the pain in his head increase, building to a pitch that was too much for even him to bear, and he slumped to his knees as a blackness swept over him.

Dimly he heard Sayid call his name, felt the man's hand on his arm. Sayid helped Falil to his feet and guided him across the roof. They reached the far corner, where the building butted hard against the corner of the northwest wall. A slender metal ladder led to the ground just outside the boundary wall. Falil was barely able to climb down the ladder. He slipped the last few feet and sagged against the wall, staring across the empty Libyan landscape.

"We must go," Sayid said, "before they discover we have left. They will kill us."

Falil nodded as the words got through. He allowed Sayid to guide him across the dark plain toward the waiting helicopter.

WITHIN THE following minutes McCarter and his team attracted fire from separate groups. They responded in kind and took out a couple of Falil's people each time. The advantage they had using the night-vision goggles hadn't registered with the enemy, who were struggling in the gloom. McCarter led the way up a flight of stairs that brought them onto the upper floor.

As they progressed along a passage, they picked up the crash of booted feet. The sound was close.

''Coming from the left,'' Hawkins said, and moments later he collided head-on with the lead man of a four-man group as they barged out of a side passage.

There was momentary confusion.

Hawkins and his man stumbled together, thumping against the wall as each struggled to gain the advantage. Both men carried SMGs, but neither could bring his weapon into play due to the close proximity they had to each other.

Hawkins swung his left elbow up and sideswiped the other's skull. The impact knocked the man's head against the wall with a solid thud. He grunted, retaliating with a hard knee that drove against Hawkins's ribs, drawing a sharp exhalation of breath. The Phoenix Force warrior wanted to end the conflict quickly. He saw no advantage indulging in a punching contest with the enemy. Repeating the elbow strike and putting a lot more power into it, Hawkins dropped his left hand and drew the Gerber combat knife sheathed at his waist. He drove the keen, blackened blade into the other man's side, burying it to the hilt. His adversary groaned as he felt the cold blade plunge deep into his body.

The moment Hawkins clashed with his man, McCarter and Encizo brought their SMGs into play. They had the advantage of being a step behind Hawkins, and that short distance presented them with a slight gain. The rattle of autofire filled the passage. The three men tumbled to the floor, weapons unfired, and the last was still falling as Hawkins dealt the final blow to his opponent.

The Briton spotted a flight of stairs and led the way. At the top he almost walked into the guns of two men guarding a door at the end of a short passage. He took a wild lunge backward, clearing the head of the steps fractionally ahead of the autofire. Bullets chewed at the walls, dusting the Stony Man team with plaster.

"The hell with this crap," McCarter muttered and fisted a grenade from his belt. He popped the pin and let the lever go. He counted off the seconds, then hurled the bomb with all his might.

The grenade bounced once as it reached the far end of the passage. The two guards were unable to do anything but watch the projectile as it speed in their direction. For them there was no place to run. Ahead were the waiting guns of the enemy. Behind them, a solid wall with a locked door prevented them from clearing the passage. The last thing they saw was the grenade as it struck the floor and rose a couple of feet in the air, seeming almost to hang motionless right before their terrified gaze.

The blast blew back along the corridor, smoke and debris curling over the head of the stairs. As the noise faded, McCarter stuck his head over the top step. The two guards were on the floor, and the condition of their shredded bodies told him they wouldn't be getting up.

With the others close behind, Encizo keeping a wary eye on their rear, the Briton approached the door at the end of the passage. The close proximity of the blast had jarred it open.

McCarter put his boot against the door and heaved

it wider. The room inside, windowless, lit by fluorescent lights, looked cold and austere. The air was cool, fed by air-conditioning.

The first thing McCarter saw was the ladder and the open trapdoor.

"Damn and bloody hell!" McCarter said. "Tell me we haven't missed Falil. Tell me the bugger hasn't done a runner."

Hawkins ran to the ladder and went up fast, vanishing through the opening.

McCarter took in the desk and the computers. He saw the main desk, with its monitor still active, e-mail denial still visible on-screen. Leaning on the edge of the desk, McCarter read the messages on the screen, a crooked smile edging his lips as he digested the information.

"Well, at least the sod didn't get his bloody way, after all."

"Look at this, David," Encizo said, and when McCarter looked down he saw the open floor safe. Encizo was on his knees, checking inside.

"Empty."

"So much for collecting data on disks," McCarter said.

Hawkins appeared, sliding down the ladder. He crossed the room, shaking his head.

"Whoever it was has gone, boss. That chopper we saw. Took off while I was up on the roof."

McCarter banged his fist on the desk.

"Damn!"

Taking a breath, McCarter glanced around the pristine room.

"Leave a couple of charges in here," he said. "Set for a couple of minutes. Let's do it and get the hell out."

WITH THE CHARGE SET McCarter led the way down the stairs. The lack of noise cautioned him, and he put out a hand to hold back Hawkins and Encizo.

"Fox two from Fox one. Somebody enforced a noise curfew?"

Calvin James's voice came back.

"It's weird. The minute that chopper lifted the whole bunch started to back off."

"How you guys doing?"

"Ben took a slug in the shoulder. I patched him up best I could, but he needs to be looked at."

"Time we called in our ride."

"Already done. Help is on the way."

"Listen, we found the control center. Falil had flown the coop. We figure he was in that chopper. So we laid a charge in the com room. Should be going any—"

The blast shook the building. Cracks appeared in the walls, and part of a ceiling crashed to the ground floor.

"—minute," McCarter concluded.

"We're heading for the north wall where we came in. Don't forget the charge we set in the bomb workshop."

"Bloody right. Fox one out. T.J., Rafael, beat feet, fellers. The big bang has yet to come."

They crashed their way through debris and smoke. Around them the main structure of the sprawling house creaked and groaned.

As they emerged from the house, the sound of an engine reached them. Headlights burst into life as someone powered up a vehicle. Tires burned against the paved area, squealing as the driver hauled the wheels around in a tight circle.

Fox 1 found themselves caught in the glare as the bulk of a heavy, white-painted Mercedes saloon bounced across the uneven ground.

"We ain't about to be offered a lift," Hawkins said as the Mercedes hurtled at them.

McCarter and Encizo threw themselves out of the way, crashing to the paved courtyard as the massive car roared by. Hawkins wasn't quite fast enough. The rear fender struck him in passing, lifting him off his feet as if he were a child. The young Phoenix Force warrior was thrown yards before he hit the ground hard, bouncing awkwardly.

Snatching up the H&K he had dropped, Encizo rolled to one knee, raising the weapon and triggering a long burst at the back end of the Mercedes. The 9 mm slugs shattered the rear window and blew out the windshield, coring into the driver's skull during their flight. Out of control, the Mercedes swerved and struck a corner of one of the outbuildings.

Pushing to his feet, Encizo ran in the direction of the stalled car as the front passenger door swung open. A blood-spattered figure slid out, wielding an AK-74.

The blood belonged to the dead driver.

The AK-74 belonged to the man named Dahoun.

Fox 2 saw the Mercedes speeding in their direction and watched as Fox 1 scattered. Moments later the sound of an H&K on full-auto sounded. Window glass blew from the Mercedes, and it went out of control, swinging in to smash into a wall.

When the passenger door opened and an armed figure climbed out, briefly illuminated by the interior light, Ben Sharon tried to pull free from Calvin James's supporting arm.

"What?" James asked.

"Dahoun! It's Dahoun. Don't let him get away! Not again!"

RAFAEL ENCIZO could still see Hawkins's flying body as he had been struck by the speeding car. He had heard the heavy sound as Hawkins hit the ground. He remembered every moment as he faced Dahoun, and he also remembered he was a professional who didn't allow personal feelings to cloud his judgment. He remembered, and there was nothing clouding his judgment as he pulled the H&K's trigger and very professionally emptied the magazine into Dahoun. The short-range effect of the 9 mm volley tore Dahoun's torso into bloody shreds, pinning him to the open door of the Mercedes so he remained on his feet the entire time it took Encizo to kill him.

DAVID McCARTER knelt beside Hawkins's still form. He gently rolled the younger man on his back. Hawkins's face was bloody. There was a deep gash above his left eye, and the side of his face was scraped and raw.

"T.J.? Do you hear me?" McCarter asked anxiously.

Hawkins didn't respond.

Rafael Encizo appeared. "How is he?"

"I don't bloody well know. Rafe, see if you can find some transport. Anything."

Manning ran to where McCarter was kneeling.

"Eight minutes left," he said. "We have to get out of here."

McCarter scowled at him. "What do you bloody suggest?" he snarled. "Maybe I should wear my underpants over my trousers and fly him out."

Manning refused to be intimidated. "No way, David. I've seen your underpants, and frankly they scare the hell out of me."

McCarter's explosion of laughter sounded all the more incongruous because of their situation and surroundings.

Encizo drove into sight behind the wheel of a dusty BMW. He drew to a halt and climbed out.

"Let's go," he said.

As Hawkins was lifted gently into the rear seat of the vehicle, Encizo caught McCarter's attention.

"I think Falil lost some of his believers. They're out of here and burning gas like it was going out of style."

They climbed into the car and rolled out of the compound.

"Maybe for now," McCarter said. "I don't think they'll be gone for long. Not while someone like Falil is around."

THEY HAD TRAVELED no more than a couple of miles when the planted charge went off and took the rest of the explosives along with it. The detonation lit up the sky for some distance, rendering the sanctuary into a heap of rubble. The pall of smoke hung over the site for hours and was still there when Libyan patrols arrived to survey the scene.

Phoenix Force was long gone. The BMW stood

abandoned in the desert, its doors wide open, drifting dust already layering the expensive leather seats.

AS THE ISRAELI SHIP made its way across the Mediterranean where it would rendezvous with a U.S. carrier, arrangements were in hand to have Hawkins taken immediately to the ship's hospital. The young commando had still not regained consciousness.

Ben Sharon was to stay onboard the Israeli ship and return home. He had work to do following up on the entire mission. He had already spoken to his superior, and an alert had gone out for Falil.

It was all they could do for the present.

CHAPTER SIXTEEN

Brooklyn, New York

Under Delacort's guidance they made the drive from Habib's apartment to the East River location in record time. Lyons drove with total disregard for traffic restrictions and ignored every red light they approached. Delacort spent a frantic couple of minutes on the phone to his superiors, asking them to keep the NYPD off their backs. Surprisingly, someone had to have pulled some long strings because they weren't challenged once during the hectic ride.

Lyons eased the car off the main street and turned down a narrow road that took them into the shadow of the Brooklyn Bridge. He braked so they could observe the area ahead. There was a concrete yard on the other side of a chain-link fence and open steel gates. One side of the yard was lined with a long row of lockups, each with its own steel shutter door. Numbers were painted on each door in large black letters. The lockup between 22 and 24 had its door raised.

Lyons gunned the engine and took the car into the yard, swinging it to a stop in front of the open lockup. As they all piled out, Blancanales spotted a man in crumpled denims watching them from the partly raised door of one of the lockups farther down the row. Leaving the others to check out Habib's lockup, Blancanales made his way to where the man stood.

"Trust us to have the tidiest damn sleeper ever," Schwarz muttered as he followed Lyons into the lockup.

Delacort found a light switch near the door and flicked it on. The light flooding the lockup revealed an empty space. The only indication anything had been stored in the lockup was a square rectangle of clean concrete where the thin film of dust layering the floor hadn't settled. The rectangle was approximately three feet square.

"So?" Delacort asked no one in particular. "What was friend Habib storing here for so long?"

"Could be anything," Lyons said. "Large explosive device? Some kind of nuclear weapon?"

"If it was nuclear, he wouldn't need to move it," Schwarz replied. "Set it off here, it would wipe out most of the city. The fallout would do the rest."

"Jesus, you sure know how to keep a guy's spirits up," Delacort said.

"There is another option," Lyons said.

They all turned to look at him. And on each of their faces registered the answer none of them wanted to hear.

"It could be a bioweapon."

Delacort sighed. Not a sound of despair. More an acceptance of something he had been expecting to occur one day, yet deep inside had always hoped never actually would.

"They've been preparing us for this for years," he said. "Like it had to happen one day. We had lectures. Descriptions of the processes. Effect scenarios. The range of these damn things. But you never really believe it because you don't want to have to imagine it happening."

"Imagine it," Lyons said. "I've got that feeling it's what we're going up against."

Blancanales appeared. He listened to what the others had come up with.

"You get anything from the guy outside?" Lyons asked.

"He saw someone fitting Joseph Haruni's description open up and back a white panel truck inside. He was curious because no one except Habib has ever come here in the couple of years the place has been rented."

"Did he speak to him?"

"Yes. Haruni told him he was Habib's cousin. He'd come to move some family property because Habib was ill. The guy, Bennie, said Haruni was real friendly. Offered him a cigarette, took time to talk with him."

"Sounds like Haruni was putting on an act," Delacort said. "How did Bennie feel?"

"He got a little nervous," Blancanales said. "Something about the way Haruni was behaving, trying to be a regular guy, but Bennie didn't buy it."

"Sounds a smart guy," Schwarz said.

"Appears Bennie was a cop about twenty years back. Got shot during an arrest and was invalided out. He still thinks like a cop."

"So did Haruni let anything slip about where he was heading?" Lyons asked.

Blancanales shook his head.

"Bennie did get the make of the panel truck and the license plate. He was going to phone it in. Would have if we hadn't shown up."

Delacort took the information Blancanales had jotted down.

"There was something else," Blancanales said. "Bennie spotted a couple of cars waiting at the top of the feeder road. When Haruni left in the panel truck the cars followed. They were too far away for him to get license-plate numbers, but Bennie was definite about the make of the lead car. It was a Buick. Late model. Dark blue paint job. One thing he was sure of. They took the bridge."

The moment Delacort got through on his cell phone he began to issue orders, stressing they be acted on without question.

"Have the local police use their aerial surveillance," he added. "We only want the panel truck spotting and the position relayed to me."

"Tell them he can't be stopped. No interference at all," Lyons insisted.

"If our suspect figures he's being watched, he might set this device off prematurely," Delacort explained to his colleague on the line. "We can't afford for that to happen. Why? Because we're not certain exactly what he has in the truck. It's a theory at the moment, but have Jake Masters put the biohazard team on standby. Oh, for Christ sake, Pete, stop fucking around. What do you expect me to do? Come in the office and sign the thing for you? Just do it."

Delacort slumped back in his seat as he cut the connection.

"Save me from by-the-book idiots," he muttered.

"Now you can see why we couldn't have that kind of restriction on us," Lyons said.

He started the car and they sat, waiting, sweating out the moment until Delacort's phone rang.

"Delacort. Yes. Okay, we'll wait here until we get a sighting. Once your people pick up the truck pass it to the chopper crew. They can track him without being seen. Thanks for that, Tony."

"The call out?" Schwarz asked.

"Yeah. NYPD has broadcast to every cruiser and beat cop. If anyone spots the truck, they call in and the NYPD airborne division will monitor the truck's progress."

It took almost ten minutes before the call came through.

"Haruni's truck was spotted on Franklin D. Roosevelt Drive about five minutes ago," Delacort said. "He's headed uptown."

Under Delacort's guidance Lyons picked up the route Haruni had taken. The FBI man was in constant contact with the NYPD helicopter trailing the panel truck, and he was able to keep Lyons moving in the right direction.

"Any ideas where he's going?" Lyons asked.

Blancanales had a map opened up, head down as he checked Haruni's route and looked for possible destinations.

"This is crazy, guys," he said. "He could choose any one of a hundred locations."

"So we follow him," Lyons said. "And when we figure the time is right we take him down."

A call from Delacort's NYPD contact added the information that Haruni's panel truck was being escorted by two cars. One had moved ahead while the second followed.

"If those guys are tailing Haruni, I'm guessing they'll be wanting to get clear before he sets this device off," Blancanales said. "And I don't see Haruni as the suicidal type."

"Right," Schwarz said, figuring out his partner's line of thinking. "That would mean they'll park the truck somewhere out of sight, trigger a timing device and then leave."

"Giving themselves time to get out of the area," Lyons said. "Even out of the country."

"As long as we keep them in sight we should be able to move in and deal with the device once they leave," Blancanales said.

"Sounds too easy to me," Lyons said.

Delacort was on the cell phone again, listening to his contact.

"Okay, but make sure you pick them up once they show."

"Show from where?" Blancanales asked.

Delacort smiled. "Take it easy," he said. "They're just going along an underpass. Be out in a few minutes."

Carl Lyons sat upright in his seat.

"Frank, tell your people to be extra sharp when those vehicles show again."

"They will."

"I mean it. Haruni is up to something."

"I don't get it," Delacort said.

"Right now the chopper can't see him," Schwarz said. "He could be pulling some stunt."

"Why should he? He doesn't know we're on to him."

"How do we know that?" Schwarz said. "Maybe he's just being cautious in case he feels someone is watching him."

THEY HIT the underpass just as the howl of a police siren cut the air. The sound came from up ahead, and would have been close to Haruni and his escorts.

"Oh, Christ, what now!" Delacort said.

He made contact with his NYPD man and listened.

"I don't believe it. Some bullhead cop decided we shouldn't wait it out. The stupid asshole tried to block off the underpass."

Lyons jammed his foot on the pedal, sending the car forward at an increasing pace. As they came out of the last curve into a section where the underpass ran straight, they saw the jam of vehicles. Figures were running in panic. The crackle of gunfire could be heard. Lyons swerved to avoid a car that was reversing away from the scene. The driver lost it moments later, and the car slammed into one of the underpass supports.

The blue-and-white NYPD patrol car was slewed across the strip, doors wide open, windows shattered by gunfire. A uniformed figure lay half out of the vehicle, blood glistening across the back of his shirt. His partner lay in the road, blood pooling under his head.

"Damn!" Delacort said. He pulled his service pistol and worked the action to cock it.

In the jam of vehicles they saw one of Haruni's escort vehicles. The occupants were firing autoweapons, scattering the spectators. There were already a number of victims on the ground.

Lyons brought the car to a screeching halt. He

kicked open his door and exited the vehicle, his Python already in his hand as he made a dash for cover behind the patrol car.

The others followed, hoping Lyons would stay put. There was no chance. His blood was up. The sight of the innocent victims was enough to galvanise Lyons into action, and when that happened it was no mean feat to make him quit. Blancanales and Schwarz could only do their best to back his play.

Lyons skirted the length of the patrol car, staying as low as he could until he rounded the front of the vehicle. Directly in front of him a young woman lay on her side. Autofire had stitched her left leg from midcalf to hip. She caught sight of Lyons and reached out a bloody hand. He nodded and mouthed at her to stay still. To her credit and despite the pain she was in, the woman did what he asked.

Raising his head a fraction, Lyons checked out the area.

Haruni's backup team consisted of two men outside the car with a third remaining at the wheel. In the short time since Able Team's arrival the terrorists had gunned down three more bystanders. They were firing indiscriminately, and Lyons figured the idea was to create enough chaos to give Haruni time to move on. Lyons wanted Haruni and his device, but he couldn't in all conscience walk away and leave the scene of carnage.

He thumbed back the hammer of the big Python, raised himself above the hood of the patrol car and triggered two swift shots at the closest gunner.

The .357 hollowpoint rounds hit the target directly between the eyes. The effect of the powerful rounds was devastating. They blew away the back of the gunner's skull, spinning him off his feet. Blood sprayed the side windows of the escort vehicle as the man went down.

The car's engine roared as the driver decided it was time to get clear. He yanked the gearshift in reverse, and the car lurched, the rear end colliding with one of the cars brought to a stop by the terrorists. Yelling in rage, the driver moved the lever to drive and thrust his foot down hard. Just before the car jumped forward, Lyons, who had already moved closer using stalled vehicles as cover, stood upright, leveled his Python and triggered two more shots. The .357 rounds shattered the side window and cored through the driver's head. One struck bone that deflected it, and the already misshaped slug tore a hefty portion of the man's face off as it exited through his cheek.

The surviving gunner, realizing that the armed response was taking a heavy toll, decided to leave. He cut through the stalled line of traffic, waving his gun and screaming in Arabic. Pedestrians scattered as he charged toward them. Others ducked in their vehicles. The man saw none of this. He was making for the panel truck and the other car. They had already started to move, but the car slowed to allow the man to catch up.

By this time Blancanales and Schwarz had circled the jam of cars and were racing along the narrow sidewalk, weapons out. Schwarz gained the lead and finding himself with a clear shot skidded to a halt. He brought up his Beretta two-handed and tracked the running gunman. He drew down, held and fired, pulling the trigger with steady deliberation.

The gunman faltered, stumbled, then lost control

completely. He took a long, slow dive to the ground, arms outstretched. When he hit, his large frame shuddered and he bounced, slithering along the ground until he came to a stop, his limbs twisted under him. He was dead by the time Schwarz reached him.

The car jerked to a near stop, heads leaning out to stare back. The dark shape of an autoweapon showed, and someone triggered a defiant burst in the general direction of Schwarz and Blancanales before the vehicle moved off with a squeal of burning rubber.

Lyons was yelling for Delacort to bring up their car. The FBI man, still talking into his cell phone, slid behind the wheel and brought the car to where the Able Team warriors were waiting.

As the three piled in, Delacort gunned the engine and sent the car along the road in pursuit of the panel truck and its armed escort.

"These guys have definitely lost it," Blancanales commented.

"I called in the emergency services," Delacort said. "They'll deal with the injured."

JOSEPH HARUNI REALIZED that his plan was slipping away from him. The Americans had located him and were following. The appearance of the blue-and-white police cruiser proved it. Even though his people had stopped both the officers, the situation had suddenly changed. The mere fact that the authorities were in pursuit lessened his chance to set the device and activate it.

He needed time to remove the safety seals before connecting the device to the timer and setting the countdown procedure. It was something that required a short amount of time, without any disturbance. One wrong move on Haruni's part, and the device might activate while he was still within the vicinity. As much as Haruni wanted the mission to succeed, he didn't want to become one of the victims. He had seen videotapes of experiments with the bioweapon. What had happened to the victims had been extreme. They had died in agony, bodies devoured by the terrible effects of the virus, flesh changing and blood leaking from every orifice. No one, not even Falil himself, had been able to view the scenes without flinching at the sheer horror of the devastation wrought by the virus. Haruni didn't relish the thought of becoming one of those victims, but if it was the will of God that he sacrifice himself, then so be it. He was ready.

The fact that he intended to release this virus over the city didn't worry him at all. This was a war he was engaged in. It was no different than shooting or bombing the enemy. In a war civilians were always involved. This time it would be the Americans who would feel the harsh realities of a war zone. It hadn't happened before to any great extent. The Americans did their killing from a great distance, not concerning themselves with the overspill. If a few civilians were killed, it would be noted as an acceptable statistic by the Pentagon planners, the high-ranking officials who never left the air-conditioned comfort of their plush offices, who saw war as a dot on a map or a blip on a radar screen. They never imagined the horror of a bombed village. A village population reduced to starving, shambling refugees. They could order the deaths of countless individuals without ever seeing one of them or concerning themselves about the aftereffects.

Falil's campaign against the Americans would have altered that balance, bringing the searing horror of the war zone to America itself. That had been prevented for the time being, but the release of the virus on New York would at least give the Americans a taste of what was yet to come.

Somehow he had to achieve that. At least one strike against the infidels would make them consider the future. Let them deal with the aftermath of a biological attack and then perhaps they wouldn't be so willing to unleash their war machine so readily.

On the seat beside him was a simple diagram of the city area he was in. It was drawn with street names and locations, and circled in red was Haruni's destination. If only he could make it with time to spare, just enough for him set up and activate his device. Once he had the device set there was no way to deactivate it without setting it off prematurely.

Haruni knew he was putting himself at risk. Once he set the device and tried to make his escape, the prevailing crush of traffic in the city might very well delay him for too long, and he could become one of the victims. That was a problem he would deal with if it became prevalent. Until then he would work on the assumption he had the opportunity to get clear in time. His devotion to Falil and the cause wouldn't waver. His own life was a mere speck of dust in the great plan. His faith would comfort him, and the loss of his own life against a great victory over the infidels was a thought to be cherished.

Behind him he could hear the crackle of gunfire as the rear escort car engaged in battle with the

Americans. In their way they were sacrificing their chance for escape in order for Haruni to move on. Their offering wouldn't be worthless.

Haruni put the panel truck in gear and stepped on the pedal, sending the vehicle into the traffic ahead. He drove blindly, ignoring everything around him. His only concern was to reach his destination. That above everything was important.

Nothing else mattered.

Nothing.

UP AHEAD the panel truck was swerving in and out of the traffic, ignoring signs and restrictions. The truck swayed dangerously as Haruni changed direction frequently. The truck clipped a number of vehicles as Haruni cut through narrow gaps or forced reluctant vehicles to let him through. The escort car stayed on his tail, following wherever Haruni went.

The panel truck hung a left, cutting directly across approaching traffic. The escort car hit the front of a swerving car and spun it out of control, sending it into a second vehicle trying to pass. Delacort hauled on the wheel, touching the brakes, and narrowly avoided the wrecked vehicles. He swung back on course and trod on the gas, sending the car forward at a reckless pace.

The panel truck braked, swinging right suddenly.

"Now I know where he's going," Lyons said.

He jabbed a finger at the large structure just ahead, a multistory parking garage.

Haruni took the panel truck along the short approach strip, jamming his foot hard on the gas. The truck hit the barrier arm and twisted it out of shape as it barged through, bouncing as it went up the entrance ramp, tires squealing as Haruni flung it around the curving lane. Sparks flew from the sides of the truck as Haruni's erratic driving scraped it against the concrete walls. The escort car, still following, fared even worse. The barrier arm, swinging loosely on its pivot, smashed against the car's windshield, cracking the glass. The car lurched, ran against the wall as it mounted the up ramp and lost most of a front fender. Metal debris rattled down the ramp, and as Delacort went through the barrier he felt the car bounce over the torn fender.

"He'll be heading for the roof," Lyons said. "Looking for a high point to release his bioweapon."

"Air currents will carry it across the city," Delacort said. "Downdrafts will pull it to street level."

"Sounds as if they've thought this one out," Blancanales commented.

"Hell, they could have been setting it up for months," Schwarz said. "Once they had the thing stored away and their sleeper in place they could take their time. Work out the best procedure. Choose their site, then sit back and wait for the call."

"What scares me," Delacort said, "is how many more there might be out there waiting their turn."

"That may be the case," Lyons replied. "All I'm worried about is the one we know about. If we don't shut this bastard down, anyone else out there might not get *his* chance."

The trio of vehicles ascended floor by floor, Haruni leading the frantic chase and gaining by driving with total disregard for his own or anyone else's safety. Nothing seemed to be on his mind apart from reaching his objective.

The roof parking level.

When the panel truck lurched to the top of the final ramp, swinging directly across the virtually deserted level, Haruni began to slow down.

Behind him the escort car topped the ramp and the driver jammed on the brakes and stopped dead, effectively blocking access to the parking level.

"Keep going," Lyons yelled at Delacort.

The FBI man didn't even pause to question the sanity of Lyons's order. He realized that if they didn't get to Haruni fast nothing else would really make much difference. Delacort figured it would be a quicker way to go out ramming the escort car than being poisoned by Haruni's bioweapon.

He gripped the wheel and floored the gas pedal, sending the car speeding across the level. The car hit the ramp at close to fifty, the rear end scraping the concrete as the heavy vehicle angled upward.

Two of Haruni's henchmen had climbed out of the rear. They heard the heavy roar of the chase car, turned and saw too late the bulk of the vehicle as it hurtled up the ramp. They tried to move clear, but time was against them. The chase car hit the rear of the parked vehicle. Metal and plastic crumpled. Luckily for Able Team and Delacort, the escort car driver hadn't had time to pull on the parking brake. On impact his foot slipped off the gas pedal, and the escort car was shoved forward, lessening the resistance. One of the men who had stepped out was hit by the solid body of the car as it was pushed sideways. He stood between the car and the concrete ramp wall and was crushed against the wall, then dragged along by the stricken vehicle.

The second man avoided the crash. He cleared the

impact zone, turning to bring his autoweapon into play. Schwarz, leaning out of his open window, triggered a pair of shots from his Beretta, catching the gunman in the upper shoulder. The man stumbled, losing interest for a few seconds. It allowed Schwarz to boot open his door and scramble out. He went after the gunman, bringing up his weapon and drilling two more 9 mm rounds into the man. This time they weren't wounding shots. The gunman went down with twin holes in his chest directly over his heart.

The others had exited the car, moving to deal with the driver of the escort car and the guy sitting next to him.

Lyons sprinted around the rear of the vehicle and caught the driver as he pushed open his door, gun in hand. The big ex-LAPD cop didn't hesitate. His Python boomed twice, and the driver slithered out of the car as if all his bones had turned to jelly.

Coming up alongside the passenger side, Blancanales fired through the window, stopping the surviving gunman before he had a chance to exit the vehicle.

"Where's that son of a bitch Haruni?" Lyons yelled.

The panel truck was in the center of the parking level, slowly moving forward. Haruni was in a bind. He would probably need a little time to activate his device, and he would lose all that the moment he stopped the truck.

"Got to stop the bastard," Delacort said, and set off at a run.

"Shit!" Lyons said.

Schwarz and Blancanales went after him.

Lyons watched for a split second, then turned and

ran to the escort car. He hauled the dead driver clear and dropped onto the blood-spattered seat. He realized the engine was still running and prayed that the transmission hadn't been taken out of action when Delacort had rammed it. Lyons yanked down the gearshift and felt the bite. He shoved his foot down on the pedal. The car lurched forward, then picked up speed. Lyons could hear a grating sound coming from the rear end, and the car pulled to the right. He hung on to the wheel and applied more power. The rear of the car slithered out of control, and Lyons fought to keep the steering wheel from dragging out of his hands.

Schwarz cut across the parking level, bringing himself around and behind the panel truck. He wasn't sure how he would manage to keep up with the truck if Haruni decided to make a break.

Haruni *did* try to break away, but he put the truck into reverse and jammed his foot down hard. With tires smoking, the truck lurched into motion, and Schwarz, who had just drawn level with its rear, was caught by its unexpected line of travel. The Able Team commando twisted to one side, attempting to clear the rear of the truck, but it caught him chest high, flinging him aside without slowing. Schwarz felt the stunning blow, then found himself in the air. He was thrown a number of yards across the lot. When he landed hard on his right side, he felt the pain in his chest and couldn't draw breath. He spun as he landed, his body bouncing over and over. Somewhere along the way he lost his grip on his pistol, and it bounced along the ground for some distance.

"Son of a bitch," Delacort yelled as he saw

Schwarz go down. The FBI agent sprinted across the roof to help him.

The panel truck came to a sudden halt, jerking awkwardly. Haruni leaned out and cut loose at Delacort with a 9 mm Uzi. The line of slugs marched across the concrete, kicking up spurts of concrete dust. Delacort zigzagged as he tried to avoid the bullets. Despite evasive training, the human form wasn't built to outrun high-velocity SMG slugs, and some ten feet from reaching Schwarz a burst of Uzi fire caught Delacort in the torso. He stumbled and went down hard, arching in agony, but still retained his grip on his handgun. As he flopped on his back, Delacort began to trigger shots in Haruni's direction. The slugs from his pistol clanged against the side of Haruni's panel truck, punching holes through the sheet steel.

Blancanales found himself in the open after the panel truck moved. He headed away from the vehicle, but Haruni redirected his Uzi and triggered a burst that caught Blancanales in the right side and knocked him off his feet.

Lyons had turned the car by this time, and he aimed it directly at the truck. He had seen what had taken place, and as far as Carl Lyons was concerned it had to end quickly, before anyone on his team took a fatal hit.

Blancanales, nursing his bloody side, was on his feet again. He picked up his pistol and ran forward. He dodged behind a couple of parked cars, quickly working his way along them until he was on Haruni's blind side. He saw Lyons driving directly at the panel truck and realized what the man had in mind.

Blancanales kept moving.

The panel truck had stalled, and Haruni was having difficulty restarting it.

When the car was no more than twenty feet from the panel truck Lyons kicked open his door and dived out. He felt the searing tear of the rough concrete as he hit. Slithering in an uncontrolled roll, the Able Team leader felt his jacket tear, then gasped as the side of his face struck the ground. Skin was torn, and Lyons felt warm blood flowing.

In the panel truck Haruni looked up as he heard the roar of the car's engine. He stared in horror as the car loomed ever larger.

Haruni, seeing what was about to happen, threw himself across the bench seat and shoved open the passenger door. He scrambled for the opening, knowing his time was running short. He didn't want to leave the panel truck, but he knew that if he stayed he wouldn't be able to continue with his plan. His only hope was to get out before the collision, then get around to the side of the truck and back inside where he might be able to set the bioweapon into motion.

For a moment he was falling, then Haruni felt his feet hit the concrete. He staggered, slightly off balance, throwing out a hand to balance himself. At that moment he heard the crashing thump as the speeding car struck the panel truck head-on. The open door swung to and clouted Haruni across the back of the shoulders. He stumbled, arms thrown before him, and saw the wounded American only feet away.

The man had a large autopistol in his bloody hands, and it was aimed at the Lebanese man.

The moment Haruni caught his balance, his

weapon plainly in sight, Blancanales didn't hesitate. He had his moment and he took it.

The muzzle of the Beretta tracked in on Haruni. Blancanales fired and didn't stop until the slide snapped on an empty breech.

Haruni's body was torn and bloodied by the pounding it took from Blancanales's volley. At least three slugs went directly into the heart. Haruni fell against the side of the truck, his blood spattering across the white paint work. He slithered along the panel then fell facedown on the concrete.

Blancanales felt a heavy weight dragging him down to the ground. He sank to his knees, and oddly it felt good. He kept his eyes on Haruni in case the terrorist was still alive. The man didn't move.

A shadow fell across Blancanales, and when he glanced up it was Lyons.

"You look a mess," Blancanales said.

"It feels worse," Lyons grumbled.

"Go take a look at Delacort. I think he took a heavy hit. I'm okay as long as I don't breathe or move."

Lyons knelt beside the FBI man. The right side of his body was a bloody mess.

"Did we get him?"

Lyons nodded. He felt something being pressed into his hand. It was Delacort's cell phone.

"Speed dial number one," Delacort said. "It'll get you my office. Just tell them to come on in."

"Leave it to me," Lyons said.

He glanced to where Schwarz was slowly sitting up. Schwarz spotted him and raised a hand. He climbed to his feet and made his way to Blancanales and Delacort.

They were a mess, Lyons thought. He looked at the panel truck and thought about what it was carrying. But at least none of them were dead. Then he made the call.

EPILOGUE

Stony Man Farm, Virginia

"This is going to take some time to tidy up," Hal Brognola said. "As missions go, it's been a tad messy."

"Am I smelling getting the blame kind of messy?" McCarter asked testily.

"Questions have been asked," the big Fed replied.

"You know one of our problems, Hal? We get kicked in the arse by nameless suits, and we don't get a chance to defend ourselves."

"Who got upset this time?" Lyons asked. "Did we break some local law?"

Brognola slumped in his seat, wishing he'd never even opened his mouth.

"Cool it, guys," Barbara Price said, leaning forward. "Don't bite Hal's head off. He's been defending your actions the last three days, and it hasn't been fun."

McCarter tapped his can of Classic Coke. "That's why they pay him more money than us. And he gets to wear a suit."

The silence hung for a few seconds.

"You want a suit, David? I can get you a suit," Brognola said, keeping a straight face.

"Oh, bloody hell, I was out of order."

There was a general intake of breath around the table. McCarter almost apologizing was something worth being there to hear.

The Briton heard the collective sound and allowed a hint of a smile to flicker around his mouth.

"The President was in our corner from the word go," Brognola said. "From what I picked up in Washington *he'd* been doing some collective ass-kicking himself. The information David brought back from Kurdistan about some U.S. agency doing the rounds and trying to warn the *peshmerga* off has caused embarrassment behind a number of closed doors. It's denial time big style, but the Man has launched an in-house investigation."

"So why the finger-pointing, Hal?" Encizo asked.

"It appears there has been a flood of complaints about U.S. interference in the Middle East. The French are more than a little miffed at what went on in Nice."

"Tut, tut," McCarter said. "You know how I feel about the bloody French. About as much use as a chocolate fire hose."

"Considering what was going on under their noses," Calvin James said, "I think they've got a nerve."

"The French are a little territorial," Katz said. "In this case it has been pointed out that they were responsible for allowing known terrorists to carry out illegal transactions within their borders. French security, it appears, had no idea what was going on."

McCarter allowed himself a murmur of disbelief.

"Haven't the Middle East countries been brought up-to-date with the information Aaron deciphered from those computers?" Gary Manning asked. "Or didn't we let them in on that part of Falil's plan? The bit where he was going to start internal strikes against pro-Western regimes?"

"We don't need these meetings," Brognola said. "You hotshots already have it figured out. Yes, we told them. And gave them transcripts of the data with names and places."

"And?" Manning persisted.

This time Brognola almost preened. "It was one of my best days," he stated. "They said it was a trick. Something we had cooked up simply to justify our actions. But it was in their eyes when they read the information. And they were nervous when they realized how close it had come. They were still muttering threats when they left. But I have a feeling that given a little time our intel will be feeding us local detail about some changes."

"Any reaction from Libya?" McCarter asked.

"Not a murmur," Price said. "The colonel has been maintaining a very low profile on this. Not even a stiff letter."

"Suggesting he knew exactly what Falil was up to," Katz said. "I spoke to Ben Sharon this morning. Mossad is monitoring everything coming in and out of the whole Middle East area, information wise. Ben said it was as if Libya had shut up shop for the time being."

"Nothing like being stung big time," Encizo said. "The colonel won't like it, but is he going to make a fuss that will link him to someone like Falil?"

"Right now Khaddafi is trying to build bridges

with the West," Katz pointed out. "Standing alongside Falil isn't going to help his case."

"Khaddafi might be interested in a little item we pulled from one of the encrypted disks," Brognola said. "We only had the translation come through a short time ago. If it ever reached him, I have a feeling he would be more than embarrassed."

McCarter's head shot up.

"Bloody hell. Not the colonel, as well?"

"From what we got it looks like Libya was on Falil's list, too. In his book, Khaddafi was selling out. Easing tension with the West. Allowing the trial of the two suspects in the airliner bombing over Scotland. We have names of Libyan sympathizers to Falil's cause."

"Talk of biting the hand that feeds you," James said.

"Hey, Katz, how is Ben?" Manning asked, referring to the Israeli's shoulder wound.

"He'll be out of action for a few weeks. He's not very happy because he's confined to office duties. He sends his best."

Price turned in her seat to catch Katz's eye.

"Has Mossad picked up anything on Falil yet?"

Katz shook his head. "Plenty of sightings from their informants, but nothing has been confirmed. Falil has been seen in France. Italy. Two different places in Portugal. As it does appear he is alive somewhere, I have a feeling we haven't heard the last of him. Falil is no fool. He's clever and inventive. This whole affair has shown that. Right from the start with the false lead about the KHP. Whatever else we feel about the man, that was a clever trick. It took our attention. Distracted us. If it had run its course we might not have picked up on Falil and his intentions until it was too late.''

''I believe we owe Aaron thanks for that one,'' Price said. ''If he hadn't exposed that trick about the KHP *terrorist* having been shot by his own people, this whole thing might not have been spotted. It was some smart deduction he made.''

''Which brings me back to what I was saying before you guys jumped in.'' Brognola interrupted. ''I realize you got a raw deal here. Information we had at the start seemed genuine enough but turned out to be less than accurate. But you came through. Improvised and took some chances. It's one of the reasons you're the best.''

''Do we know what was in that device Haruni was trying to set up?'' Lyons asked.

Price checked her file. ''Preliminary findings are suggesting it was a strain of the Ebola virus. CDC and USAMRIID have both been analyzing it. Where Falil got it from is anybody's guess. Ex-Soviet stock. Chinese. We don't know. Maybe some former biochemist doing contract work. It seems this particular virus was transmittable by air. Once it had been released it would have drifted across the city. People would have breathed it in and the cycle would have started. Three, four days the symptoms would have started to show and we would have had dying people all over New York.''

Calvin James sighed. ''Man, they really meant it.''

''Yes, they did,'' Brognola said. ''And this virus would have had the body count hitting the ceiling. We've all read the papers on the Ebola virus. What it can do. How it jumps from host to host, adapts, spreads. Hell, we can't begin to imagine how bad this might have been. Thanks to Able Team, it didn't get that far.''

"Hey, Carl, I'll buy you a pint for that,'' McCarter said.

Lyons looked at him. "A *whole* pint?''

McCarter considered for a moment. "Okay, you talked me into it.''

"Couple of downers,'' Brognola said. "The unfortunate incident at the Ghosh farm in Canada. Problem there was our need to move fast and not knowing the local law had decided to stage its own raid. Barbara, see what we can do for the future.''

Price nodded. "Liaison with the FBI in New York went well. Too bad those NYPD patrolmen decided to jump the gun, though.''

"How are they?'' Lyons asked. Being an ex-cop himself, he hated to see police officers go down.

"They both died from their wounds,'' Price said. "So did four civilians. Three more are in hospital.''

"Talking of casualties,'' Schwarz said, "what's the update on our people? And that includes Frank Delacort.''

"Delacort is still recovering,'' Price stated. "His injuries are going to keep him in hospital for a few months. The guy was hurt badly, but he'll recover.''

"We owe him big time,'' Lyons said.

"Pol?'' McCarter asked.

"Spoke to him earlier,'' Price said. "He's doing okay. The head nurse told me he tried to date her yesterday.''

"That's my man.'' Schwarz grinned.

James stirred restlessly in his seat.

"T.J?''

Before Price could answer, someone said, "Why don't you ask him yourself?"

All heads turned as Jack Grimaldi pushed T. J. Hawkins into the War Room in a wheelchair. Hawkins's head was swathed in bandages. The impact from the speeding car had left him with a fractured skull and a blood clot had formed, adding pressure to his brain. Only the swift action of the surgical team on board the U.S. carrier had brought him out of danger. Hawkins was over the worst but was being forced to rest until the medics declared him fit enough to return to duty.

"How's it going, buddy?" James asked.

Hawkins brightened at the sight of his friends. He still looked pale and he needed rest. Today was special—he had been allowed out of the hospital for the first time in a week.

"Good to see you, guys."

For a time the War Room was noisy with greetings. They were all glad to see Hawkins was recovering, all aware it could have been any one of them in that wheelchair.

Or worse.

The day could yet come when their number might be lessened on a permanent basis, when one of them failed to return from a mission. And on that day the survivors would breath a silent prayer that it wasn't their turn.

David McCarter caught Katz watching him. The Israeli had passed the responsibility of Phoenix Force to the Briton. Now it was McCarter who carried the weight on his shoulders. Katz knew they had made the right choice. McCarter could handle the burden. He would do it in his own way. It would always be unique. There would be times when he would still irritate them. Do things completely out of left field, but he would always get the job done and bring his people home.

Grimaldi rolled the wheelchair to where McCarter was sitting.

"Hi, boss," Hawkins said.

McCarter eyed the younger man, casting his gaze over the wheelchair.

"Things you blokes will do just to get a few days off. Tell you something, Katz, they don't turn them out as tough as they did in our day."

"Here we go," James said. "Hearts and flowers time again."

McCarter grinned. "Welcome back, T.J. It's bloody great to see you, pal."

Switzerland

JAMAL SAYID TURNED as the door opened. He recognized the director of the private clinic.

"How is he?" Sayid asked, forgoing any greetings.

"Much better today. Still weak, but he is gaining strength every hour."

"Have the results come through yet?"

The director crossed to his desk and sat down, gesturing for Sayid to be seated, too. The doctor picked up a large envelope and slid out a number of X-rays. He held them up to the light and indicated points as he explained them to Sayid.

"This is the original photo. As you can see, the tumor had expanded dangerously." He picked up a second print. "This is the one we took yesterday.

The area is clear. The operation was a success. Mr. Haleem is a lucky man. If you hadn't brought him to us when you did, I do not think he would have survived for much longer.''

"Thank you, Doctor. Have you informed him yet?"

"No. I thought you might like to do that. He is able to have visitors today."

Sayid stood and shook the doctor's hand.

"Thank you again, Doctor. We are in your debt."

In the corridor Sayid smiled to himself as he walked to the private room where Falil lay. He silently thanked God for his greatness. For saving Falil. For allowing them a second chance. He knew it would take time for Falil to recover fully. During that time, they could review past events and start again. There was much to do. Many things to put right.

The great disappointment as far as Sayid was concerned was the failure of the final strike in New York. The Americans had even prevented that from happening. Joseph Haruni had died in the attempt, and the bioweapon had been confiscated by the Americans. If only that part of their plan had succeeded, at least Sayid would have been able to bring good news to Falil. He decided to skirt around that for the moment. Falil would learn about it eventually. It wasn't something he needed to know right now. The priority now was to get him strong and well again.

Sayid reached the door to Falil's room. He paused for a moment, then pushed open the door.

Here was where it all began again....

James Axler

OUTLANDERS®

TOMB OF TIME

Now a relic of a lost civilization, the ruins of Chicago
hold a cryptic mystery for Kane. In the subterranean
annexes of the hidden predark military installations
deep beneath the city, a cult of faceless shadow figures
wields terror in submission to an unseen, maniacal god.
He has lured his old enemies into a battle once again for
the final and deadliest confrontation.

In the Outlands,
the shocking truth is humanity's last hope.